# Knight's
# By Summer Devon

He agrees to her challenge, but only if she's the prize. And this dragon never loses.

Sarkany has collected a fine hoard, including much of a small New England city.

But Miranda knows his true nature. To drive this dragon from her home, she issues Sarkany a challenge—give it up or get out.

He's more than ready to play her game, but only on his terms. After all, what could be better than to add the beautiful knight to his collection?

Warning, this title contains the following: explicit sex, graphic language, greedy dragon.

# The Dragons' Demon
## By Marie Harte

A prank gone wrong throws three unlikely partners together: A demon. A dragon. And an egg.

In the ordinary world, forces are at work which keep the balance of the universe in order. Enter Eve Sinclair, a higher demon with a mission—to sway those souls on the brink of Decision, to push them toward heaven or toward hell, as they are meant to go.

After a prank played by her brothers, Eve finds herself holding the proverbial bag, accused of stealing a precious dragon egg. Worse, it's a royal egg, as she learns from Ranton, the furious commander of the dragon legion.

Not a creature to have on one's bad side, Ranton shifts between his human and dragon forms, keeping Eve off-balance and off her game. Normally a master at manipulating males, Eve finds that Ranton is more than a match for her...as is his brother, the new dragon king. In their arms, she's mere putty.

And soon they're not only molding her desires, but her heart.

Warning, this title contains the following: explicit sex, graphic language, ménage a troi, and steamy dragon love.

# Wings of Change
## By Bianca D'Arc

One young woman could be the miracle that heals a dying dragon—and unites a family with her love.

Lucia, born a lady in a foreign land, now waits tables for her keep. When she sees Sir Reynor wasting away, she storms the Castle Lair seeking help for the dying dragon. What she finds is a dashing rogue, a mighty dragoness, and a contrite knight who blames himself for his dragon partner's injury.

Marcus is enchanted by the foreign beauty and intrigued by her mission. Few women will go near dragons and fewer still can communicate with them. Marcus recognizes Lucia for the treasure she is and knows she is meant for him...and for Kaden.

Kaden is wracked with guilt over the injury that has grounded the dragon—possibly forever. He knows Lucia is special, and he wants her. Lucia just might be the missing piece they all need to form a family. But with Reynor unable to fly, how can any of them be happy?

To make this family whole, they need a miracle. And love—the greatest miracle of all.

Warning, this title contains the following: explicit sex and ménage a trois.

# I Dream of Dragons I

*Summer Devon*
*Marie Harte*
*Bianca D'Arc*

A Samhain Publishing, Ltd. publication.

Samhain Publishing, Ltd.
577 Mulberry Street, Suite 1520
Macon, GA 31201
www.samhainpublishing.com

I Dream of Dragons I
Print ISBN: 1-59998-807-0
Knight's Challenge Copyright © 2007 by Summer Devon
The Dragons' Demon Copyright © 2007 by Marie Harte
Wings of Change Copyright © 2007 by Bianca D'Arc

Editing by Angela James
Cover by Anne Cain & Scott Carpenter

Knight's Challenge
First Samhain Publishing, Ltd. electronic publication: September 2007
The Dragons' Demon
First Samhain Publishing, Ltd. electronic publication: September 2007
Wings of Change
First Samhain Publishing, Ltd. electronic publication: September 2007
First Samhain Publishing, Ltd. print publication: March 2008

# Contents

# Knight's Challenge

*Summer Devon*

# Dedication

For Laurie Adams because she deserves something for *her* dedication.

# Chapter One

Sarkany's newest assistant, Pettifer, stood at straight-backed attention, a posture left over from army days, no doubt. Pettifer coughed and the subtle pulse in his throat increased. The man must carry bad news. But when he managed to speak at last, he didn't divulge any great surprises. "She isn't willing to come see you. Sir."

"Miss Benson is a nuisance." Sarkany selected a chocolate and allowed it to melt in his palm before licking his hand clean.

Pettifer apparently didn't like Sarkany's cruder practices. He showed his discomfort now by averting his gaze and staring at the painting of a mountain range that hung on the office wall.

Sarkany didn't bother telling Pettifer that chocolate against his skin tingled. He didn't tell any of his assistants the reasons for his odd eating habits. He never explained himself to anyone.

Sarkany wiped his hand with a linen cloth. "Did she tell you why she has been buzzing around me or hunting for a way to cause me harm?"

Pettifer shifted his weight from foot to foot. "No, sir. Though I did ask. She, uh, only said she didn't need to report to you."

Sarkany was almost amused at the man's nervousness as well as the woman's defiance. He fished out another chocolate and tossed it in the air before catching it in his teeth. Rather like catching prey, or the closest he came these days. "I am her landlord. I am her employer, or close enough." He swallowed this chocolate almost whole. "What else do I need to hold over her before she understands that prodding me and then ignoring me is not in her best interest?"

11

"She might not know you own her building. Do you want someone to reveal your ownersh—"

"No, I don't think so. She'd find some way to weasel an advantage." Hands in the silk-lined pockets of his trousers, he walked to the window and stared down on the busy street. His realm—but he didn't feel the usual satisfying glow of surveying his possessions. Miranda was more interesting at the moment. "I imagine she'd make threats about safety inspectors or some such rot. She is not a subtle creature, this Miss Benson. Did she say why she attacked me? Again? And do you know what her next attack will be?"

"Um. She has some idea that you are responsible for the mess at the nursing home."

He turned around to examine Pettifer. "Interesting. I don't even own that property."

"She thinks you could somehow step in and solve the problem."

"I should have more of a sense of *noblesse oblige?*"

"Yeah, that's about it. Sir."

Pettifer shifted from foot to foot again and took a few shallow breaths. Apparently the subject made him nervous. Sarkany made a guess. "Tell me. Did you use your looks with Miss Benson?"

"Sir?"

"Your manly wiles. You are an attractive specimen. Did you attempt to placate her with a winsome smile?"

The assistant frowned. "No, sir, it didn't occur to me."

He was a bad liar.

Sarkany knew Pettifer enjoyed pretty women and Miranda Benson fit any description of pretty. Her skin glowed like pearls, her eyes were bright as emeralds, though not that uninteresting color, her hair bright as gold. He considered the notion, and decided not gold. Lustrous like gold, yes, but the color was more a tarnished silver, rippling to her shoulders.

Her good looks might explain the foot-shuffling. Perhaps Pettifer'd been caught by her attractions and he'd listened to the female—and even agreed with her. Pity if he'd have to sack the man, but more than one assistant had been tossed out for going over to the other side.

Sarkany grinned at a sudden thought—and ignored Pettifer's tiny whimper of fear.

Could the other side actually be the guild?

Miranda might be one of *them.* Silly not to have thought of the possibility right away, but he hadn't faced one of their foolish knights for more than a hundred years. The guild kept itself quiet, just as Sarkany did.

He could easily stop the threat of Miranda Benson, but he'd been bored lately. Simply smashing her efforts wouldn't be amusing.

"I will go to her," he announced and saw Pettifer's pulse increase again. Not guilt—lust. Strong enough to influence a weak man.

Perhaps Pettifer would eventually join her efforts to undermine Sarkany's small but sustaining hoard of buildings and wealth in this unimpressive New England town. He'd find out from Miranda Benson. She had an expressive face, incapable of hiding anything, especially from him. He'd take it upon himself to examine her very carefully.

ಬಎಲಿಅಚಿ

Miranda waited.

Linus was convinced that soon the devil would come to her. If Sarkany did, well, she didn't have an enchanted sword, but she and her friends had gathered some weapons even a powerful creature like that couldn't defeat—she hoped. Linus said the creature had a propensity for illegal drugs. They all watched his kingdom carefully looking for slip-ups like drugs or zoning laws violated. They acted as gadflies and wrote indignant letters to the editor of the local rag about Sarkany's misuse of power. Linus had Miranda sign almost every letter they composed, part of a plan he didn't divulge. The guild leader enjoyed his secrets.

The letters finally had an effect. Sarkany had sent a hulking idiot, who'd first threatened her then made a come-on. Neither of Mr. Pettifer's attempts worked, and now Miranda paced her apartment. Honestly, Sarkany should hire more impressive henchmen—he could afford people nearly as dangerous as himself.

There was a sharp rap at her door and she almost reluctantly went to the peephole. What new weirdness would she find?

She had eventually expected to meet the man himself—or rather the creature. But already? It was a shock to see the tall, rangy, dark-haired figure in the slightly too formal clothing.

Miranda muttered a curse. If only Linus were here. He knew the best way to deal with Sarkany. He'd devoted his life to discovering the secrets of Sarkany's kind. *Calm the breathing*, she reminded herself and she counted to ten before she opened the door. To avoid meeting his eyes, she looked down at expensive leather boots, black and surprisingly scuffed.

"Come in, if you must," she said.

"Miranda." He held out a hand. "So pleased to meet you at last."

She shook his hot, dry hand. Smooth skin. No scales.

*Sarkany*. He didn't even hide his nature. Hungarian for dragon. She could feel his silver eyes on her. That must be why her skin prickled and her heart stuttered. She'd always felt his attention from a distance when entering his presence at city council meetings or charity events they'd both attended, but she'd never looked into his dangerous face. Photos showed him handsome and lean, with near-black hair and sardonic brows above pale grey eyes, irises rimmed with pure black—a dragon's spellbinding eyes.

"Miranda?" He moved to her sofa and sat, then patted the cushion next to him. She walked to the back of the couch and stood behind him.

"You are not a very good hostess," he said.

The amusement in his voice, along with the way he treated her apartment as if it were his own, would have infuriated her if she weren't being so very careful to not allow herself to grow angry. A knight must keep emotion at bay when battling the dragon or she forfeited any advantage.

Miranda followed Linus's advice and immediately revealed her knowledge of Sarkany's nature. "May I offer you some sake?

I hear it was invented by the Japanese to lure your type when you were being nuisances. I won't bother warming it. You can heat it yourself."

He laughed, and shifted on the couch. He looked at her and she didn't turn away in time. Disaster.

She met his gaze.

At once she forgot her mission, forgot her reason for aggravating him. She'd been using herself as bait and in that second their eyes met, she was caught. What a mistake to fall into the spell of that silver gleam—his power tugged at her. Heavy lust seized her. She gazed back, immobilized by desire. Dear Lord, he'd gotten her too easily, within a minute of entering her house.

The bottomless irises made promises.

*Let me stroke you. Do you know what I can do with heat? Can you imagine? Taste me. Let me taste you. Your skin, your mouth, your sex. Heat. Miranda. Take the heat I offer. Thick honey we devour together.*

Her body ached to respond and her mouth opened to answer the dragon's call. She almost leaned to him, over the couch, to that mouth. Silver eyes that created a hunger so strong it made her hands clench and her womb grow heavy.

She had to do something. Something—the sirens used music and the sailors stuffed their ears with wax.

*Shut your goddamn eyes.* She forced her lids closed.

He laughed. "What a pity. You don't want to flirt with me? I should feel insulted." He spoke in a smooth rumble as seductive as those eyes. "Shall we talk business? How much do I need to pay you to stop harassing me? Ah, now I can see the indignation in your face, even with your expressive eyes closed. All right. If you are too noble to take money for yourself, then allow me to contribute to your favorite good cause in your name. Assuming, of course, it isn't one devoted to destroying me."

"No, no pay." She folded her arms over her breasts in case the tingling in her nipples meant they had visibly hardened. "No. We'll win. If not me, then another member of the guild."

"Oh, heavens. The guild?" His loud laughter sounded genuine. "I suspected as much, yet still, I'm amazed. It has

15

been so many years. I must say you are hearkening back to the worst of your primitive ancestors, young woman."

"The guild is strong." She felt foolish standing, arms crossed, eyes firmly shut.

"Do your members still make oaths in blood? Do you still carry shards of bone?"

She shook her head, but didn't answer. He *couldn't* know Linus insisted she keep the precious small object with her every minute of the day.

"You know it's all nonsense. The peasants stopped fornicating in the fields to bring forth good crops centuries ago."

"Okay. Some of it might be nonsense, but I—I know you are a dragon." Her voice cracked.

"Open your eyes. Do you see any sign of fire? Scales? Claws? You are a superstitious, silly woman. Now that I know what sort of nonsense you're up to, I can stop wasting time on you. A pity, because I thought you might be more interesting than the usual opponent. You're just a small dog yapping at my heels."

"I'll yap until you go back to your own kind. You are a dragon and don't care about anything human. You only use us to gain wealth."

He sniffed. "And how does that make me any different from any other businessman?"

The answer came to her, simple and perfect. A challenge. Dragons were vain creatures and hated to be bested in any contest.

"You're right. You aren't any different, are you?" She tried to imitate his amused indifference. "I mean, you're just exactly like any regular old idiot of a human."

He chuckled again. "You know, I've changed my mind. You are still rather intriguing." Her heart sank at his next words. "I can see your game, of course. Baiting me is an old trick."

The couch creaked as he stood and only a stir in the air and his voice told her he moved closer. He walked silently. "But I don't mind playing. Tell me the terms of your challenge. If you win, I'll vanish. Not into the hills, mind you, I'm not ready to rejoin the rocks. I enjoy life as a human too much at the moment. But I'll leave your city."

*Life as a human.* He'd admitted his real nature. She tamped down a wave of panic. A authentic dragon stood next to her and she was expected to face the danger—and not run away screaming. She exhaled carefully before asking, "And if you win?"

"If I win, you stop playing the role of nuisance ants at my happy summer picnic of a life. And you play another role for me. You'll be my treasure."

She held her breath as a warm hand firmly cupped her chin. A finger brushed over her cheek, sending shivers straight through her and down her spine. Horrible, delicious shivers she couldn't hide plummeted directly to her lower belly. He gave a satisfied purr and removed his hand.

"I wish we were back in the bad old days," she said, and the unfortunate quaver filled her voice. "I want some better weapon than the law. Something sharp and silver that I could use on you."

He stood so close she could feel the heat radiating from his body. "You guild members always were a bloodthirsty bunch of heel-nippers. I'll have you know it has been quite a while since I cared for a fight. A very long time since I have touched human flesh." He leaned close and whispered, "For anything other than pleasure, of course. My pleasure and yours."

His touch, his warm breath on her cheek, made her pussy throb. She forced her muscles to stay still and didn't dare open her eyes. Her skin felt drawn tight. Thin-skinned. Far too aware of the pleasure he'd promised. Oh God, desire seemed to thicken her blood.

He pulled away, and she could breathe again. His finger very lightly touched the side of her throat. Of course he could read her pulse. She cursed herself for not wearing a turtleneck.

"Perhaps you would like to reconsider your challenge?" He laughed, softly this time. No doubt all this laughter, though it sounded real enough, was to rile her. "I'll give you a day or so."

"No," she said.

Never give a dragon time to reflect, said Linus. They reached choices slowly, and knights must take advantage of a human's faster nature. "I don't need to. You accept? No matter what?"

"Miranda." He made her name sound decadent, even obscene. "My dear girl. 'No matter what' is not a very pretty oath. You guild members have lost the baroque beauty along—"

"Do you accept it?" she asked, impatient. She was tired of the dragon's playful nonsense designed to intimidate her. Impossible goal because if she'd been any more afraid, she'd faint.

He was silent a moment, then quite seriously said, "Yes, I do. I shall win you, and I'm looking forward to what I shall do to you. And with you."

She again held her breath to stop her gasp, not the sound of anger, but pure, eager response. All of the training with Linus and she could barely control her body when at last confronted with a true dragon. Still, there was some compensation for her weakness. He wouldn't win this one, no matter which course he chose.

# Chapter Two

As Miranda tried to arrange the words in her head, the dragon taunted her. "You're frightened of me. That's why you're not saying anything."

She shifted her weight to lean away from him. "Yeah, of course I'm terrified of you. But I'm not going to let my fear stop me. And I won't be seduced, either."

"Are you issuing yet another challenge?"

"No, I'm not stupid. I know what you can do to me." Pain, as well as more mortifying reactions. The thought of her own response to him forced her to pause so she could clamp down on the fresh wave of arousal. She knew he could smell her excitement.

Miranda opened her eyes. She wanted to watch Sarkany as she spoke, and she reminded herself not to look higher than his lips. "Sarkany. I don't want to pick unnecessary battles with you. I have only the one challenge." His well-defined mouth slanted into a smile when she licked her own lips. *Damn. Of course he knew how much she wanted him.*

She didn't look away. "Listen. My test is simple. The goal is to show you're more than a simple greedy human, okay?"

His hair brushed softly against the collar of his shirt as he nodded. She wished she could be less aware of his every motion.

"Okay, then give it all away," she said. "As soon as possible. All of your hoard. The buildings, the jewels, the possessions, the money. It's either be left with nothing and stay here. Or keep it all and move far away from this city. Oh, and you have to allow me to choose the administrator or manager of the properties once you go."

He gave a low whistle. "I should be more careful," he said, apparently unruffled. "I forget that you guild members have no pity."

"Fine, I won't be ruthless. You can keep five hundred dollars so you can buy a passport and plane fare."

"No, my Miranda, that makes no sense. I will have won, and will have the right to remain here. With you. You will have room in this apartment for a very poor dragon. Or perhaps because you'll be mine, I'll take possession and force you onto the streets? So many choices I'll have to make."

Oh, damn. She should have thought of that, but he sent her thoughts into a whirl, sucked her awareness to some part of her body that shouldn't be clamoring for attention at the moment, thank you.

He chuckled. "You should have considered what's going to happen when I win this. This is delightful. I haven't had a decent challenge for quite some time. Going around the world six times was tiresome."

His wide mouth and his very white teeth showed in a grin.

"You can't just give the money to—to one of your underlings," she warned. "It won't count unless you give it to someone you don't know or someone who can't be threatened by you."

He idly brushed her arm with the side of his thumb. "Of course you try to add stipulations after the fact. You are an inexperienced young knight. It's rather like playing cards with a child who tries to take back his wrong moves. But to prove I am an amenable man—"

"You are a dragon," she interrupted, and then wondered when he could have possibly played games with a child.

"Amenable *man*," he said firmly. "I agree to your limits. Any more?"

She was about to say no, when another scenario occurred to her. "You can't give it to me."

He chuckled again. "Oh my, you are good. Not good enough, of course."

"I know your assets, dragon."

"Really?" He sounded interested, still not alarmed. "Did you bribe one of my employees?"

"No. Taxes accounts at city hall, tax returns and your insurance policies."

"Ah, so you bribed my accountant?"

She shook her head again and then, because she feared for the accountant's life, said, "A guild member acted as his secretary until last month. Her name is Liddy. Check it if you don't believe me."

"I can see you are telling the truth, Miranda. I'm satisfied. Or as satisfied as I can be for now."

She didn't see him move, yet suddenly his large hands rested on her hips.

He whispered, "Close your eyes again, if you insist, but I will seal our challenge."

"Not with blood," she warned. Her hand went into her jeans pocket where her sliver of dragon bone lay. She didn't know what it would do to him, but it was all she had.

"Mm, no, with a kiss."

She couldn't refuse—Christ, she didn't want to. Dry, soft and passionless, his lips brushed hers, gently. The simple kiss triggered a response that seized her whole body. She groaned and couldn't hide the sound. His mouth returned to hers, and for a moment the kiss flashed into something potent. His arms tightened around her and then he stepped away, leaving her breathless and rubber-legged.

"Oh, I am glad I came here today," he said.

She wondered if he told the truth. No one could tell when a dragon lied. Their skill at creating lovely falsehoods was legendary. Seduction and lies until they sucked the humans dry and moved on. Or made the swooning victims into their dinners.

"I'm glad, too," she lied. She rested one hand on the back of the couch to steady herself.

"No, you're not. But you will be, Miranda."

Before she opened her eyes, the door creaked and he'd left. He moved so fast and silently. But even if she hadn't heard the soft sound of the door closing, she'd know he was gone. His presence had filled her and now his absence seemed to deflate her. Thank God.

With shaking legs, she walked around the couch and collapsed onto it. In a few minutes she'd call Linus and he'd scold her for acting without first speaking to him and the others. In the meantime, she practiced deep breathing, trying to bring her heart rate down to a reasonable speed.

# Chapter Three

Sarkany usually enjoyed humans. For many years, they'd provided him with treasure, and once upon a time, the occasional snack. In the more violent confrontations, they'd entertained him by pretending they weren't afraid of him when they tried to turn him into some sort of trophy.

In the less violent encounters, he liked their malleable morals, and in bed he adored their soft skin and had been intrigued by their delicate yet rather conspicuous sexual parts. He'd transformed his semblance into one so long ago, he considered himself near-human, much of the time.

He felt a thorough alien at the moment.

Leaving the knight's apartment, he took the stairs rather than the elevator. Anything to keep moving and bring his body back into complete control.

Outside the apartment building, he dismissed his driver. The day was cold, but he didn't mind weather, and this would give him a chance to walk past many of his buildings and bid them good-bye, for now. He intended to slough them off like an old skin.

He'd try to walk off the strange mood created by his encounter with the knight. The Miranda female reminded him of how unhuman he was. Not inhumane—it took one of them to be so dreadful. She reminded him of human strength, a stirring power he'd rather admired, usually in books, rarely in the flesh.

She was the first genuine knight he'd encountered for centuries. Many men—and even a woman or two—had challenged him, called him out from the rocks in his natural form or accosted him in his human guise.

Miranda's heart was strong and true and she, unlike all the others, might bring about his defeat. She had no notion of it, of course, and it wouldn't be her silly challenge that would do it.

No, he'd had an answer to that challenge almost before she'd finished adding her addendums.

His sister, Tia, could crush him into a grease spot if he kept his present form. To fulfill the terms of the challenge, he could give Tia all of his worldly goods and expect to get many of them back.

And really, he'd only have to hand over the possessions the guild and the U.S. government had discovered. Sarkany owned much, much more, including land on his favorite mountains not far from the peak of Shisha Pagma in Tibet. The ant-like humans could toil up Shisha Pagma but no human was allowed to climb his sacred mountain.

Sarkany walked quickly. He dodged around a bike messenger then stopped in the middle of the road when he realized the truth. He'd even give away at least one of his mountain lakes, if it meant he could possess the knight Miranda.

Touching her had been a treat. Miranda was as warm and sweet as the best chocolate against his hand. He couldn't wait to taste her—and that was the core of her power over him. Dragons can always wait. Always. But when he thought of her, impatience bubbled inside him and made him wish he could roar and set something ablaze with a strong blast of fire.

When he touched her mouth with his, her unexpected power surged through him. His heart gave a strong lurch. The effect was almost as dramatic as changing skins. Exhilaration poured through him and he felt nearly as skittish and excited as any human.

He was intrigued by her manner as well as her delicious flesh. She'd admitted her fear, and she'd set him to a task though she would gain nothing from it. Refreshing. She didn't want his dragon hoard for herself. Rare, perhaps unique, in his encounters.

"Hello, Mr. Sarkany. What an unexpected pleasure to see you," someone called out to him, a man in a blue suit.

"Good afternoon, Mr. Blair." Sarkany smiled mechanically.

Blair started to cross the street, but a bus blocked his path. Sarkany walked swiftly, turning a corner so he'd be out of sight before Blair could track his progress.

He was in no mood for sycophancy, which was what most people wanted to offer him. In exchange they wanted him to give them jobs, money, prestige, homes, happiness, a reason to live.

As he strode along the sidewalk, he wished he could shed the ill-fitting clothes. No matter how carefully tailored they were, his garments never seemed to fit him comfortably.

When he stopped at the light, he realized he'd promised to get rid of the garments and the people who nagged at him when he agreed to the knight's challenge. No human would bother with him if he shed his money, properties and influence. No need to hire heavy-breathers like Pettifer.

His enemy had cleared the way for some interesting, albeit temporary, changes. The idea made him laugh aloud, startling a man who also waited for the light to change. "What's so funny, mister?" The man's grumpy question was rhetorical, but Sarkany answered anyway.

"Following rules," he said. "An intriguing idea, don't you think?"

The man took a couple of side-steps away and didn't answer. Sarkany, to amuse himself, turned and met the man's eyes. The stocky businessman went still as a statue, obedient and ready. Far too easy.

Sarkany thought of the shows he sometimes encountered on television featuring men toying with fish. They enjoyed the sport. So did he. He wanted more fight, more play.

Miranda.

Once upon a time, a beautiful maiden like her might have been chained to a rock as a sacrifice for a dragon. This method of dangling her in front of him, defying him, was far more to his taste. Give her a sporting chance.

౬০৪০গ৪৪

They met in the nearly deserted boarded-up industrial area, no doubt slated to be another of Sarkany's projects. The room smelled of mold and sweat and Miranda supposed it always would. The basement remained damp, no matter how long they ran the dehumidifier, and they used the large space for their exercises. They spent hours improving what Linus called their frail human bodies, learning how to fight. All of them, even the stout Garth, were in good physical shape.

Linus pressed his mouth tight and picked a pimple on his lean cheek as he clicked through his vast store of information. At last he rolled aside so the others could see the monitor. A woman with long black hair and grey eyes stared out at them. "His sister. She calls herself Tia. I suspect that's from Tiamat, which is a Babylonian name for dragon. She's not afraid of him. Sarkany could give it all to her and she'd return much of it to him. And if she didn't, well, she was a dragon. Therefore just as bad as he is."

He clicked on the screen and the woman slowly melted into an image of a silver serpent with the same grey eyes. Linus enjoyed dramatic effects on the computer. Miranda suspected he enjoyed drama of all kinds and that formed his early interest in dragons as well as his intense hatred of them now.

Linus drank some of his bottled water and said, "She's an even nastier specimen than Sarkany."

"Oh, damn." Miranda sighed and slumped on the beaten and lumpy brown armchair. "What have I done?"

"Delivered yourself and the city into the hands of a ruthless creature. Most of the city is already in his claws. It's you I worry about." He cast a sidelong look at her and Miranda ignored his obvious glimmer of lust. At least she wouldn't hurt his feelings. Though they both knew he had the hots for her, both of them disliked the fact.

"We are weaker when we indulge in the animal sensations," he'd told her early on. "Therefore, we shall overcome them. If I should ever attempt to seduce you, please refuse me."

She hadn't told him that she would have refused him even if sex weren't out of the question for guild members. Linus was smart, interesting, dedicated, and not even remotely her type. She could have overlooked the permanent acne, but not the permanent lack of humor.

Linus impatiently drew fingers through the strands of lank brown hair that fell across his face. He leaned back in his chair.

"We'll have to find all of the weaknesses in your challenge and try to get them shored up. After the fact."

She was reminded of the dragon's remark about playing cards with a child.

Hogarth, the tallest and oldest of the small group, was sharpening a Bowie knife. His precisely cut, short gray hair and clean but dull clothes made him look like a police officer off duty, although the scars on his hands and arms gave him the look of a construction worker. Miranda could only guess, because they did not share their other lives. Too risky.

Without looking up, Hogarth said, "I think you should explain why you had to take action, Miranda. I thought we'd agreed to continue the campaign to bother him until he did something illegal to stop us. You were the tethered goat, but you weren't in danger, right?"

Miranda had already explained, but understood that Hogarth wanted to find holes in her story. They all knew people under dragonspell were dangerous. She took the proper step of telling the same story, using different words. "He came to see me almost immediately after he sent the henchman. I thought he'd wait a day or two at least. I wasn't sure if I'd have the chance again. Have his attention."

Linus scowled at the screen. "Which is another thing. I wonder why he's moving so much faster than dragons usually operate."

She shook her head. "I think he'd been planning to see me for a while. I have had a sensation of him watching me when I go to places..."

Even Hogarth stopped scraping blade on stone to look at her.

Linus slapped the arms of his computer chair. "Aha. So what he said about making you his treasure wasn't just a spur-of-the-moment desire to teach you a lesson. He's had his eye on you." Linus sounded triumphant. "Just as I thought he would. That's why we sent you into the meetings and had you write the letters. Well, this could be good after all. See if you can spend time with him while he addresses your challenge. Dragons who are greedy for an object not yet in their grasp might expose some weaknesses."

Miranda took a deep breath and rolled her head. "This tethered goat wants to know why can't we be straightforward? Let's skip luring him out and dig for more evidence of his evil side. If even a quarter of what you've told us is true, we could find enough to have him thrown in jail. You've said again and again when it comes to trickery, no one can beat a dragon at his own game."

Linus answered with exaggerated patience. "We don't have enough weapons and we haven't found enough evidence. Ruining his image isn't going to bother him. He doesn't care what humans think of him. He's never going to run for any sort of political office, so he doesn't need to worry about his public image."

Miranda folded her arms and looked around at the others. "Why are we so certain he won't try for political office? He's on boards of directors and that's not such a huge leap. Politics might amuse him. He likes playing games with people."

"He doesn't crave power, just possessions. He just buys the politicians and lawyers," Tina said. She peered suspiciously at Miranda over her bifocals. She had a right to be annoyed— Miranda had blown one of Tina's names. The guild would have to buy Tina new identities, and she was the guild member least proficient at disguising herself.

Hogarth went back to sharpening his knife. "The only way to get him is going to be with a weakness we haven't uncovered." He smiled down at the blade and Miranda remembered her own longing for a good sharp sword when she'd met the dragon.

But the guild wasn't going to attempt that sort of straightforward attack. "What if he only commits a crime because we pushed him to?" she asked. "I mean, what if we're entrapping him? It seems so underhanded...so dragonish." She rubbed her eyes and wished she'd kept quiet. Linus squinted at her and she knew she was still under suspicion.

"The ends justify the means. He's a dragon and therefore his essence is evil." Linus paused. "You've talked to him. Didn't you sense that?"

"I sensed power."

Chairs squeaked as they all leaned forward to listen. "That all?" Linus asked.

She had the urge to tell them to go visit the dragon themselves if they were so interested.

Linus must have felt her impatience. "You have to be honest about this because it would help us understand if you've been put under any sort of spell."

"Okay, okay. So about the dragon. I sensed danger. And um, a basic irreverence about humans and the guild in particular. He mentioned us."

Murmurs and smug smiles greeted this—the dragon knew them. Rather exciting to have a powerful enemy recognize your existence.

"But evil?" She shook her head. "I didn't smell it or however you put it once, Linus. The misery he creates. I know he's responsible," she said and allowed her anger to show. Her old neighborhood, so many old neighborhoods and small businesses, lifestyles and jobs, gone, carelessly wiped out by the dragon's greed. A whole town's character destroyed. "I know. But now I think it's just..." She tried to think of the right words. "It's a by-product, not what he's aiming for."

Garth, who rarely spoke, said, "Sounds like he's got a splinter of control over you. Not a lot, but we'll have to keep close watch careful. Particularly if you're the one who's going to be with him. Gonna have to make sure you don't take part in bigger plans from now on. You even let slip Tina's role."

"I had to protect the accountant, you know that. I didn't use her real name." She bowed her head to hide her frustration. "I don't like it, but I get why you're saying that. Just don't give spring any surprises on me if I'm involved. Fair enough?"

"Of course," Linus said at the same time Garth responded, "Dunno."

Garth got up and ambled over to where she sat and awkwardly put a ham-like hand on her shoulder. "We shouldn't guarantee nothing. You know? Don't want to lie to you, Miranda."

She glared up at him. "So I watch my back with the dragon and with my own comrades. I get it."

Garth frowned, his blunt Nordic face wrinkled in thought. "Sorry. But it'd be true of any of us who'd had face to face with the dragon. And you're gonna have more contact. It'll get worse."

He was right. She nodded wearily.

The guild had been her friends and family ever since the neighborhood had been bulldozed under. Soon after her mother died of heartbreak, Linus had discovered Miranda weeping in the public library. Later on he'd told her he'd been watching her, knew her history.

He bought her a cup of coffee and convinced her that Sarkany was the worst kind of predator, the type with no connection to other people.

When Miranda had blurted out "it's like he's not even human," Linus had slowly, masterfully, revealed the truth.

Miranda had once believed the group was her city's best hope—before she'd met and talked to the dragon. Tonight they looked like a motley crew of misfits, barely able to organize themselves, certainly no threat to a power like Sarkany. The guild seemed almost...comical. Perhaps a shard of poison had been lodged in her thoughts by the dragon.

No doubt about that.

She didn't admit to them the fact that every time she closed her eyes, she saw his expressive mouth quirked into a half-smile. She had memorized the lines of his lean strong body, and it had only taken that half an instant to fall victim to those grey eyes. Amused, bright eyes that almost melted the disciplined resistance she'd slaved over so long. Gone, vanished in a puff of air, his warm breath on her, his hand and mouth touching her skin.

Shit.

She couldn't tell her friends because she suspected they'd banish her entirely if she talked about the heat he created inside her body. No way could she explain that, sure, she might feel the effect of the dragon, but the mesmerizing attraction wouldn't stop her, any more than she'd ever allowed fear to get in her way.

# Chapter Four

The next morning as she dried her hair, someone knocked on her apartment door. A man stood right outside her door, not downstairs. She guessed he had a keycard to the downstairs door, and when she saw his dark uniform, she knew who'd sent him.

Playtime with the dragon had begun.

When she opened the door, the chauffeur took off his hat and informed her that Mr. Sarkany had sent a car for her. The driver was smaller than Sarkany's obnoxious assistant, Mr. Pettifer, more polite and probably would have taken no for her answer. But why bother? She would march right into the heart of the creature's lair.

She even allowed the chauffeur to open the car door for her and she tried not to shrink back into the leather-covered corner of the seat when Sarkany himself opened it at the destination.

She ignored his hand and climbed out of the car.

"You issue a challenge, you witness it," he said.

"I have to go to work."

"No, I'm firing you."

She shut her eyes tight. Of course, she'd forgotten he was part-owner of the crafts factory where she worked as a shipping foreman. That was the job she'd had to get when rising living expenses and a sick mother meant college was out of the question.

He went on, "I'm rehiring you in the capacity of special observer. That certainly sounds impressive enough to be a job? Shall we go upstairs to my apartment and get some breakfast for you?"

"No thanks."

"Don't trust me, eh? Smart."

"I'll grab something here." She swung into the coffee shop at the bottom of the building. Strong hot coffee. Linus said dragons hated the stuff, but Sarkany didn't seem put off by the scent.

He waited for her outside. They rode the elevator up to the top floor. He'd have the penthouse, of course. She sensed he watched her, so she returned his bold examination—at least up to his neck. Hands in trouser pockets, he leaned against the back of the elevator, completely at ease under her scrutiny. She quickly looked away from the swelling in his trousers that he made no move to hide.

"I do enjoy this unpredictable human form," he murmured.

When the doors slid open, she bit her lip to hold back a gasp. The huge room looked even larger with the floor-to-ceiling windows on three sides. A dizzying view.

"Being up high remind you of your mountains?" She wanted to insult him, remind him of his animal origin.

"Yes, it does. I miss them sometimes," he said, and the serious answer shook her. She recalled Linus's warning. Sarkany would try to show he had emotions, even a soul.

She sipped her paper cup of coffee and, ignoring the dizziness of acrophobia, forced herself to walk to the window. "What is on the agenda?"

"We'll work on that together. I have drawn up lists, and you look them over. You help me decide which organization or individual should get which property."

A shuffle of papers, and she turned away from the window to face the dragon. Either view felt dangerous to her, but only one truly was—the handsome creature. He held out a sheaf of paper. Manicured fingernails couldn't disguise the brutal strength of his hands. A white scar crossed the back of his knuckles. Did he carry that from his dragon days?

She took the papers. "Why are you doing this?" If only her hands didn't shake—but he already knew she was frightened of him. No point in trying to hide any secrets from a dragon. He probably even knew about the shard of bone in her pocket, the bit of a dragon Linus once mentioned had been called Flame.

"A challenge," he said, lightly. "I like to do them well. I do many things well."

"Uh-huh." She looked down at the list of assets—she'd memorized what he owned—and slowly ran her finger down one page and the next. She flipped through the whole list. It was all there. Every property and even the objects in his apartment and private office. Quite a few objects and one property were new to her.

She looked at his chin. "Who suggested the charities and organizations?"

"I knew of a few of them. My assistants gave me a list. The Internet. I'm not entirely cut off from human affairs in my realm, you know. I choose to live in this building among you, after all, when I could go inhabit some sort of country estate with a large wall around it."

"You just want to be able to look out over everything you own."

"Perhaps. Yes." He sat down at the large polished granite table that took up much of the room.

When he didn't stand so close, she breathed a little more easily, and she took the time to examine the room. The only personal touches were a few paintings on the one wall that wasn't windows, and some rugs on the polished marble floor. Otherwise there was a sense of wealth and nothing else.

"May I see the rest of your lair?" she asked politely.

"Certainly, on the condition that you look into my face occasionally. You are behaving like a shy young virgin."

"Never mind." She pulled out a heavy carved chair—an antique, she realized—and sat down to read over the list again.

"If I promise not to attempt to seduce you?"

"A dragon's promise?" She shook her head.

He leaned forward, moving more of his body into her view. Broad shoulders. "In blood, just like your guild oaths. Hey?

How'd that be? I'd put the blood on a piece of white cloth and you could keep it with your bone shard. Nice little collection you'd have then. And if I broke my promise, you could burn the cloth. That would give me a terrific headache. You know that from your lore?"

She didn't look up and hoped he wouldn't notice her blush. "No, I didn't know. Why do you care so much about whether or not I look at you?"

He laughed. "I have no idea, my young knight of the guild. It amuses me. I'd like to see the true quality of your eyes, for instance."

She flipped a page of his list even though she had no idea what she'd just read. "Hazel. Not blue, not green, not brown. Bags under them from not sleeping well. I haven't for a long time. Not since you paid off city hall to have Point Green destroyed."

"Your old home, I presume? Is this the only reason you hunt me? Or has the code of the guild truly entered your heart?"

"And then when you built the overpriced condos where the affordable rental units—"

"I tire of the subject and I'm disappointed that you are acting from a sense of vengeance. Pfah, typical. And it's ancient history, Miranda. Because of your challenge, I enter a new era. Although I do have one question. Why do you persist in blaming me when the politicians go merrily along with my plans?"

She stopped pretending to read and pushed the papers away. "You have far more wealth and power than they can resist."

"You resist it with no difficulty. Allow them some responsibility. Why should you be the only incorruptible human?"

"They don't know your true nature. You seduce them with—with magic."

"Dear me. This is dull, familiar territory. I might allow you to leave after all." He rose to his feet and paced. "The blood offer is real, you know."

"If I don't play your game, you'll get tired of me and let me go?"

"Exactly. You are perceptive. But you have been told to watch me, haven't you? Take the drops of blood. Hoist them up as a flag at your basement headquarters."

Her heart sank. How did he know she'd been told to watch him and that they met in a basement?

"God. Is one of the guild a spy for you?"

"Yes, you. You've just told me all I've guessed is true. The guild rarely changes from generation to generation, you know. They'd meet in shabby outbuildings or even dungeons when there were no basements."

She sighed and slowly bent forward until her forehead rested on her hands that lay on the table. A gesture of defeat. The granite was cool against her chin. Why the hell did Linus insist she do this work? She was not clever enough.

She wished she could recall if Linus had ever said anything about dragon blood or blood oaths. He remained so secretive about dragon lore and dragon lures, saying he didn't want information to fall into the wrong hands. Still face-down, she made her decision. "Give me the blood." She sat up again, but remained focused on her hands. "Put it in a plastic bag, please. Make that two plastic bags."

Sarkany laughed. Unlike his usual smooth, practiced chuckles, this was a delighted, loud shout of laughter.

He went through a door and soon reappeared with a wickedly sharp silver knife, a white cloth and two plastic bags. "Watch," he commanded. "You don't want me to cheat, after all. I could pass off chicken blood as my own."

She felt slightly sick as he carelessly cut a gash into the top of his elegant, long finger. "Doesn't that hurt?"

"Certainly," he said. "It'll be worth it."

The blood, deep red as her own, dripped onto the cloth. He wiped the knife and his finger, and efficiently tucked the cloth into one bag and then that bag into the next.

"You are so good at that. Do you give out your blood to every visitor?"

"I never have." He pushed the bags across the table toward her.

Her heart beat hard, and she knew that despite her turtleneck, he could see her pulse. No reason to believe his words, but she did. "Why are you giving it to me?"

"I've always been certain I'll know what the humans around me would do with the blood. You, I'm less sure of."

"I thought I would hoist it like a flag."

"I'm not entirely sure, actually."

"Less certainty means I'm more amusing?"

"Exactly. You do comprehend me, my pet."

She couldn't bring herself to touch the bag. "Ugh. Don't call me that."

"Because it will soon be the truth? Very well, Miranda. You have my blood," he said. "Now look at me."

She yanked the bag towards her, thrust it into her back pocket and looked up. After all, she'd managed to close her eyes the day before.

Grey eyes, amused, sharp and gorgeous stared back at her. No whisper of seduction, beyond the obvious and unspoken, yet she was lost, examining his thin, aristocratic face. Oh, no, the smile was kind? That was too much because, God help her, she felt herself responding only to a compelling face and a pleasant smile. *Taste his mouth, run your hands over his skin. Feel his dark hair.* That urging came from her, not him.

"Hello," he said softly. "Very nice to meet you, Miranda Benson."

She could only nod. The dragon poison filled her, she was certain of it. She would have to phone Linus, arrange to not meet guild members in person and try to forget what she knew of the guild. The attraction that filled her was far too potent to ignore.

"Damn it." She rose to her feet. "Show me what you have, please."

# Chapter Five

Sarkany let the knight go first because he loved watching her walk stiffly, as if fighting every nerve in her body. She stalked from the room, into the place where he slept, the heart of his nest. No need for a bed because he didn't require much softness and he never brought back his human lovers to this spot. Should he first have her here? Not yet. He wanted to seduce her with crude, human methods, nothing easy—unless she proved too obstinate. He'd risk the headache of breaking the oath, though he'd far rather strip her and take her naturally pliant.

In the meantime, he'd play by her rules and tell her truth, usually. Though lying had never struck him as particularly odious, she, like most real knights, seemed to dislike it, oddly enough even in herself. Sarkany would try on a new skin, see what it felt like to be a knight, without the bother of a real change.

She shifted uncomfortably as she looked around the nest. *Bedroom,* he corrected himself. Even without the bed. Was she imagining herself lying naked on the cool pile of treasure? He was.

"It doesn't feel as if anyone lives here," she said at last. "I wonder, do dragons have a personality?"

His turn to experience discomfort. In all his years, no one had asked a question like this, and an answer didn't come easily to him. Not even a lie. "I'm not sure I understand you," he said at last.

She waved a hand at his collection of objects. His treasure. "You have a lot of valuable things, but they don't seem to be important to you. They're just there in a jumble, as if it were a store, and not for looking at and enjoying, I mean." She shrugged.

Sentimental nonsense. He had more personality than any short-lived human could imagine. Personality. What the hell did that mean? New-age twaddle. But far inside him the tiny spark had ignited again. The tiny part of *being human* that he admired. Was it personality? Was that the word? All part of the silly admirable bravery?

He didn't have any wish to discuss this with his opponent, for she was that, of course.

"Miranda." He put as much into the word as he could, without using magic.

She started and turned to him, even took a step closer to him. The light coming though the window shone on her hair and clear skin, and he resisted the urge to run his hand over the soft texture and feel the tingle of her. He loved human hair and wished he could bury his face in the waves. Soon.

"Do you know I have never invited anyone into this room? Not even the cleaning staff. No wonder I've kept it secret. The first woman to enter tries to tell me where I've failed as a human. Shall I show you where I excel, my dear Miranda?"

She grinned and he nearly fell over. The female had a gorgeous smile. Why on earth didn't she use it more often? She must know it held power. "Dragon. Thank you for showing me your private space. Let's finish the tour of your lair and then we will work."

She'd turned him down, and easily, too. And she'd taken charge. He'd allow it for now.

Her pulse was nearly steady now and her breathing calm. Something had caused her to relax. This could be good, but he wished he knew what had done it. His nest and its lack of... Blast, he wouldn't obsess about the word any longer.

He led her through the rest of the place. Kitchen, bathroom, nothing particularly interesting but she was fascinated, walking into the shower area, opening the cabinet over the sink.

"So you use soap? And shampoo?"

"I am as human as you are, silly woman. In fact, I believe I am growing some gray hairs. You're responsible, I'm sure."

She pulled out the bottles of cologne people had given him and, closing her eyes, inhaled each of them deeply. "No," she said at last. "None of them smell like you. They're all too sweet or fruity."

The thought that she knew his scent created a strange sense of elation and the impatient excitement deep in his belly. New sensation was always interesting, though he rather resented the fact that a human was responsible.

"Oh, and what do I smell like?"

"Your soap, of course. I thought you'd smell like a snake, but no. You've got the scent of the wind off a mountain, mountain air in winter," she answered at once.

Was she trying to seduce him? Lovely to know she'd been thinking about his scent. Bad that the fact only increased his interest...oh, foolish Sarkany. He almost laughed aloud. Of course she'd gotten that twaddle from dragon lore. He really had to be careful.

In the kitchen she opened and closed cupboards and held the dainty wineglasses and fragile china up to the light. "They're so pretty," she said. "Do you use them? Do you eat off plates?"

"I am capable of your version of good manners."

"I see chopsticks, but no silverware?"

"Yes." Sarkany decided not to tell her that the flavor of metal spoiled food for him. Wood he could tolerate. Ivory or most other bones actually lent a savory hint. But bitter, biting metal... No. He didn't need to remind her how different he was from her. He led her back to the first room and waved a hand at another door. "There is another meeting room, like this with fewer windows, and then the rooms for my assistants. They're there now. Shall I introduce you?"

"I met one of your drivers and Mr. Pettifer, and I'd probably recognize some of your other, um, servants. Not now, thanks. Maybe later."

"Yes, if you manage to destroy me, they'll be no threat."

She winced. His campaign to capture her sympathy might be working. Really, humans could be manipulated easily, even the ones with strong moral codes, though he rarely bothered with them.

In fact, this was the first time he'd attempted to seduce a female by evoking her compassion for the poor, lonely dragon. It had struck him as beneath his dignity but perhaps it could be fun. No human he'd met understood the dragon's notion of dignity, though he wondered if this one could. Perhaps once he had her firmly in his possession, he'd experiment with explanations.

She'd probably no longer interest him after he won the challenge. He'd set her up in one of his domains as a servant. It would serve her right if he put her in a lair he'd locate in her city—a lair he'd purchase later because, of course, he would win. A bitter lesson that she should not attack a power she could not comprehend.

Her back was to him as she stood examining the painting of the mountains, her hands stuffed into the back pockets of her worn jeans, one hand only partway in because of the bag with the bloodstained cloth.

He enjoyed their interactions; perhaps that's why he didn't feel the usual thrill of satisfaction to think of her conquered and added to his collection. Although then he'd dress her in fine silk or nothing at all. He'd be able to taste her and feel her naked skin, and play with that lovely moist opening to her body any time he wished. Kiss every one of those lovely moist spots of hers. Yes, that would be satisfying.

He detected her sex now and again, and her sweet muskiness of desire. The aroma had increased, even when he didn't attempt magic. Pleasant to know he'd drawn excitement from her with no real effort on his part.

He wondered if she shaved her feminine parts. A silly habit. Rough or silky, curling human hair was so delicious and held scent so—

"Mr. Sarkany? I think I'll go downstairs and get another cup of coffee if you don't mind." She'd turned from the painting and was examining him, her mouth quirked into a half smile.

He frowned back at her. "When did you start calling me 'mister'?"

"When you didn't answer me the first time I said something."

"I'll go with you."

He obviously needed fresh air.

She shoved the papers into her jacket pocket and seemed impatient to go. He waited outside while she bought her coffee and apparently some food.

"We could take a walk." She licked a dollop of cream cheese from her finger and he forgot to answer for a moment. He looked forward to the taste of her skin—he imagined her fingers against his tongue. Ah, not just fingers, no, she would be utterly delectable everywhere.

She zipped up her nylon jacket, a cheap and shabby garment, though the blue did match some of the light in her eyes. "We'll go to one of the last parts of the city you haven't bought yet. Do you want to bring a bodyguard or something?"

"Oh, I might be in danger, but I doubt it. I'm a very popular man in this city." He smiled at her scowl.

"Then why do you employ bodyguards? It's hard to imagine you'd be afraid of humans."

"I'm not afraid, but I don't want to be arrested for murder. I could get carried away."

"Oh." He could almost hear the words she didn't say. *Bloodthirsty animal.*

"I am jesting with you. I keep my assistants so I won't have to interact with any more humans than is necessary. I'm solitary by nature, as you must know from your studies."

She shivered, and this time he supposed it was with cold. He nudged her arm. "Let's walk." He couldn't help teasing her some more. "Did you know that other cities court me? They want me to pour my money into their rotting downtowns. They beg me and offer enticing tax breaks so I can build a stadium or a project."

"I'm not surprised." She strode along, keeping up with him easily. "From the outside, your projects are like you. Beautiful. It's inside that there's...nothing."

"Clever woman," he said approvingly. "You would tear down my self-esteem and force me to weep confessions of my sins to you."

"No." Her eyes widened and she looked appalled. "I would hate it if you did that."

He put it on his to-do list at once.

"Instead of visiting the signs of my greed, let us find one of the institutions that might get the money I'm to give away."

"The challenge again." She gave him a puzzled look.

"Yes?" he asked.

"I don't understand you at all. I know you don't operate on whims. Dragons are usually the least whimsical creatures there are. But why you took the challenge, and so quickly, and why you're doing this..." She shrugged.

She had a point.

"Perhaps I have worn this human form so long I am one of you."

She laughed, but the sound wasn't ragged with dislike or mockery. He suspected she'd begun to like him. This should be a nice advantage for him until the moment she realized the fact herself. Then she'd have to punish him and herself.

"We'll go this way," she said, and they walked down a steep hill where single-family houses still stood, some boarded up, almost all in need of a paint job.

They passed several people and she smiled at them. This knight might contain power but she had a propensity to be warm-hearted. Not a useful habit for a warrior.

"Predictable location," he said, already bored, as they reached the bottom of the hill and pushed through the door of the Community Life Center.

"You've been here?" she asked.

"Of course not."

"No, no treasure here," she said mildly.

"Precisely." The scent of ammonia and unwashed bodies was far from delectable, but he was practicing meek and sympathetic, and decided to remain quiet.

Inside, three old silent men slumped on a bench. They'd probably occupied that spot so long they'd become part of the it. None of them looked up as Sarkany and Miranda walked down the hall.

A younger man, shaggy with beard and unkempt hair, shambled towards them. One of the homeless served, no doubt. The bear put out a hand and grabbed Miranda. Sarkany felt a growl gather in his throat, until he saw she returned the man's hug.

"Mira, Mira, how've you been doing?" The man snuffled on her shoulder in just the manner Sarkany wanted to. Sarkany could sense the man growing sexually excited. Miranda's body didn't change, not like it had the day before in her apartment or even during the tour of his lair. But he could imagine her radiance blossoming for this bear-man who didn't even call her by her proper name.

"It's great to see you. I'm fine, Pete." She pulled away but didn't let go of his hand and the smile on her face showed some of her glow. Sarkany felt a fierce stab of greed. He wanted that glorious smile for himself. Next time she looked in his eyes, he'd just insinuate a touch of command to get it.

No, no. He was absurd to break his own rules so quickly.

Miranda's smile vanished as she turned to Sarkany. "Pete runs the Center. He's been working here for almost ten years and he says in the last five years the numbers of homeless have tripled. They can't keep up with the numbers who need—"

The bear-man was gaping at him. "Jesus, Mira," he interrupted. "I mean, uh, sir."

Sarkany knew this wasn't a member of the guild, but the man recognized him. Plenty of people did. Sarkany extended his hand. "How do you do?"

"This is Mr. Sarkany." Miranda sounded as if she were apologizing to Pete.

Pete beamed at him and clasped his hand in both of his rather damp ones. "It's an honor, Mr. Sarkany. You've come to visit our facility at last."

"Only because of a bet," Miranda muttered under her breath so only Sarkany could hear. Clearly the bear-man's groveling annoyed her. She'd have to get used to unctuousness

43

once she was his. She might even try a little herself. He'd enjoy watching that.

"Would you like a tour?" Pete asked. "Please, please, let me, I'll just...I have to..." He scurried off to a cubbyhole of an office near the door they'd just come through.

"Seen enough?" Miranda said. Her hand made a generous circle above her head, indicating the walls. "So this center is number one on my list. Pete's a great administrator. Give them, oh, a few million. And maybe half your buildings."

He grinned at her flip tone. "You are a piece of work, Miranda Benson. How many more of these public servants do you want me to turn into...what are they called? Fat cats. That's what happens to most of them once they taste money and power."

He expected her to defend her large friend, insist that he couldn't be corrupted. Instead she shot him a sidelong look and said, "Oh, yeah, speaking of cats, I thought you might give money to build a home for stray felines. Three homes."

He gave in and played along. "What about the dogs?"

"Three for them, too, of course."

"Miranda. I beg you to take this challenge seriously. You saw the assets I must dissolve and distribute. It will be a tremendous task. And I warn you, almost every bit of it is in private holdings, yet many people will be seriously annoyed."

She cocked her head to the side. "Every now and then, I actually believe you'll do this. Usually I wonder what we're doing and why you're playing with me." She bit her lip and looked around. "And when you're going to finally get tired of the game and pounce."

"I thought I made it obvious why I'm playing." He had to tamp down the urge to grab her and yank her against him. The shabby little hallway was not the right place. "I can't stop the game midway through, you know. Not at all *pukka sahib,* as the Brits used to say."

She lost the troubled frown and looked at him with curiosity. "Did you know colonial India?"

"Of course. Think of the treasure."

Pete hurried over to them. He'd put on a crooked tie and a rumpled jacket that might have fit him when he was twenty or so pounds lighter. "Shall we start the tour? How about, um, the top floor? We have the job training unit and, um, GED classes."

Sarkany started to refuse, but realized Miranda watched him and expected him to say no. "We have a great deal of work to do, but if Miss Benson wishes to visit a particular area?"

"The kids," she said. "You mentioned something about kids, Sarkany."

He did? He couldn't recall. "Very well. Lead on, Mister..."

"Oh, yes. I'm Peter Leonard, sir. I'm sorry. Right. The children. Most of them belong to the students working upstairs and some of the, ah, homeless. Who haven't been tested or, ah, placed in the right schools. Right. Okay." Leonard strode ahead and Miranda caught up with him.

Leonard leaned close to her ear and murmured quietly—probably a range humans wouldn't hear. "You shouldn't be so rude, Mira. Do you know what that man's worth?"

She didn't bother to hold her voice down. "Oh, Petey. What is it you always say? Since when does money make someone worthy of respect?"

Leonard glanced nervously over his shoulder at Sarkany. Their eyes met and Sarkany took the opportunity to send a message... *She's mine. Don't touch her with sexual intent again.* He sent it politely, of course. His smile showed all of his teeth.

Leonard pulled away from her and almost broke into a run.

Miranda sniffed and allowed Sarkany to take her arm. "Known him long?" he asked.

She didn't answer. Sarkany went back to composing his list of confessions he'd pour into her ear while he wept. Maybe she'd take his head in her lap and stroke his hair.

"You look satisfied with yourself. Like you've just pillaged a surprisingly rich village," she said.

"Mm," he agreed and felt her shiver just a little bit. Exquisite hunger coursed through him. This was more fun than pillaging two villages.

The room full of children fell silent when they walked in the door. Bright light streamed through large wire-covered windows. *Not such a bad space,* he thought. *Perhaps too many little imps and not enough keepers.*

They walked through the room, stepping over plastic toys. The noise level slowly rose. One of the young ones whined. An older one snickered, at the out-of-place adults visitors, no doubt.

The stench of ammonia and false pine was gradually drowned out by one almost as obnoxious. Sarkany smelled disease and wondered which of them was ill. He'd long ago learned that young humans tended to spread ailments quickly but this was a particularly strong, abhorrent scent. He looked around the room and picked out the likely suspect, a listless creature sitting at a table with a picture book propped up in front of her.

"That scrawny one in the hideous pink nylon sweater. Yes, the one with the upside-down book. Why isn't she in a hospital?" he asked quietly.

Leonard and Miranda stared at him, and he realized he shouldn't know this sort of thing. All the more reason to avoid humans and suffering.

"Why do you ask?" Miranda whispered.

"She's sick. Surely even you can see it." The child's skin was yellow and pinched, her face too small or her eyes too large, and something worse than the usual infection lurked in her.

"She goes in for treatments," Leonard said, too loud, though the girl didn't appear to notice him as he went on about kidneys, livers, insurance and her expensive care. Sarkany had heard the sort of story before and paid no attention.

The book slid to the floor. The girl sat and stared at nothing. Sarkany made a disgusted click of the tongue. "They obviously don't even bother with enough medicine to drown the pain. And you call me inhuman," he muttered at Miranda, who didn't answer.

Leonard, too nervous to remain still, had moved onto another subject. He bustled over to another part of the room to point out some cracks in the wall. *More bleating for his aid,* Sarkany thought sourly. His life had been filled with meaningless cawing for his attention.

He gave a polite cough to attract the girl's notice, and the pain-blurred eyes met his. *Strength, you little bag of flesh and bones, don't let the bastard illness wear you away. Claw back. Wear vigor like a dragon's heart. You will be strong.*

The girl didn't smile, but her mouth twitched and perhaps some of the lines relaxed. "You said bastard," she told Sarkany in a sing-song voice. "That's a bad word."

"Is it? So sorry." He gave her a clipped nod and walked across the room to look at Leonard's dripping sink.

When he glanced back, the girl had reached for the book that lay at her feet. She propped it on the table and leaned her thin arms on the pages.

"I didn't hear you say 'bastard,'" Miranda murmured as he caught up with her. "What did you do to her?"

"None of your business," he said, annoyed by the whole thing. "I'll write a check and we'll go elsewhere."

A boy tossed a ball and, without thinking, Sarkany caught the object flying in the air in front of him. Too hard. It popped in his hand. "Damn," he said under his breath. He held up the flaccid blue object between two fingers. "Sorry, kid."

At once the boy began to howl and the other kids started talking excitedly.

Sarkany turned to Leonard. "Look, I need to get going, but let me just leave you with something."

Miranda had gone to the sobbing boy. An attendant hurried over, too, and the two women sank to their knees to talk to the boy.

Sarkany watched their useless efforts as he pulled out a checkbook. What had she said? Half of it? He grinned at the thought, but knew that the cash wasn't there. Yet. He could write something large enough to make Leonard scream like a little girl—or like the little boy who was still sobbing, although with less strength, now that Miranda was doing something clever with a hand puppet.

He ripped out the check and handed it to Leonard, who went pale.

"Two million dollars?" Leonard didn't scream. He tugged at his tie and seemed unable to get a good breath. "Two million? Oh, God. Sir. But. Ah, do you. I can't take this without some planning. The board. Oh. God. Earmarked. Where do you want it to go?"

"Get the boy a new ball and get that skinny one something for her pain. She needs it. Let's go, Miranda." Sarkany wanted away from this surfeit of gratitude. Often he'd enjoyed and even basked in creatures' delight, but he was not in the mood at the moment.

Leonard hurried along beside him, his voice still coming in little pants. "I have to call the papers. This is amazing and we can use the publicity for our halfway homes for—"

Sarkany stopped. "No," he said. "Don't."

"We shouldn't use it for the homes? Okay, sure. I understand. How about—"

"Don't call the press. Just spend the damn money anywhere you want."

# Chapter Six

"That was very odd," Miranda said as they went out into the fresh air. "Why did you do that?"

Sarkany purposefully misunderstood her. "You're the one who set the challenge."

"No, I suppose you wrote the check to show me you're serious. I mean with the ball. And the girl."

"The ball was pure instinct, and I did nothing to the girl." He should have told her. No doubt she'd approve, but he didn't want to allow her to see too much. She was his enemy, he reminded himself. He'd learned not to underestimate enemies.

"Do you know, I've heard that dragons are excellent liars, so there must be some reason you're trying to pretend you don't want me to know."

"Now, that is hard to follow."

"Liar."

"Miss Benson, I believe you're flirting with me."

She pondered this for a moment. "You might be right. I think I'm less afraid of you, too. I wonder why."

"My charm?"

She laughed—a raucous sound, not even close to the practiced polite titter of the polished women he interacted with. "I think it has to do with the way you looked so appalled after you popped that boy's ball. Not your charm. Your charm is one of the most frightening things I've ever run across. Especially that thing you do with your eyes."

Damn it. "You have nothing to fear. Remember? You hold the blood oath in your back pocket."

"I have to look up that oath thing," she said, sober again. "On the walk over here I remembered reading that dragon blood would burn me, so I know you didn't give that cloth to me for my sake."

He smiled and grasped her arm again. "Smart girl," he said approvingly. "Do look it up, though. I'm sure there's something about blood oaths. Very common habit between serious enemies like the guild and my kind."

She wrinkled her nose. "Surely you have other things you should be doing instead of telling me this nonsense."

She liked plain speaking so he decided to indulge in some. "Yes. Let's go to your apartment," he said. "I'll make phone calls and send faxes to start the process of giving it all away and then we can make love in any room you wish."

"Make love?"

"Certainly. I just gave your favorite cause two million dollars. I deserve a kiss or two. I would love to taste your body. Kisses everywhere you like. It doesn't have to be flat-out fucking, you know, though that would be exquisite. I'm very amenable when it comes to making love. I'd be content with feeling your sweet flesh under my hand."

She made a squeak he knew was supposed to register disgust, but it was unconvincing. He'd have her soon.

"Have you lain awake and wondered what a dragon as man's body looks like? What it feels like?" he asked, delighted by the red that had risen to her face. "My skin is warmer than yours. I possess less hair than your friend Pete. Is he hirsute all over?"

She pulled her arm away and managed to turn businesslike. "Sarkany. I am not interested in discussing this with you. We'll return to your apartment and you can do your— your work or whatever you have to do there. Unless you want to see the other locations I have in mind."

He wrinkled his nose. "One reason I enjoy high altitudes is that I can avoid crowds. I can still watch the interesting creatures but I don't have shove my way through them."

"A pity not everyone has that choice."

He wished she didn't wear such a high-collared shirt, but still, he could rest his hand on the nape of her neck. "Yes, indeed a pity."

Under the cloth, her pulse quickened nicely at his touch.

"I know," he said. "Let's get the car and drive to your old neighborhood. You can tell me all about what a scoundrel I've been."

She stopped dead on the sidewalk. "It's not funny," she said, sounding almost apologetic. "You have no idea what it was like, fighting against the tide of your machine. Heartless. Useless changes."

"Why do you say that?"

"Our city was fine." She tucked her arms tight around herself as if sealing out the cold or the awareness of him. "Not grand or beautiful. But it wasn't dying. And then you killed it."

He laughed. "You make it sound like the inhabitants are my prey."

"Believe me, trying to survive here has felt like that sometimes. Come on, I'll show you." She grabbed his hand, no doubt to give him an impatient tug, but she clearly felt the sudden burst of sensation. His blood fired, too, as fingers and palms touched, wrapped together.

Miranda froze. She looked down at their clasped hands and then into his eyes.

"Yes, you are showing me." He inhaled deeply and looked away from her wide, startled gaze because he wasn't sure he'd be able to stop himself from mesmerizing her. "Very nice."


Miranda and Sarkany walked next to the several-acre site that was to be a multiplex and shopping area with lovely tall structures of arching glass. Who wouldn't admire such buildings? He didn't bother asking Miranda.

She told a good story. She talked in a quiet voice about the dead neighborhood, pictures of human activity that Sarkany had never witnessed. He found the descriptions amusing—block parties, bike races, people washing cars on sunny days.

"Over in that deep pit with the big pipes—" she waved a hand, "—that was my best friend's house. Her parents had to leave the area when their furniture store closed down. They couldn't afford the rental prices you charged—and everyone else charged when they saw what you got away with."

She grabbed the wire fence and stared through at nothing. "You did nothing to help the people who'd spent generations here. The money they got was pathetic. I don't know how much you paid the politicians. Every one of your projects is eminent domain abuse at its worst. And the newspaper? Your puppets own that, too, so there's no one left to protest."

He nodded and listened. He even felt a twinge of her sorrow as she described the way her mother had desperately tried to find ways to hold onto their life. But at last she was silent.

His turn.

And he suspected that because she'd been overburdened with a sense of fairness, this would be easy. "Do you know what was here before your row houses?"

She looked out of the corners of her eyes. He did enjoy those sidelong examinations of hers—Miranda trying to hide her fascination with him. She thrust her hands into her pockets and continued to stroll next to the wire fence. "What?"

"I find it interesting to learn the history of my domains."

"Tell me," she said. Her shoulders hunched as if she knew what was coming and tensed herself against it.

He assumed the manner of a lecturer. "We shall start with the first humans. Indian tribes that showed up, oh, about eight thousand BC. The later natives who lived here and left their trails and records called the area the Meadows, although much of the land a few blocks north was swamp."

"Yeah, I remember this stuff from fourth grade." Her back relaxed slightly.

Not for long.

"Do you, then? Perhaps you recall how the wetlands were destroyed, and the creatures that lived there were driven out. Did your teacher tell you if the settlers did anything to help the other humans adjust to the huge changes? The people who'd lived here for generations?"

She stopped walking, and looked up at him. Something like panic filled her eyes as he continued, "The human tribe died out. Most of them died in the winter of 1670 when they were driven off their lands without enough supplies to last the winter. From what I understand, the squirrels and raccoons are really the only creatures remaining that thrived once your people took up residence. And dragons flourished, of course. "

He smiled at her and waited. She opened her mouth. Then closed it. "Forget it," she said. "Forget the whole thing. I can't do it. Someone else will have to go hand-to-hand with you." She blinked and looked away again, over at a huge pile of dirt and an empty bulldozer.

He frowned. "What? You're talking nonsense."

"You win. It's that easy. Damn it, just give it all away and move into my life or don't give any more of it to anyone and whatever you do is fucking fine. Forget the stupid challenge." She strode quickly away from him. He scowled after her for a moment, then went to the construction site, where he found her leaning against a wall, her face buried in her crossed arms.

"What kind of weakness is this?" he said, disgusted.

She wasn't crying, but her face was drawn tight when she looked up at him. Despair. "Sarkany. It was bad enough when you used the dragonspell of attraction. And then when you did whatever you did with the girl at the center. It made me think you had actual feelings. But this is the worst of all."

"What?"

"You're right." Tears came into her eyes. "The creatures, the people who lived here before. No one cared about them. We are just as bad as you. We are as ruthless. Worse. We destroy our own species."

He gave a click of impatience and pulled her away from the wall, into his arms. She wrapped her arms around him and leaned against him. Her embrace felt even better than he'd imagined, but he was too irritated to enjoy it at the moment.

"Fight, dammit," he said. "You're no fun if you don't fight."

She stiffened. "Perhaps being fun for you isn't the main goal of my life."

"That's it." He patted her on the back. "Get angry again."

She sniffed and rubbed her face against his shirt. "You're being nice," she said, and he was glad to hear the note of surprised laughter.

"Am I?"

"Yes, you're hugging me and you're being nice."

"I like holding you. You're a perfect size for this shape of mine." He pulled her a little closer. "See?"

"Yes." She sighed. "Hell if I know how you do it. I was so determined. Focused. And you've reduced me to this." Her arms around him tightened. He forgot his irritation.

He put his face in her hair and breathed in the enchanting scent. He pressed his hands up and under her shirt. Ahh, the flesh he found at her waist was sweet to touch.

Once, long ago, he'd discovered swimming, and the first time he'd dived into the icy lake and felt the ambrosial water surround him he'd wanted to swoon with pleasure—though dragons don't swoon.

The feel and scent of her reminded him of that experience. He hadn't dived in yet. Oh, he couldn't wait. But he wasn't entirely satisfied. This part was too effortless. She was something of a disappointment, how easily she caved in.

What had she said? Her kind was just as ruthless and horrible as he was? This wasn't really a conquest, yet. Ha, he'd rid himself of this realm and show her how considerate he could be—without showing his secrets. He wanted her to worship him, to look at him with the same light she'd looked at Pete Leonard and those children.

But first he'd take her home and turn her into his wanton creature. He wondered how much sexual experience she had, though he didn't particularly care as long as she'd regain some of that strength of hers. He longed for a more strenuous battle with this knight.

Her apartment, he decided. He'd only take her in his lair after he had a proper mat to protect her fragile human form from the hard marble of his nest—and once she really had been properly defeated. This didn't count. This couldn't because he wasn't done playing.

He tore himself away from the delight of her skin. They both sighed.

"I offer another challenge," he murmured. "There are still people you care about who're displaced, yes?"

She nodded slowly. The spark in her eye had returned.

"You allow me in your home and allow me to touch you any way I wish, and I will stop construction on the Meadowglen."

"You have to give it up anyway. The original challenge stands."

"I'll build something first and use my considerable influence to change the project into whatever you please. No stalling around, the way another developer might have to. And then I'll hand it over. Such a generous move to allow your old neighbors to prosper, and all because you allowed me access to your lovely body. No pain. No trickery. Just a sweet exploration of you. I gave the blood oath."

She rubbed her face with the palms of her hands. "You're giving me an excuse, aren't you? Because you know I want to."

He grinned. She would surprise him again and again with her lack of guile. "If that's so, why don't you give in?"

A slight breeze ruffled her hair. "I don't want your dragon poison."

"Nonsense, I won't put poison in you, but I fully intend to put something of mine in you." He had to pause as sharp desire roiled through him. "Oh, you will enjoy it, my Miranda. And so will I. I'm sure your guild members would tell you that you must appease me and my harmless whims."

She snorted. "Harmless? They would tell me to run—or run you through with something sharp."

He smoothed his hand over her hair and allowed his palm to brush her cheek at the same time. "What will you do?"

She closed her eyes. "I can't think when you're near me."

"Don't think, then. Just let yourself enjoy."

"Sarkany," she whispered, and he knew this battle was nearly won, too, though he couldn't bring himself to regret this easy win.

They walked in silence to her apartment. For once the dragon didn't push, didn't touch her or tease.

She excused herself and made a call on her cell, hidden in her bedroom.

"Linus, I need help." Without going into any other details, she described the blood oath.

She could barely stand the glee in his voice. "He gave you one? God, this is better than I expected, and I had faith in you and the...well, anyway. Don't touch the cloth. It'll burn you."

"I remembered that."

"Keep it hidden, Miranda. In a dark place. Oh, fantastic work. Anything he links to that blood oath will cause him pain to break. You're doing great."

She went to the living room where he waited, no sign of impatience on his unreadable face.

With a trembling hand she unzipped her jacket. "The apartments. Low income." He took a step toward her and she held up a hand. "Not yet. Make the calls. Promise on your blood oath. And..." Her voice trailed away. "Yes. I'll let you touch me."

# Chapter Seven

A half hour later, Sarkany put down the phone, and across the room, Miranda clicked the extension off, too. "They think you've lost your mind," she said without dropping her steady gaze.

"I have." He stood and walked to her, slow careful movements. A predator trying to keep the prey from starting and running. Her heart thumped hard but not just with fear. God, at last. At last.

For an hour, she'd said.

"An hour with the blood oath not to cast any sort of spell on me or harm me."

"Nothing more than you've done to me," he whispered in her ear. "My sweet knight." He slid his flattened hand along her spine. His voice died away as she found his mouth and pulled him into a kiss, greedy hot followed by more kisses. Hands explored and each touch brought a gasp.

She ran her fingertips along his muscular side, over his belly, pulling out his crisp shirt. No hair, silk over the iron muscles. "You were right. So warm. I love the feel of you, Sarkany. More."

He tightened his hold, pressing her so close she couldn't breathe. She squirmed in his grip. He loosened his hands at once and mumbled, "Sorry."

She even believed he meant it. Grabbing his hand, she hauled him to her bedroom. "I want you. No more clothes."

"Miranda." He reached for her shirt and yanked it off her body. She lifted her feet one at a time as her shoes, her jeans, were all shucked expertly.

She sprawled naked on the bed. He lay next to her still fully dressed except for jacket and tie, which had gotten lost somewhere near the couch.

"Time for you to get naked," she said, unbuckling his belt. "Please."

Sarkany pulled away. He smiled, but his eyes glittered dangerously. "You don't honestly think I'd expose myself to a member of the guild, do you? The scale remains secret."

She was confused for a moment then recalled the lore. Another bit of information that Linus had right, apparently. The single scale he retained for his power. "I forgot." She laughed without humor. "Unbelievable, Sarkany. I only thought of this and this." She touched his mouth with her fingers, and reached to stroke his belly and through his trousers his long, extremely hard cock.

He groaned and pushed against her fingers.

She moved closer to him, impatient to feel the heat and shape of his body. "Touch me, then. Your skin on mine where you want. Anything you want." She closed her eyes, moved in for another kiss, only pausing to sadly smile and ask, "Have you ever in all your long years met a worse knight?"

"Never." His kiss was almost tender. The next tasted more demanding. And then he slid down her naked body. Swift, relentless and determined in his apparent goal to savor every inch of her with his fingers, and mouth.

He licked her belly. "Hold still," he commanded

She twisted from his loose grip on her thighs. "No. I can't. I don't want to. Dragon, come up here."

He ignored her pleas and grabbed her legs again. She relented when his warm hands coaxed her legs apart and he flicked his tongue over her clitoris. "I've dreamed of this, my morsel," he said and went to work, sucking and licking with relish. "I've promised myself a feast of knight. So rich. Yes, curls."

The tingle of his stroking tongue added to growing waves of relentless pleasure. "Dragon," she cried out. "Here."

He kissed her knee. "Oh, very well. I obey."

And the kisses worked slowly back up to her mouth.

He'd managed unfasten his trousers, and his hard cock grazed along the trail left by his mouth.

He rested much of his weight on her, and their kisses began again, saltier and wet now. Her eager writhing had turned serious. She pushed against him, growling with need.

"Now." She reached down and grabbed his thick, unyielding cock to put it where she needed him. He slid over her, teasing, but not into her pussy.

"Beg," he whispered.

"I have, dammit."

"Give yourself to me."

"Sarkany." She reached between their warm bodies and squeezed him tight. His cock throbbed and swelled in her hand, grew warmer.

His eyes staring into hers narrowed. She whispered, "You beg me."

He said nothing but gently, persistently pushed. She wanted him too much, so she moved her hand and he sank slowly into her. Her breath went ragged as he pushed so far inside her. Lord. She would never be able to escape. "Never. Oh. Never. Beg. Please." Nonsense words she barely noticed speaking poured from her, as she writhed, impaled, skewered, penetrated by solid heat.

He cupped her butt, his large hands holding her as he relentlessly pressed deeper, filling her. He stopped at last. Each made tiny tentative motions that made the other moan. Inside her he seemed to grow, pushing her to the verge of too much again. She opened her mouth to bellow against his cloth-covered shoulder. But then she tilted her hips. More.

"Wait," he commanded, and then something shifted, no, a tangible shiver passed between them, warmth rising from where he lay unmoving, buried deep inside her. As if he'd orgasmed and the heat from his come spread. But he hadn't. This must be something different.

The tingling in her skin grew, and every inch he'd kissed felt the touch of him again. More than tactile sensation, her body opened to something more. Taste? Scent?

"Oh, it's perfect," she moaned. If he moved again, the sensation would throb through her. She craved it. Greedy as a dragon, clutching for it, she hitched her body up and down as far as his hands holding her firmly would allow her to move. Just out of reach.

"Dragon, dragon. Give more to me."

Sarkany couldn't believe it. The first and only time he'd allowed his natural urges full rein with a human, the seasoned whore had screamed and passed out.

He hadn't made that mistake again. When he kept his senses restrained, his cock wouldn't grow too large or release the dragon's essence of *vishaya* that sharpened the pleasure for him and his partner.

He'd intended to intimidate his delicious knight, make her feel the taste of his power, only a hint of the *vishaya* that could be poison. He craved her heat around him, but he also wanted to push her to a swoon, watch her weakness. When she reawoke, he'd gloat and they'd retreat to the pleasant, less passionate or punishing love play he enjoyed with humans. But she wanted more?

He hauled himself up on his arms and pushed tighter. Harder. Not checking his motion. Her cry was nearly a shriek, but instead of passing out, she wrapped her legs around his, wiggled around him, even thrust up to meet him.

He cursed in an almost forgotten language. Not since Flame had he allowed his body such lease. With one hand, he reached down and pushed off the trousers that hampered him. The sensation of skin to fragile skin was too irresistible and he fumbled with the shirt and yanked it over his head, ripping the cuff-linked sleeves.

Her heart thudded against him, throbbed from her body straight into his.

They rolled, writhed and cursed as if locked in battle. Her arms tightened around his torso, so hard he exhaled with a grunt. He rubbed his face against her neck and bit the tender spot at her shoulder. She cried out and he felt her pussy spasm.

He shuddered as her sheathe tightened around his cock and her thighs gripped his human form harder. But he still held back, and the tension made him tremble with the need for release.

"Sarkany, oh God." Tears streamed down her cheek.

He slowed to a more gentle pulse in and out of her.

"I hurt you? Miranda?" He was dismayed to discover true concern that he might have harmed her. He began to pull out of her. Slowly, carefully, though all he wanted was to drive into her, bury himself in her flesh.

"No, no. Stay," she gasped and her heels pounded against his ass. She arched up again. He must move deep inside her.

Less than a minute later he wouldn't have been able to stop even if she begged him.

He gripped a handful of her lush hair and devoured her mouth, to stop his roar of triumph.

"I feel it," she yelped and then babbled. "You're coming. It's wonderful, hot. I didn't know. I didn't know."

He didn't, either.

She murmured something about "wonderful" and tucked her head against his chest. Her body seemed to fall into a swoon. Still deep inside her, he could feel the throb of her heartbeat around his cock.

"I love your skin. I worship your lovely body, your sweet cunny. You have won this round," he crooned, but so quietly she couldn't hear. When he managed to untangle his limbs from hers, he revisited his favorite discoveries of her body.

Sweat-slicked skin tasted sweet beneath the salt, he decided as he sampled her nipple, which hardened against his tongue. Such a charming shrinking of the areole into hardness, he had to play with those nipples until she moaned and moved, restless again.

Her fingers curled through his hair. "I did this to get over you," she said. "I wanted to satiate the hunger and move along. It hasn't worked. Dragon, I can't be lost this easily."

"Why not? I have been captivated by you, too. Turnabout."

"I vowed to defeat you. I can't believe I'm that—that vulnerable."

She sat up and he rested his head on her thigh, close to the darker curls covering her pussy. He breathed in the feminine musk of arousal and completion. And now arousal again. The scent he left in her only added to the best of cycles.

"You vowed to rid your city of a nuisance. I've agreed to go."

"Why?" She put her hand in front of his questing mouth, but he thrust his tongue between her fingers. She giggled but he hadn't distracted her. "Why has this been so easy?" she persisted.

Very well, he'd allow his hands to taste her. She leaned over him, her eyes wide. "I feel that now. It's as if I can feel you touch me. It's—it's…" She groaned. "You put a dragonspell on me. Either that or I'm a poor excuse of a knight to give in just for a little pleasure."

"Why should you be any different from any other mortal creature? We appreciate our pleasure and those who provide it." At last he managed to nose past her fingers to her slick opening, the sweet flesh of her thighs. "You have also pleasured me with your power. You are the best of knights, my Miranda."

He tasted and smelled her delicate flesh again. Ambrosia.

She whimpered and shifted to reach her hands under his arms. He allowed her to distract him again. He forgot to worry about his scale or his enemy. He only wanted more.

They explored each other's bodies at a slower pace. She licked and sucked his cock then stopped to stare at him. She stroked her fingers over the round head.

"Am I too exotic for you?" he asked.

"Large, but not abnormal." She licked again. "Very tasty, but I wonder if you'd mind—"

"Please. Be my guest." He held his impatience at bay as she slowly climbed his body. The wonderful female could do this again—obviously she possessed a rare strength. He would allow her to take the initiative because he didn't want to use her up—yet.

Gingerly she held his cock and lowered her swollen pussy onto it.

He could feel her pain almost the second she did and her pleasure as she did. The sweet, slight human body was filled with sensation, and he wanted to explore each shiver and throb with her until the desire was too much and he forgot himself, plunging so hard they cried out together.

# Chapter Eight

Sarkany seemed to doze, so Miranda took the opportunity to sit up and examine his body in the gathering gloom, a stealthy exploration at first.

She wasn't even sure what the scale looked like.

Why did the guild care about the dragon's scale? She suddenly understood she wouldn't tell Linus even if she knew where it lay on Sarkany's body. She'd say nothing—at least until she knew what kind of weapon it meant against Sarkany.

Her goals had shifted. She didn't really have any, other than revenge for the end of the life she'd known. Her loyalty to the guild had melted away as if it had never existed. No, it was more she could not allow them to kill the dragon—even if he proved capricious and tricky, as she supposed he would, even if he managed to hurt her, as she knew he planned. She had made her vow to destroy him back when she thought of him as a mindless hoarder and nothing more.

She had her doubts about her vow as they visited the center and had abandoned it when he'd murmured that he worshipped her body. She knew he hadn't intended her to hear, he didn't understand what he'd created inside her. Every part of her, every nerve had soaked up the startling heat. Now the sparks had died to a warm glow but she felt changed. Renewed.

Giving up the hunt for his scale, she leaned back to admire the long lean limbs, and wondered if his strength and muscles came from this form or his true one.

"My heel," he said without opening his eyes. "Take a look."

She didn't bother to pretend not to understand. Instead she moved to him and ran her hand along his hard thigh, kissed his calf and, sure enough, a blue scale lay flat, yet jewel-like, on his heel. She traced the skin and the smooth surface of the scale. He watched and shuddered.

With a smile at his response, she rubbed the scale, tapped it, even put the tip of her tongue to it. It tasted of him and was only slightly warmer than his human skin, though harder.

She lay back down and snuggled into his arms. "I like the way it feels."

"While I'm alive, only I can take it off," he said in a warning tone.

She suspected that wasn't true, but she wasn't interested in stealing it. "In your other form? You're covered with that?"

He nodded. "Various shades of colors, but yes."

And you're larger?

"Much."

"I wish I could see that."

"No more challenges."

She sighed. "You must be lovely, though."

He frowned at her. "Are you all right?"

She shook her head. "No. I lost. I'm lost. Filled with dragonspell. You better go, Sarkany. We'll meet again tomorrow."

"No," he said. "I'll let you sleep and make some calls. We have our work to do."

She rolled onto her back and stretched her arms overhead, enjoying the ache of her well-used body. "It's late. Nearly nine p.m. We played for hours."

"I will reassure my people. They're not used to my unexplained absence. And I do business when I wish, Miranda. I am not a slave to the clock."

"Why do you want to stay?"

A small smile twitched at the corners of his mouth. "I enjoy this new game of human lover. Why should I stop?"

He put his hand on the curve of her breast, and rubbed his thumb over her nipple. She arched her back in invitation, and his clever mouth was on her breast, greedily tasting her, swirling and sucking.

He didn't start work until ten.

With a computer and the phone line, and a visit from a couple of his assistants, he had no need to leave. And apparently no desire.

Pettifer brought over fresh clothes in the morning and some documents to sign.

He glared outright at Miranda, who refused to look away.

Only Sarkany's cough flustered Pettifer, who left a thick folder along with the laptop.

Sarkany opened the laptop but watched her instead. "This is like existing in the back recesses of a cave. No windows, no views. Ah, wait." He leered at her breasts under a T-shirt. "I am wrong about the view."

She saw the direction of his attention and pulled off the thin white shirt. Closing the laptop, he stood and walked into her bedroom.

He slipped under the covers and lay on his back, his hands behind his head. "I rather like it. 'Cozy' is the word, isn't it? I hadn't comprehended the appeal, but with you in here, I appreciate the soft nest you make."

"You wouldn't fit in my bed, would you? In your proper form."

He gave her a sideways look. "You do seem to dwell on the subject, my pet. I suppose there's no reason I can't show you."

Panic filled her, and she sat on the edge of the bed. "No, please, I didn't mean it."

"I'm not going to transform, Miranda. But I can show you. If you'll allow me to access your mind."

"Huh. What you did that first day." She touched his muscular arm. "And what you did to that little girl, I'll bet. You put thoughts straight into our heads and we have no way to keep you out."

"Do you want me to stay out?"

She closed her eyes. "I don't know. But I'm a fool so..." She lay down next to him. "Yes. Show me what you look like. Hypnotize me. More than you already have, I mean."

"You have no faith in me," he said.

"Are you kidding? I'm such an idiot, I even trust you." She moved over him and kissed him, a slow and lingering kiss. A loving kiss. She couldn't help it. "Show me."

Clear and bright as glass, his silver eyes caught and held her gaze easily. She didn't fight him and stared back—but thoughts didn't worm their way into her mind. Then she realized the body next to hers was growing, changing form and color. The bed didn't shift, so she understood it was only an illusion. Otherwise the strange and terrible change seemed too real.

She looked at the large haunches near her shoulder—and the form melted back into a human body.

"You can't look away. You can only catch glimpses." His hand brushed her cheek to turn her face to his again.

"More than enough," she breathed, but stared into his face again.

Almost at once he grew and filled the space, the room, her whole vision. A monster and the most beautiful creature she'd ever seen. She reached out to touch him and felt soft human skin. The hunger for him sliced through her, and she closed her eyes and reached for the whole of Sarkany, dragon in human form.

For the next couple of hours, he worked. Sarkany hadn't lied when he said people would protest his plans to divest himself of his property.

"You owe me more of that luscious thing you do with your mouth," he said after he got off the phone at last. "There is some balking at changing the plans for Meadowglen. I had to promise exorbitant sums of money to all sorts of corrupt politicians. You are not a popular person with my assistants."

"I'll survive," she said and wondered how she would.

For two days they did nothing but make love, rest and eat. Sarkany turned off his phone, and then her answering machine filled up with messages for him, so she turned that off, too. She only left to pick up some food and, without telling Sarkany, she went to talk to Linus.

They met at a coffee shop. Linus bought her a cup of decaf, and even before they'd sat down at the rickety table, began asking questions about the dragon's scale and if she'd seen any special powers at work.

She bit her lip when a sudden image of the huge aroused dragon came to her mind. "I don't know where the scale is," she said. "Why do you want to know?"

He frowned at her. "You do know where it is. You've been poisoned by him."

She doubted he could read her face, but she'd decided to be honest. "I am probably under the dragon's spell, but that's why we're meeting here and not at the headquarters."

He didn't answer and she went on. "I know about the important goals. You probably do, too, if you read the public records. Heck, even the newspapers are reporting that he's divesting himself of local properties. He will leave, I'm more certain of it every day." She wondered if he'd drag her with him. And how she'd feel if he didn't.

"How much time do you spend with him? There are rumors that he's disappeared from sight."

"Getting rid of his worldly goods in this domain takes a lot of time. He's busy." And kissing every inch of her skin and screwing her brains out. And allowing her to sleep in his arms.

"Look," he said. "You be careful. You know he tried to burn you with his blood."

*He's burned me with worse than that.* She nodded. "I know he's a creature filled with tricks. He likes deception."

"Just keep that bone close to you and he'll be less likely to harm you, okay?"

"What does it do?"

Linus picked at a pimple. "It's a charm. I'll recite a poem." Very softly and with careful pronunciation of the strange old words, he spoke, *"The skinne scales of a dragon holds all brand of power for its kin and kind*

*"The blud burns enemies of his yet binds his oath*

*"The bone beckons to its proper mate and acts as a charm*

*"The tough flesh is of no earthly use to any one"*

She sniffed and picked up her coffee. "Not much of a poem. More like a guide to uses of a dead dragon."

"It's proven true. From what I can figure out, anyway."

The tough flesh was more than useful to her. She ached for it now. She swallowed the coffee and put a hand on Linus's shoulder, an affectionate farewell. "I'll be okay." She rose to her feet. "I promise. And if I'm not, at least I know the city will be."

He glared after her but didn't try to stop her.

She walked away quickly, fingering the smooth bone in her pocket, wondering what it did to Sarkany.

He'd never had a proper mate, Sarkany'd said grudgingly, giving into her questions one night. "I've come close," he'd added. "But no one remained in my blood." His smile had distracted her from that conversation.

She wished she could comb through Linus's files. She wasn't safe or sure enough to ask Sarkany. Not yet.

৪১৪১৫৪৫৪

Sarkany didn't need as much rest as his human did and he watched her sleep, greedily admiring her body. The curves, the marvelous soft skin. He stroked her hip and she burrowed toward him.

He eased away from her and got up. Instead of going to work, he took his time to look carefully at her belongings. Perhaps clutter wasn't to her taste, but she'd grow used to it. A dragon felt secure with his objects. Like her. She'd be one of his prized objects. He waited for the thrill of possession, but it wasn't as strong. She didn't fit the lists he drew up to gloat over.

He had to find where she fit, because he was on the edge of winning her challenge. Only two more buildings and few hundred thousand dollars remained to his name.

He'd appeased his advisors by transferring much of his property and treasure to Tia, who, he promised, would be as greedy as they were—and wealthy in her own right.

Was Tiamat an American citizen? They needed to know.

Of course. Just like Sarkany, Tia was a citizen of wherever she landed.

Miranda had rolled her eyes when she learned of that transfer, and he pointed out that he hadn't broken the rules of the challenge.

"I'd expected this," she'd only said. "I'm glad you gave the most to people like Pete."

For some reason he was glad, too. After all this time, humans and their concerns had gotten farther under his scales. He'd examine the reasons another time. Just now, he'd take a closer look at Miranda's *personality.*

He found photos on Miranda's shelves and on her computer. Smiling people, usually posed outside a shabby row house—no doubt the place his construction company had knocked down. He stared at the photos of people, laughing together. Humans were pack animals. He'd occasionally envied such creatures. Dogs, lions, humans. When he saw them at play he envied them most.

He clicked on Miranda's computer and easily accessed her privacy code. She'd kept notes on him for her guild, but then it had turned into a sort of journal. His body expanded with ridiculous joy when he read how she adored every self-important bit of him, Sarkany. He restrained himself from going to her and demanding she say the words aloud to him.

He scrolled back to the earlier entries and read more. And then he found entries about the bone—not a sheep's shank after all. An honest dragon's bone, that Linus insisted she carry. She had thought it nonsense—perhaps Sarkany had put that thought in her mind at their first meeting—but now she wondered what charm the bone held.

He read it again, his joy dissolving.

He only skimmed the rest. She was reassured that her love, her dragon, her Sarkany could not be susceptible to such a spell. The binding of what? He'd had no mate.

He sighed and clicked off the computer. And went to wake her up.

"Miranda. We have been tricked," he said as he slid down next to her. "The things you say about me aren't true. I'm not a pure-hearted lover."

She smiled at him. "You are a snoop, Sarkany. I love you anyway. And I don't care if love is an illusion because it makes me happier than I've ever been."

"It's like the drugs you humans seem to enjoy," he grumbled, but the sorrow in his heart was real enough.

"Yes, exhilarating like drugs. Like the tingle you enjoy when you eat chocolate. Or when you touch me or I touch you. It's the view from your mountaintop. It's all love but, oh, love with more. Another layer. So many more layers."

She kissed his neck. "So. You've gotten me to admit it and I like to say it aloud. I hadn't before, you know, to anyone else. I love you. I love you, my dragon."

"You are my knight?" he couldn't help asking.

"Of course." She studied his face and must have seen the pain. In a low voice she said, "I'd die to protect you."

"I've paid people to defend me. Lawyers, usually. My assistants. I don't want their love, just their protection."

"Too bad, I love you."

He wanted to talk her out of this, but had no idea where to start. "I don't want one of my possessions to love me."

This seemed to lighten her mood, not make her angry. "Possession. Ha. I looked through your list, but you don't have living possessions. Servants, yes. Minions, I'd believe. But you don't know what to do with me."

He started to speak but she interrupted, "And I certainly don't need your permission to love you." She stretched and yawned. "Why are you so afraid of this?"

"Chemicals," he said sadly. "Spells. It's the same thing, really."

"Is it because you've never had a mate? Sarkany, you needn't worry. I would never be so silly as to ask for promises. I am content to be your knight."

He didn't answer. Now was the time to end it. "I didn't tell the entire truth. I nearly had a mate," he said at last, watching her. "A dragon who called herself Flame."

A simple name.

Miranda went entirely still. All color drained from her face. Her lips parted but no sound emerged.

He understood the truth and now, apparently she did, too. He merely watched as he waited for her to speak, though he wanted to weep and rage like any human lover. Demand the truth from her.

In a faint voice, Miranda asked, "I—I am not sure how your kind bond. Why weren't you formally mates?"

"She died."

A whisper now. "How?"

"In the Alps she grew fond of domesticated mutton and raided the herds once too often. An enterprising shepherd with dreams of knighthood muddled the story of the wise man of Krakow. He dressed up as a sheep. She swallowed him, they both died when he set about her insides with a sword."

"Oh, Sarkany." She sat up and searched his face, frantic. "You loved her?"

"We planned to make hatchlings together. I treasured her company. There was none of this desperation that seems to accompany your version of love." He knew the answer but asked anyway, "Why do you look as if you're going to be sick, my pet?"

"Would something like a bone from her have power over you?"

He didn't answer. She studied his eyes for a long minute and was the first to look away.

"Shit." She sat up and her hair slid from her shoulders. "I've entrapped you. Sarkany, I must have. I didn't know. Truly, I hadn't understood. You are right. You—you haven't been attracted to me. I think. It hasn't been me after all." Honest and straight to the point.

He half-smiled. "Yes, I know."

She went to her drawer and pulled it open groped around for something. In her hand lay the gleaming white shard. "Flame," she said simply. "Linus once mentioned the name of the dragon this was from. Do you see? It hasn't been me. He knew your history. He knew you'd be attracted to her."

His laughter hurt his throat. "I never imagined I could be manipulated so easily."

"Why should you be any different from any other mortal creature?" she quoted his words back at him. "Oh, God,

Sarkany. I didn't know. Please believe me, I didn't. He wouldn't tell me a plan like that because he knew I wouldn't allow myself to be a part of it."

She walked across the room to him, and he knew what would come next. He hated it.

Lifting his hand, she opened his clenched fingers and put the bone of his ex-lover into his palm.

"It is disgraceful, all of it. I'm sorry." She stood shivering, but her chin was high. "Tell me what you want from me and I'll be glad to perform it. Even treachery for you, Sarkany. I meant it when I said I love you. Every part of you, especially your dragon heart. Your, um, affection for me has been forced from you, so I see why you'd renounce it." She reddened and murmured. "I hope you won't harm me."

She dropped to one knee, elegant and naked. She bowed her head. "Dragon, I pledge myself, my heart, my soul to you."

Once long ago, days ago, he'd imagined her groveling to him. The reality felt nightmarish. He supposed this meant he'd won the game. Without any magic—on his part at any rate. Only at the moment, he didn't remotely care for the entertainment of the challenge.

He pulled her to her feet and brushed his fingers across her forehead. When he touched the tear on her cheek, it burned even hotter than the bone in his hand, the bone that had created this interesting brief obsession with a human female.

Deep inside him lay the essence his dragon nature. He couldn't call it up without burning off his human form.

He couldn't do such a thing in her apartment. Outside, then. Time to be going. He had almost nothing left here, thanks to his own stupidity.

She gave a low moan but didn't follow him as he walked away from her.

He walked slowly down the stairs and outside clutching the last of Flame. He could almost picture her flexible dragon form. But in his imagination, as she turned towards him, she didn't have round silver eyes. They were blue-green and oval. Human.

"Blasted spell," he growled.

He realized he couldn't go far, nearly naked, so he walked to the alley behind Miranda's apartment. The scale on his heel stung briefly as he pulled it from his skin. He slid it over his throat, and his dragon blood scalded his tender near-human skin.

With a roar he sent out the blaze deep in his gut, and before the agony drove him mad, fire burned away his human form. His dragon self rose, dizzy from the pain and delight of freeing himself. The fresh scales covered him, hardening almost as soon as the heat died.

He still held the last of Flame. It took the strongest fire to burn a dragon's bone. He had enough of the human left in him to care about not setting the building ablaze, and he put the bone inside a large metal dumpster before loosing that heat. He blew hard. The bone flamed up, and the dumpster glowed orange and slowly collapsed in on itself.

He waited to feel the release from an enchantment—he'd been under them before—but still the ache remained where there had been something important. Hazel eyes looked at him with something he hadn't seen before. The radiance.

Enough. The end of Flame's bone should have brought about the end of the knight's hold on him.

No, not her spell. Linus was the name she'd mentioned more than once. If he weren't so tired and hollow, he would have visited the misbegotten Linus and reduced him to ashes.

He spread his wings and gave a tentative beat. The wind puffed around him as he raised and lowered his wings again.

From far away he heard the strange siren call of fire engines. Time to go. Past time.

But he wanted to shout his farewell to the realm he'd owned. He'd say good-bye to the strange victor, the only one who'd beaten him. Linus's second-rate scam? No, not him—the knight who'd made a mark on Sarkany. She deserved a farewell keen.

A few slow flaps took him to the top of the tallest building he could find. He roared his finest song to the woman. And then he left these haunts, beating lazy measures against the air, for it would take a long time to cross the world to his mountain, especially in his weakened state. He might have been newly hatched. His full strength would not return for weeks.

As he flew he remembered the truth. He'd actually won that encounter. She'd pledged herself to him.

If he'd won, why hadn't he punished her?

He flapped too hard and flew too high as he thought of his pet, his knight. She'd given herself to him, providing him a feast of passion. He couldn't recall exactly why he'd left her behind.

The answer was dragon pride, of course; he'd been caught by deception. Not that he minded a few lies, but these had nearly undone him and he didn't want to be reminded of that ignoble event. She was a pawn, yet so was the mighty and foolish Sarkany. Made silly by the madness of love, created by an old bone. Flame would have been extremely annoyed by the whole thing.

He stopped often on his flight back to his mountain the peak near Xixabangma in the Himalayas.

For a day he visited Flame's old haunts in the Alps. A crowded place now. Humans everywhere, pushing all other creatures out of their way. Why shouldn't he have pushed them around a bit, too? He argued with Miranda in his mind.

As he started again the next night, his thoughts still dwelt on the knight. The fever she'd caused should die away. The magic spell had been broken.

Then why did the image of her naked human form fill him with longing and a most embarrassing erection? She didn't even hold a form he should desire in his present skin.

Love, she'd said. And he'd been on the edge of believing until he understood the truth, that he'd been a moth to the flame, his long-dead Flame.

More than a hundred years ago, he'd swooped down and given his lost mate a proper end—except for the one tiny bone from her claw he'd missed, damn his careless scales. The mourning period for Flame had been long and painful, but it had faded. The spell of her bone should break far more quickly. Yet he still craved the female knight, and not as a snack.

Home on the lovely cold cliff, he relaxed his aching wings. He looked out over his favorite domain and recited words from his favorite human poet: "'Madam, you have bereft me of all words. Only my blood speaks to you in my veins; And there is such confusion in my powers.'"

He wasn't sure if he addressed Flame or Miranda, but he thought of the sweet pliant lips of a human on his mouth. The heat hadn't come only from Flame's bone, then. And he'd held Miranda afterwards. The one time he'd had the urge to stay and sleep and breathe with a mate, it had been her, not Flame.

Ah, well. He'd had won and lost treasures before. He still had the fine pile of possessions in his mountain realms where the sharp, thin air would cleanse human concerns from his mind and body.


The anger remained lodged next to the longing. Both of them were deep aches he wished he could heal by ripping off a scale or two and rubbing on the afflicted area. His groin or his chest or his head? But despite his morose mood, he didn't look for a cure. He told himself that would be as lazy as using magic in the wooing of his knight. That blasted bone was a bitter lesson to learn that deception in love created pain. He'd recover using his own strength.

And if he created a small nest of cloth and pillows in his lair, it was only a way to say farewell to that short, interesting episode.

# Chapter Nine

He'd arrived at the start of summer, when the rainy season pushed over the Jugal Himal. Nights and days of rain fell, turning his favorite meadows lush.

Within a month his sister tracked him down. She came to him as he lay sunning and brooding on the rocks by a lake far below his cliff dwelling.

Tia wore the form of a moth-eaten wolf. "No, not mange, merely shedding," she informed him with hauteur. She dug at her ear with a back paw and changed the subject. "You're sulking. That's a new unpleasant habit."

With her bothersome teasing, Tia soon infuriated Sarkany enough to reveal most of the story. He hoped he didn't say much more than a knight had gotten the better of him and he'd behaved like an idiot. He changed the subject from the knight to complain how he'd once been content as a dragon. The piling of possessions, the occasional flight and admiring the lake. He'd been happy.

Tia shook herself until the fur flew. "Nonsense. If you loved this life so much, why'd you grow restless enough to take on the human form? And then why, when human, did you take such a ridiculous challenge?"

And so he explained Flame's bone.

She laid her ears back in disgust. "Oh, you are as blind as a troll. Blaming poor lazy Flame's bone for your own stupidity. And the bone couldn't have caused such craving all these years later."

"Blast your fire." He sighed and rolled onto his back. His sister padded near him, circled and settled. He scratched behind her ears gently with his dagger-sharp claws.

"Not so hard," she barked. "You forget your strength. What will you do with yourself now?"

The wretch wasn't done plaguing him after all. He snorted a plume of smoke. "Remain here. Watch the sunset. Collect and steal treasure whenever I can. I'll be glad to abandon that frantic speed of the humans. Really, the whole rushing life. No wonder they die so soon."

She stood, circled again and rested closer to his warm belly. "Perhaps your foul mood is a sign you should find another mate. Did you ever think of that?"

"The process makes one into such a fool."

"I hardly recall you behaving like such a fool when you and Flame flew together. There was no indignity in that courtship. Besides, she was far too indolent for drama. Never mind arguing, Sarkany. Just tell me what your excuse is for your behavior now that you've destroyed the bone?"

He shrugged his wings.

The wolf showed her teeth and growled. "You are dull as lead. Do you believe that passionate love can occasionally be a permanent or at least serious condition?"

He yawned. "Love is fiction."

"So are dragons. You might be doomed. From what I know of you, my formerly chatty brother, you have been changed. Go and seize your treasure and retrieve your tattered soul."

"Do you suggest I destroy her?" He forced back a gust of insane and angry fire.

Tia only panted at him, a smirk on her doggie face.

Every scale on his body shivered, as he understood the truth. "Tia, oh, Tiamat. I couldn't kill her. I think I'd rather kill you. Or myself. Dear skies above, I must love her."

"Huh. Did you honestly believe any thinking, living creature could escape the trap? I mean any living creature, since *thinking* obviously isn't necessary."

He rolled away from her and plunged into the lake for a swim. When he came back, the wolf stood dewclaw deep in the water, a fish flapping in her sharp white teeth. An indignant crane watched from across the water.

She carried the fish to shore, ripped and gulped it down. After her meal, she drank some of the cold lake water, then continued her harangue.

"We might not run in packs in our usual form, but our kind isn't as solitary as we like to think. I'm delighted a soft little creature like a human has snared you." Water dripped from her muzzle as she looked up at him. "I'm tired of fur, and the pack is tired of me. Do you know their alpha male has driven me out twice? He's smart enough to know my real nature. A wolf guild member. Tell me more about your human female."

"No. You are annoying me."

"I see. You are clutching her as tight as any favored treasure." Her ears perked. "You've never been so reticent. What was her name?"

She must give up pestering him. A few more questions and he'd turn her into a charred wolf. "Miranda," he growled.

She scratched at a flea, then bit at the base of her tail. "I expected as much. It's a familiar name. It's appeared in an official human letter or two. Or were they emails?"

He forgot to be annoyed. "What are you talking about?"

"The property you insisted on giving me. They've tried to pull me into some sort of mess you left behind. My human assistants tracked me down and said I had to answer questions about your disappearance. And the main suspect is a female named Miranda Beesom or something. Why else would I escape to wolf form?" She yawned.

He resisted the urge to swat her, dagger claws out. "Miranda Benson. She's a *suspect?*"

"Yes, in your murder. I told them, nonsense, you're not dead. But they persist in believing you dead. Some sort of fire."

"They think Miranda killed me?"

"You are repeating yourself. Yes. That's what they think. But she's since vanished, too."

He loped across the lush meadow to the highest point and spread his wings.

"Going immediately?" His sister's tail wagged furiously. "This is interesting."

"Feel free to steal from my cave, although I've hidden the best from you." He pointed his face to the sun and tested the breezes that always blew this time of year.

"You still have the ring of Eustace?" she shouted, bounding after him.

"Yes, I'll fetch it first. But not for my knight."

He took to the sky and flew, pushing through the nights, and days, too, until he arrived at his old human realm on the other side of the earth, the small, shabby city in New England.

Weary from constant flight, he rested, then changed form in the barren wasteland next to the highway, hunched among the beer cans and other debris. He'd forgotten humans were such messy creatures. As he painfully peeled off each scale, he thought about his knight and hoped she wasn't a slob, but it hardly mattered. He'd been tamed and collared and tagged by her. He wondered if she still felt bound to him.

Pity if she didn't. To distract himself from the pain, he thought of possible challenges she'd pose for him and he'd pose right back for her. Nothing simple this time, he hoped.

At long last only the two scales remained on his bloodstained, healing body. They lay on his belly this time, where a sharp-eyed guild member might detect a scale. Ha, he'd go see about that Linus.

After he recovered from the change, he looped Eustace's arm ring over his wrist and found some clothes outside a gas station.

The fresh bare skin prickled and stung and itched with the touch of the rough cloth. He cheered himself with the idea of the sleek, usually well-dressed human Sarkany showing up barefoot and dressed in a mechanic's coveralls. At least they didn't reek of gasoline and other hideous automotive products.

He didn't have any of the proper key cards for his lair, but it only took one roar of anger before the chauffeur came rushing out to open the front door.

"It's you! Thank God, sir. It's been almost two months and—"

Sarkany pushed past him and jabbed at the elevator button. His feet ached from the transformation and from the long walk into the city.

The questions wouldn't stop, though. "Where did you go, sir?" Two other assistants remained. Apparently everyone else on staff had gone in search of other work. Only three had been retained to maintain his home.

"Your sister didn't know where you'd gone. Were you kidnapped, sir?"

That seemed as good an answer as any. He nodded. "I escaped."

Pettifer said, "That Benson woman. She was part of it."

He stopped and turned to face them. "Miranda Benson had nothing whatsoever to do with my disappearance."

The three men went on babbling and interrupting each other.

"The fire—"

"But she admitted she'd seen you—"

"We have to call the police at once and—"

He held up a hand and they fell quiet at once. "Call whomever you want but leave me alone for the rest of the night."

"What do you plan to do, sir?" They'd lost some of their training after all, the way they kept prodding after he'd silenced them.

"I will take a shower. Good night."

After a half hour under hot water and a reexamination of his human skin, he went to his office, where an astounding pile of mail covered the large desk. Opened and neatly stacked by subject, most of it appeared to be invitations to gala dinners in his honor. He was used to the pleading notes—he'd rarely seen the happy results of pleading rewarded. Giving away buildings and money had made him the most popular creature in the city.

The other stack was all about his disappearance.

He found Pettifer and told him to throw most of it away and to inform the mayor he most certainly did not want a street, a bridge or a park named after him.

At last he allowed himself to ask, "And what has happened to Miss Benson?"

A flicker of triumph in Pettifer's face. The assistant's thoughts were obvious: Sarkany didn't know and so Sarkany was stupid to protest her innocence.

"She disappeared, sir, soon after you did. And the group she'd been associated with turned out to be dedicated to destroying you. The leader disappeared at the same time she did." Pettifer did a poor job of hiding his disdain for the boss who'd been seduced by a hot female.

Sarkany ignored Pettifer. He understood at once: Linus had Miranda. He wondered if the dragon-hater was protecting her because she was some sort of suspect or if he was holding her prisoner.

His tender human feet already ached, but he wouldn't order the car to go explore the battered area near one of his projects. She'd mentioned a few details of this place to him—not on purpose, of course. During their brief time together she had eventually given every part of herself to him, but nothing of her fellow guild members. Not consciously, at any rate.

It didn't take long for him to discover the guild's headquarters. The unpleasant room was abandoned, empty, but he still had his sense of smell and he used it, hoping no one would see him occasionally kneel and try to pick up the scent. Just the smallest hint of her fragrance. He allowed himself a moment of dizzying lust as the vivid memories poured into his body along with her scent.

Back to the search. He squatted again. Linus was the sort who would stay close by—perhaps the man was even waiting for Sarkany.

He hunted until daylight, and then decided he'd best not be seen prowling the area.

At his lair, his assistants, lawyers and accountants wouldn't leave him in peace, so he was exhausted when night fell again. At least the calm, windless weather meant the scents stayed strong.

He'd rest and then pay a visit to the old triple-decker apartments where he suspected Linus lurked. Fresh scent of the man, not so new of Miranda. Damn.

Unfortunately, Linus would probably have learned of Sarkany's reappearance. The spokesman for the police department had accepted his bribe—the promise of a generous gift to the retirement fund so the authorities stayed quiet.

Someone else, however, didn't keep his or her mouth shut and alerted the local press. The newspaper decided to put his triumphant return on the front page.

Sarkany slipped from his lair early and went to the apartment house where he'd traced Linus. The first two floors were empty. The third. He pressed an ear to it and heard voices, a man and a woman. Miranda's angry shout.

He knocked and put his face next to the flimsy door. "I'm here. You've been expecting me?"

A sudden racket broke out inside the room. Shouts, rattling, clinking. Sarkany kicked the hollow door, which gave way with a giant crack.

Miranda.

He wanted to shout with relief. And then with anger. She wore nothing but a large man's dress shirt. Shackles on her ankles and wrists were attached to chains bound to the wall.

The cause of the noise was immediately obvious. One of Miranda's arm chains was wrapped around the throat of a thin, well-built young man.

"I came to rescue you, Miranda, but I should have known you wouldn't need me." Sarkany moved closer to the struggling pair.

The man snarled, though his face was red and he looked like he was on the verge of passing out from the pressure of the chains.

Miranda stumbled, and the man, who had to be Linus, whipped out of her grasp. He lunged for a huge sword and hauled it up over his head.

"Sarkany!" The man roared an impressive war cry. The silver gleamed as he raised the sword high overhead.

The clatter of chains against sword was startlingly loud.

Miranda wrapped her chains around the sword and yanked down. Judging from her agility with the chains, she'd been held prisoner for too long.

Linus swiveled to face her, swearing. "Miranda. Stop! You're still under the dragon's spell. Don't fight me."

Sarkany picked up a wooden chair and brought it down hard on the guild member's head.

Miranda dropped the sword—an even louder clatter—and she fell into Sarkany's arms. "You came," she sobbed against his neck.

The chains that touched him were clammy and burned against his skin, but she felt like heaven. He gently pushed her away.

He squatted and pushed Linus over to search his pockets. The room and the man reeked of male arousal and human sperm. No scent of female excitement, however.

Sarkany froze and looked up at Miranda. "Has he... Did he assault you?"

Jingling and crashing, she slowly slumped to the floor. "That's the first thing you ask?" she whispered, then shook her head. "No. He is a pure knight. He wouldn't touch me. Made me wear this stupid shirt though and stared at me until my skin crawled."

Sarkany continued the search. "Must wank off frequently then."

She sighed and stretched her legs. Small bruises patterned them. "I suppose it was to keep from touching me."

Sarkany found a ring of keys. Miranda wearily held her arm up so he could try the different keys, and he eventually discovered the one to unlock her shackles.

"I regret your troubles," he said as he released her legs from the chains. "My disappearance has proved a nuisance."

"It's your reappearance that made him do this." She waved a hand at the pile of chains on the linoleum floor and the crude restraints attached to the wall. "Before that, I was fine. Hiding, yes, but that felt more like a vacation than anything else."

She rubbed her wrists and ankles. Then to his dismay, she crawled over to Linus and pushed the lank hair from his eyes, far too caring a gesture to waste on such a fool.

She pressed her fingers to his neck, then felt the back of his head. "Good. His skull is okay. And his heart's strong."

"That's good?"

"I don't you to be a murderer."

He rose and dusted his hands on his trousers. "Would you turn me in?"

She stood and with wobbly steps walked to Sarkany. With a quiet sigh she sank to the floor by his feet. "No, never."

He thought about pulling her into his arms but dismissed the plan because he suspected her touch would prove distracting. Later. "How did you end up chained to the wall?"

"Linus showed up the night you left, when he heard about the fire. For once he didn't ask any questions. I guess the smoldering mess of the dumpster was enough and he thought you were...gone. The police wanted to take me in for questioning but Linus found a lawyer who pointed out there were no charges filed. And then he took me to a place in the country. He left me there and went off for a few days at a time. I think he was making plans to trap your sister if she came here." She wrinkled her nose.

"Tiamat can take care of herself. Why didn't you leave? It seems to me you allowed the idiot to decide your fate for you."

"After you left I was, uh, sad. And well, actually, I'd never spent time outside this city, and I loved it there in the woods."

That explained the golden skin, the sense of the outdoors that clung to her, despite the clammy apartment.

"After a while I was tired of hiding and wanted to come back to the city. We had an argument about it. Two nights ago, Linus must have put something in my food, and I woke up to find myself here and in chains. I suppose he discovered you were alive and back here and didn't want me to find out."

"You are all right?"

"I'm pissed off at myself for being careless. But yes, I am okay."

She rose to her feet again, collected some clothes from a plastic garbage bag on the floor and disappeared into the bathroom.

He considered following her, but decided to keep an eye on his captive.

Sarkany pulled the thin golden circle from his arm and slipped it onto Linus's. He waited and watched, though it would take hours.

She came out of the bathroom, brushing her hair. Color had returned to her face, which was thinner than he recalled.

The sight of her in shorts and a thin T-shirt that molded to her curves made his breath catch, but all he asked was, "Are you ready?"

She nodded. "Where will you take me?"

He didn't like this passive female. "I must deal with him."

"Oh." She went pale and her eyes widened. "Don't kill him."

Ugh. Perhaps she'd beg for the useless Linus's life. That would be repulsive. "Of course not. I have far worse plans for him."

"Please, no." She bit her lower lip and glanced at the sword. Perhaps she contemplated doing something to defy him. He supposed he should be pleased at any show of strength.

"It's too late." Sarkany pointed at the circlet on Linus's arm. "He's going to feel how it is to be hunted by the guild."

Miranda moved close to the unconscious man. She frowned and skimmed a finger over the circlet but didn't ask Sarkany what he meant. Instead, she went to three computers lined up on the wall. Calmly and methodically she lifted up each machine and smashed it against the floor.

"Why are you doing that?" he asked.

"He had hundreds of files about dragons and a bunch about you in particular. I wish I had a good magnet or at least a screwdriver," she said.

She wasn't so weak after all. He wondered if she was putting on the show to impress him.

When the computers lay in pieces on the floor, Sarkany gathered Linus up and easily slung him over his shoulder. "No point in waiting for him to wake. He'll be out for a while longer. Go ahead of me and see if anyone's around. There's a deserted warehouse near here that will do nicely."

She nodded and bounded down the stairs. Whatever Linus had done to her hadn't sapped her physical strength for long.

"Okay." Her voice echoed up the stairwell.

They walked quickly, almost trotting. Sarkany shrugged the weight of the young man further up his shoulder and shifted him so Linus's unconscious grunts didn't sound in his ear.

Miranda ran ahead to look around the corner towards the block of warehouses. She nodded and jogged back. "No one in sight. How long will Linus's transformation take?"

"Ah. You've heard of Eustace's ring. I wondered why you didn't ask."

"The last couple of days, whenever Linus went out, I looked at his computers. He didn't have a connection to the Internet but he still had a lot of information. I saw the story of the ring on there. He won't be a true dragon, will he?"

Sarkany slowed his walk. The dead weight on his shoulders was making them ache. Go through a transformation, miss a couple of nights' sleep and the human body went weak. "Semblance only. No fun powers."

The knight's face reddened—she was obviously was thinking of some of the fun they'd had with his powers.

Sarkany hid a grin. "If he's strong enough he'll be able to fly, and if he gets the ring off, he'll revert to human. Not such a terrible punishment, really. I restrain myself for your sake, of course."

Her step faltered and she glanced into his face—though she looked away again at once as if afraid of his eyes. "Oh, Sarkany. Thank you. Does that mean you've forgiven me for the deception?" Her tone was too eager.

He wondered if he disliked her groveling for her ridiculous friend even more than her passivity. "I didn't say that."

He tightened his grip on the unconscious man's ankle. Good. It was already thickening. Sarkany would be glad to leave Linus to his fate.

# Chapter Ten

Miranda couldn't stand another second of this wintry Sarkany. She jogged ahead again to the building he'd described. "There," she said, pointing into the narrow, weed-choked passageway between two old buildings. "If we go around back it should be easy to get in the building."

The side door was halfway off its hinges. Inside the echoing, empty corrugated walls, Sarkany dumped the sleeping Linus on the damp concrete floor. After a hesitant glance at Sarkany, Miranda found some old newspapers and shoved them under Linus's head.

"I'm only staying here until I see he can't get the ring off," Sarkany said. "I have no interest in lingering with this fool."

"May I stay with him?"

He looked as if he were about to say no, but instead gave her a cool glance with a trace of disgust in the set of his mouth. "You do whatever you wish. I am nearly done."

"You need the cloth with your blood." She stood and wiped her hands on her shorts. "I hid it in the floorboard my apartment. I'm sorry, I wasn't sure how to get rid of it so it wouldn't cause you pain."

"I'll find it and destroy it." His arms folded, Sarkany leaned over Linus. "I see his arm is swelling. Shouldn't be long, and then I'll be on my way."

She wanted to howl and beg and shake him, challenge him to a real fight. With his superior strength he'd knock her flat, but she longed to at least attempt to turn this bored creature into something more like the passionate man she recalled. Instead, he matched the file on Linus's computer. The one that described dragons in human form as cold, unmovable creatures.

The spell of the bone had been broken and the heat had died. But she'd felt his fire and wouldn't forget it. No one who'd had a chance to taste love with a dragon would regret the experience.

He was beyond her reach now, literally and emotionally, so she decided not to make a fool of herself after all. *Let him go.*

"Good-bye, Sarkany," she said quietly. "Thank you for helping me. I am grateful. I am sorry all of this had to happen to you."

The door slammed. She blinked to erase the useless sorrow that blurred her eyesight. She settled cross-legged near the now-snoring form of Linus.

"I don't want your gratitude."

She jumped up. "I—I thought you'd left."

"I changed my mind. I wanted to tell you that if you say thank you again, or apologize again, I'm going to rip that ring off his arm and jam it on yours."

"But I have to say thank you. You did me an enormous favor coming back and helping me."

He scowled at her as he moved closer, obviously hostile. Better that than indifferent.

She gave a helpless shrug and went on, "And saying I'm sorry makes sense, too. I caught you in a spell that destroyed your plans for your future."

"You *wanted* to destroy my plans."

"No. Maybe. But not like that."

She realized she was backing away from him, into a dark corner of the warehouse.

"Fight me. Raise your voice."

She tilted her head back and tried to read his glittering eyes. "Why should I fight?"

"Because you're a warrior woman."

"Please, Sarkany," she said. "I've shown I'm anything but. Please. Don't mock me."

"There's another one, no more saying please. Don't be such a cringing blob. You look like you're going to faint, Miranda. Where is the knight?"

"Sarkany," she said sharply, trying not to sound desperate. "Ple—I mean, enough. I don't want your scorn."

"Tell me why I should listen to you."

She swallowed. His contempt stung and she said the first thing that came to her. "Do you know that you lost my challenge?"

He stopped his steady approach and put his hands on his hips. "I did?"

"Yes. You still own two buildings at least and a substantial bank account. Linus said the papers reported that. Today. "

"You're right," he said. "I didn't finish my part of your challenge. Well, well. Such a shame we dragons rarely hold up our end of such agreements."

Anger flooded her. Her heart felt as if it lay in pieces, and he was still insisting on playing cold and deceitful. "You're lying now," she said in a steady voice. "Linus's files said dragons' pride wouldn't allow them to renege on any challenge."

His brow furrowed. The corner of his mouth twitched. She wasn't sure if he smiled or sneered. "I am glad you destroyed those files. Stupid to have the information lying around where anyone can access it. Very well, if I agree I lost, I will allow you to assign a manager to my remaining properties and I'll leave. What will you do?"

She studied his silver eyes but still could read nothing in them. He'd come back to save her, but he hadn't allowed her to embrace him. His manner had been a strange mix of off-hand and formal.

She gave up trying to figure out Sarkany's response and told him the truth. "I've fulfilled my oath to protect my city from you. I have no reason to stay here. You didn't win the challenge but then again, I made a vow to you and...and no, it's because I want to. I'll follow you."

"Ah." He rocked back on his heels. "To the ends of the earth? That's where I often go."

"Yes. To the ends of the earth."

"Well, then, I shall have to go more slowly than usual so you can keep up."

Her heart, suddenly whole again, leaped. "You're serious. Yes. You want me." She clamped down on her pure joy. "After all that happened?" Perhaps he was toying with her, and would crush her hopes. She watched him carefully as she asked, "What do you want to do, Sarkany?"

He showed every one of his white teeth in a smile. "I shall eat you."

"What?" She backed away.

"You will enter my lair, and I will lay you down and do what I want with you."

"Oh, my," she said softly. "Yes."

At long last he opened his arms and she went to him, breathing in the crisp scent of him. She never wanted to move again.

"You smell like autumn," she murmured. "Clean and perfect."

"You smell like sweat and fear. Earthy."

"Ugh," she said but didn't move from his embrace.

He kissed her hair and then gave a small chuckle. "Ah, but now I detect something a little more interesting in your scent."

"That's because of you, and you know it." She pushed even closer to him, soaking in his heat, enjoying the reawakening of craving flowing through her body. "You are a conceited dragon."

"You sound fairly self-satisfied yourself, Miranda."

"Yup, I am. The only bones I have are my own and you still want them. You want me." She circled her tummy against the growing bulge in his trousers and inhaled at the lovely ache of awakening lust that coursed through her. "Mmm."

In the corner, the lumpy shape that had been Linus groaned. Miranda sighed and pulled from Sarkany's arms. She walked to Linus.

The guild leader glared up at her from strange rounded eyes. "Traitor."

"Yes," she said sadly. "I suppose I am."

He rolled onto his back and writhed. "What did he do to me? I'm on fire." He didn't appear to notice the strange low quality of his voice, but he must have spotted the circlet on his arm. Linus gave a shriek that was no longer entirely human. "Eustace's bracelet! I'm doomed." He gave another shriek that ended in a hiss.

"Nonsense," Sarkany said. She hadn't heard his footsteps, but he stood beside her now.

"I'll send along some keepers—assistants, I should say— and they'll find you a pleasant garden where you can spend your days contemplating your bizarre desire to destroy my kind."

Linus opened his mouth and a lower growl came out.

Sarkany appeared to understand him. "It will probably be less than a year, but to be honest, I've never employed the circlet before. You won't stay that way forever, I'm almost certain."

Another hiss.

"I believe a strictly vegetarian diet will make you sick but you do what you feel is best. Good-bye, Linus." Sarkany turned away from the animal that had been Linus and gave Miranda a nod and the flash of a smile. "Miranda, you know where to find me."

He strolled away without looking back.

Miranda squatted and touched Linus's swelling arm. It felt hot under her fingers. "Are you in pain?" she asked.

He twitched away.

"Would you like something to drink, or um, maybe an ice pack?"

He growled and she stood. "Linus, I won the challenge after all. Sarkany will leave the city."

She gave a nervous laugh then kept talking, mostly to drown out the strange sounds coming from Linus. "I'm not sure what will happen. Since he still owns some property, I suppose that will make him an absentee landlord."

He twitched and tried to climb to his feet.

She readied herself for an attack, but after a second he crumpled into a moaning heap.

Miranda resisted the urge to lay a comforting hand on him. "Making Sarkany leave this area or even leaving human habitation wasn't really your aim, though, was it? You want to kill him—and I won't let you do that."

He didn't move.

She backed away. "Good-bye, Linus. I'll make sure Sarkany doesn't break his promise to keep you safe."

His final snarl sounded like an obscenity.

She turned and went out into the bright sunshine.

# Chapter Eleven

He hadn't waited outside the warehouse. He wouldn't, of course. She would return to her home and then go seek him, a knight's errand to enter the dragon's lair. She wondered which weapons she should bring and decided a shower and her favorite short red dress would be enough—and the cloth with his blood.

Sarkany met her at the door of his lair. "What have you got there?"

Miranda swung the knapsack off her shoulder. "My favorite worldly possessions. And here." She pulled out the plastic bag. "Your blood oath. I don't need it any more."

"You are confident, aren't you?"

"Yes. You came back for me."

"Maybe I was hungry."

"I'm counting on that." She pushed past him and dropped the backpack on the floor. "So what end of the earth are we visiting first? I'm suddenly filled with wanderlust and can't wait to travel."

He eyed her for a long minute, then pulled off his shirt. She admired his lithe muscular torso, the line of his collarbone and his throat, and then she noticed the shimmer.

"Two scales," she said and reached to touch the faint blue against his belly. "And they're right there." Her mouth went dry as she brushed her fingertips over his skin again. Her dragon. How could her body have forgotten this astonishing contact?

He grabbed her hand. "I was feeling reckless. One scale was for you, but I think not. Flying takes some practice, and your precious, crowded city isn't the spot to learn."

"A scale for me? I don't understand." This wasn't in any of the files she'd read.

"You are one of my kith and kin now, you would be transformed and not burned."

"Kith, I guess. Whatever that is. Not kin."

"No," he agreed. "Not kin. But when we touch, you feel it. To the center of your body."

She remembered and grew dizzy with the flood of lust. "Yes."

"You want to see my lair." He smiled and the silver eyes were warm. "I made a place there for you, soft with cloth and pillows. I've thought of you naked on those pillows. Pettifer will deal with Linus. Let's go."

He unbuckled his trousers and a few seconds later stood naked before her. She moved close to touch the tall sinewy figure. Tentative at first, she ran her fingertips over his skin and scales and rising cock.

He pulled her into a kiss, rough and full of demanding appetite.

He backed her slowly to the wall, tugging up the hem of her dress, massaging her belly with his other hand then cupping her breast, sliding his fingers around to hold her bottom.

At the wall, he bent his knees until his erection pressed to her flimsy, wet underwear. He rocked against her. She instinctively spread her legs and, with a grunt of satisfaction, he straightened and hauled her up in his arms, his hands molded to her ass. The length of his powerful body against hers and his cock nudging at her swollen sex made her breathe a sigh of momentary satisfaction, but a heartbeat later she wanted more.

Bracing her against the wall, he supported her with one hand and with the other fumbled with the scrap of silk clinging to her wet pussy. He hooked his finger in it and ripped the fabric.

She gasped. "Here?"

"Yes." He found her clit and gently strummed it with his thumb. "Yes, here." His palm curved over her sex, and his fingers sank deep into her slit.

She panted and whimpered against his neck, and he growled in her ear. "Here and now."

He leaned over, his erection still pressed firmly against her, and he teased at her nipple, nibbling until it stiffened. She arched her back, offering up her breast, an invitation he understood because he sucked greedily, pulling at the nipple with his mouth and clever tongue.

"Now." Her turn to be demanding. He nudged and pushed and thrust home. With a trembling gasp he waited as their racing pulses calmed. Wedged against the wall, unable to move except around the cock that impaled her, she could only writhe, trying to release her frustrated craving.

"Now." She licked the tender satin of his neck then nipped him. He flinched and grunted, but she knew it was with desire, not pain. And he pushed until their bellies met. He sighed and the spreading sensation of Sarkany filled her. She teetered on the edge of elation, drunk on sex and love and the strange dragon essence. But the tension and need still thrummed through her.

He plunged hard then, in and out so hard he pushed the air from her lungs in little huffs.

His eyes grew unfocussed and dark silver, and she caught a glimpse of the creature beneath the civilized surface. The vision pushed her close to fear, and danger sharpened that thick desire seizing her lower belly. She grabbed handfuls of his dark hair and pulled him down to her face.

A kiss with the remembered taste of him would reassure her. His tongue met hers. He shifted his hips where she straddled him. The slight motion chafed her clit as well as swelling something deep inside. That stroke and the kiss—familiar but still laced with danger—broke the agonizing, wonderful tension at last. A few more tiny movements and...

She came, falling into an orgasm as astonishing and as fierce as their fucking. As the raw sensation crashed through her, she squealed, twisting in his arms and on his cock. He reached for her ass again, his fingers held her tight and still as he thrust into her. His head went back, and his throat worked.

She wiggled free of his tight grip on her and undulated around him, still savoring the thick heat inside her, but, oh, she wanted to push him to the same desperate edge she felt. Yes. She was winning. He shuddered deep inside her. She loved the moment of his helplessness and squeezed tight around him.

He shouted her name and convulsed. Hot pleasure, the flashes of lightning, pulsed through her. His weight pinned her to the wall and he panted against her neck.

A few moments later, still clutching her in his arms, he crouched, then lay flat on his back. She gave a squeak at the chill of the marble floor that touched her legs and her palms. He gathered her onto his front, his penis stiff and deep inside her.

Another battle, and they'd both won. He kissed her forehead and she wrapped herself in his body as if she could somehow merge into him.

She rested her head on his chest, listening to his breath and the slight gurgles of his human body.

"You're relaxed?" His voice rumbled beneath her.

"I am a cooked noodle," she told him. "You're on the cold floor. Want to move to that bed you promised?"

"No. I'm happy here for now."

"Good," she murmured. "Me too," and dozed off but not before she heard him say, "We'll both rest. And then, yes, certainly we'll move to my bed."

The sound of the assistants' voices in the adjoining chamber woke her. Before the men could come in and discover her sprawled on their naked employer, her dress up around her armpits, she climbed to her feet. Sarkany grinned as if he read her embarrassment, but he too stood and reached for his trousers.

"Be right back." She dragged her backpack into the bathroom and cleaned up. She considered the sad remains of her panties and tossed them into the trash. No need to change her rumpled red dress. Soon, she hoped, she'd be naked.

He waited for her in the large room, staring out the windows. He wore only his trousers, unbelted. The door to the assistants' area was partially open. They had been through. She wondered what he'd said to them about her.

"Come on," he said and held out a hand. "Let's go look at the bed. Or rather, pillows."

She expected him to pull her to the main bedroom, but he led her to some dusty stairs instead.

"Where is this bed of yours?" she asked as she followed him up the steps.

"Near Tibet." He pushed open a door, and they were out on the roof. A wall hid them from neighboring buildings. He slipped out of the trousers and stood naked again. He stretched his arms high over his head and bent from side to side as if warming up for some sort of exercise.

She glanced back at the door that she suspected had locked behind them. "But you said you wanted—"

"I want to take you in my favorite lair. No need to look so stubborn—you won't be trapped there. Not for long at any rate. Once you learn to fly, you'll be able to come and go as you please."

"I'll be a dragon?"

He shook his head. "No, no more than I'm a man. You'll have your human essence."

"But the skin? The semblance? Do you mean I'll be like Linus?"

"No, not Linus. He's a poor imitation." He looked up at the nearly cloudless sky, gradually turning the purple of a late summer evening. "Are you ready?"

She folded her arms. He wasn't explaining this change very well and she wasn't sure she should give in. Even if going after him was her idea. "Sarkany. Wait. I'm not your possession."

"Of course not. I lost your challenge." The corner of his mouth went up. "Since I lost, I shan't give up any more of my possessions here to your causes, by the way. We'll want to visit your home now and again, and this building will provide a place to stay."

"And who will you leave in charge?"

He shrugged. "I gave instructions to Pettifer for now. Don't frown at me, woman. I know his weaknesses, so he's a good choice. He likes animals, so he'll treat your friend Linus well enough. You may select another supervisor, but later."

She couldn't resist putting her palm flat on his chest, then she had to move near so his heat mingled with hers.

After a long sweet kiss, he pulled away and rubbed his fingertips over his belly and the flexing muscles of his upper arms, as if testing his own skin—or saying good-bye to it.

She wet her lips. "You're going to transform now, aren't you?"

He put his hands on her shoulders and nuzzled her neck. She reached for him, suddenly anxious. "Let's go downstairs again. I like this lair."

He shook his head. "I want to show you my mountain and my lake. You said you wanted to see the ends of the earth." He pointed to a corner. "Wait there. Don't stand too close for a few minutes."

She walked to the wall, peeked over the top to see the far too small cars and people below. With a groan, she huddled down. Craziness. She was scared of heights, and she was considering flight on the back of a dragon?

A loud curse distracted her. With strong fingers, Sarkany tore at himself. The scale pulled free with a ripping sound.

She gasped as the blood trickled down his bare belly through the scant hair to his penis. Some dark blood dribbled down his thigh.

"The worst of it comes now," he said calmly. And a moment later he followed the path of the blood with the scale. His face squeezed tight with pain and she had to stop herself from running to him. Smoke rose from his skin and he gave a roar of pain and something more as the flash of flame burst around him, so bright she had to look away.

When she looked back he was in his true form, the shimmering scales slowly deepening in color, iridescent blues, aquamarine, shimmering jades, midnight sapphire.

"Sarkany," she whispered.

"Yes." Stronger, deeper, almost too vibrant, but it was his voice, and she went straight to him. His scales were hot to the touch.

"They'll cool," he said. She looked into his eyes and saw the man—or rather, the being she knew—smiling back. "I have done this quite a bit lately. All because of you, Miranda."

She walked around him and admired the gleaming scales and large, lithe form. His claws were tipped with opalescent blue talons, almost too beautiful to be frightening. The curve of his belly sloped to massive thighs—and an impressive organ. She tilted her head and considered it. A cock? A penis? He was altogether too imposing for the words she knew.

He stretched huge dark wings, also tipped with talons.

After a time, she tentatively stroked his side. Beneath the lingering heat was something more. The shivering that soaked through her skin and aroused her again. She pressed her cheek to his side.

"If you are ready," he said. "We won't go far today."

She raised her head. "Ready?"

"Climb onto me."

The breeze caressed her bare legs and reminded her she wore nothing under the little red dress. "Oh. I'm not dressed for it. I should put on jeans or something."

"On the contrary, your bare legs will stimulate us both. "

She pressed her lips tight. "Sarkany, this is crazy."

"Mmm?" The splendid creature bent low. She gave up protesting and slid a leg over his back, where his neck met his shoulders.

"Oh God," she moaned as her entire inside leg made contact with the scales of the dragon. "I thought you'd feel like a snake but it's more like...like gold. Living gorgeous gold."

Very carefully, like a woman entering a hot bath, she spread her legs to straddle him. Her curls brushed him. Desire sparked through her. And when she sat, her wide-open sex abruptly pressed to him.

She gasped, flooded with need. "Oh, wait, oh God," she panted and ground convulsively against him.

He growled. "Curse it, I didn't know you had no undergarments."

She collapsed against his neck and clutched him. "Whoa. You feel so wonderful. Everywhere."

"Yes." His voice was rasping and thick. "I didn't know. It's because we haven't touched after so long." He growled again. "I can control the air rushing at you—so we'll fly fast. I want you too much."

"Couldn't we try? I might be able to use my hands, for your...uh. To help you come." That wouldn't be much help, she thought, considering his enormous form. She had stared at that part of him for quite a while.

"I'd kill you. Don't laugh. I'm serious. But please, my little morsel of pleasure. You feel free to enjoy my body. I can wait. I am a dragon, so I have patience."

She laughed again and wrapped her arms tight around his neck. Her laughter turned into a screech as the wings spread and he beat the air and swooped high.

The rooftop dropped away too quickly. "I thought you had patience. Must we go so fast?"

"I lied about patience. I dislike having to wait to touch you."

"Did I mention I'm afraid of heights?" she yelled as her city dropped away beneath them.

"Lie as flat as you can. Yes, your legs wrapped like that. Yes, good."

She pressed every part of her body to him, holding tight, and listening to his dragon crooning.

Eyes shut. And the thrumming infected her body again. Her breasts, tight against him, were caressed as his muscles stretched and contracted. She shifted in her seat, and the contact with him caused her pussy to swell. Her slick moisture must have touched Sarkany, for his rumble grew even deeper and his wings beat faster.

She teased him by grinding small circles with her pelvis. It occurred to her she couldn't stop—she had to move. "Dragon dancing, pole dancing, about the same," she said into the wind.

She'd forgotten about his superb hearing.

"When we land," he said. "I want to be able to see this dance of yours. What is it called? Dry-humping, but aha, I don't think it is so dry."

She gave a snort of laughter and tried to keep her body still.

"Don't stop," he ordered. "You are making this the best of all possible flights."

"Sarkany." She pressed her face to the hot, smooth scales of his neck. "You smell like wild thunderstorms."

"Poet," he mocked, but affectionately.

The muscles of his back rippled under her, stroking her in just the right spot, and she shouted with surprise at the force of her response and the growing hunger.

Her body rocked as, groaning, he moved the muscles beneath her slowly and deliberately. She stopped clamping down on her hunger and twisted and rubbed her swollen clit against the warm flesh of her dragon.

She leaned forward and put her mouth on him and tasted the windy flavor of wild dragon. She enjoyed his scales but craved more. "I wish you could kiss me. I want you. I want you inside me again. All over me."

She'd have to do with plastering herself to him. Her bare arms around his neck squeezed tight, she kneaded him with the tender skin inside her thighs, her legs, her clit, her bare soles, all of her skin—and then the orgasm washed through her at last, and almost made her lose her grip. Heavy spasms of pleasure dragged another scream from her and an answering moan from him.

She opened her eyes again when something jarred her. They'd landed on a field with a thump. He stopped and twisted so she rolled off his back. He caught her on the velvet of his wing and slid her to the ground.

"I've changed my mind." His claws feverishly raked along the scales on his side.

She sat on the damp earth, ignoring the tall stalks of grass tickling her legs. "What are you doing?"

"Looking for a scale for you to transform. I need to be inside you."

"You said you are a patient dragon." She stood up on rubbery legs and supported herself with a hand on his neck. "I saw how much heat you gave off. I want to be near water for my first transformation. What if it goes wrong?"

"It won't go wrong, silly female." He sighed, blinked and, craning his elegant neck, looked around. "I see rooftops. Ugh, and telephone poles. I suppose we should wait until we're in a less human inhabited area. Climb back on." He brought his nose around and deftly pushed it between her legs. "Yes, that's a sweet scent." His dexterous dragon tongue licked her once, twice. She stumbled and groaned, still dazed and inflamed from so much stimulation and her orgasm.

"Lie down with your legs apart," he suggested.

She leaned against his side. "Inhabited area," she reminded him.

"All right. Get on, then," he grumbled.

She hauled herself onto his back and lay face down on his scales. Gradually she slid her legs around him, enjoying the rush of physical pleasure brought on by direct contact with her dragon. A little adjustment and "Whoa," she squeaked as her swollen sex brushed and settled on him again.

"Mmm," he purred and rolled his shoulders. Teasing her again. Once she had her dragon form, payback would be wonderful, she reflected.

Her breath hissed through her teeth and she closed her eyes. "We're traveling for days?" she said, faintly.

"Yes."

"Don't use me up."

A laugh rumbled through him as he took to the air again. Her head didn't swirl as they reached the clouds and her body grew accustomed to the strange passion the touch of his true body evoked. A good start. Her own transformation would be a terrifying, wonderful climax. No, she corrected herself. Making love in midair with her dragon would be the best peak. She held on for the long ride.

# About the Author

Summer Devon is the alter ego of writer Kate Rothwell. To learn more about *Summer or Kate*, please visit http://www.summerdevon.com or http://www.katerothwell.com or her blog at http://katerothwell.blogspot.com. She loves to hear from readers—you can write to her at *summerdevon@Comcast.net.*

# Look for these titles by
## *Summer Devon*

*Now Available*

Revealing Skills
Learning Charity

# The Dragons' Demon

*Marie Harte*

# Dedication

To the Nailiim, and what your future holds

# Chapter One

"There's no way I'm paying you when you haven't proven a damned thing. I mean, come on." Eve Sinclair crossed her arms and scoffed at her older brothers through the haze of smoke covering the dark, crowded bar.

James eyed Duncan and grinned, then took a large swallow of ale, staring at Eve over the rim as he drank. With a loud thunk, he slammed the glass on the wooden slab of a table and sighed. "Never thought I'd live to see the day that our little Evil Evie welshed on a bet."

Eve scowled, not amused. Others had leaned closer when James raised his voice, and in just a few minutes the entire pub would be rumoring about her "cheating ways". Not a great way to ingratiate herself into the community, and James, damn him, knew it. She turned her glare on Duncan, who met her stare with a shrug.

"Truth be, Evie. When have we ever failed to deliver as promised? You owe us, and you know it." His blue eyes crinkled with laughter, mirroring his twin's. And without meaning to, hers smoked with heat. "There's our Evil Evie coming to the fore. Now pay up, sis. I want the redhead in the corner, and James prefers the blonde."

"The man or the woman?" she snapped, seeing the pair he referred to speaking quietly in the hazy corner of the taproom with a blond man.

"Good point." Duncan turned to James with a wicked grin.

Instead of rejecting any interest in the male, James appeared thoughtful. "You know, I've been thinking of expanding. Why not try both?"

"Sure, why not? Just shut up, James." Eve felt the heat burning behind her eyes. Her brothers, those jerks, riled her on purpose, constantly needling the youngest Sinclair with the least amount of control. She blinked down at the napkin on the table, and it started to smoke.

*Shit.* That's all she needed, to foster another tabloid report. "Demons Invade Conshy," *News at Eleven.* And wouldn't that piss off her father even more than he already was? Her father's number two rule—blend in with the human populace and never, ever invite attention to the demon world. She'd violated that rule once...once more than she planned to ever again. Memories of the pit swam heavily in her mind.

She took a deep breath and waited for her inner fire to recede. "I'm not welshing on a bet since I didn't lose."

"Yes, you did." Duncan leaned back and nodded.

"No, I didn't."

Duncan waved a hand at their waitress, who zeroed in on him despite the crowd. Red hair streaked with blue, brow piercings and a studded tongue accented a face garish in black make-up. Finishing the package, a tribal tattoo raced across one breast, up her neck and over one cheek.

"Dark and slutty, much more your type," Eve muttered, wishing her brother would just once lose his temper. But he never did. The most easygoing demon in all of Philadelphia.

Duncan ordered another drink and winked at the waitress, sending her into a tailspin and causing her to trip on her way back to the bar. "Come on, Evie. You know I can't approach the good girls. All I need is for you to bring them here, let them make their own choices."

"Right." She didn't bat an eye. "I bring them here and you and James *charm* them into bed. Then I'm double-damned to eternal punishment. You think Dad won't know who helped you break the covenant yet again?"

James pursed his lips, considering. "That may be, but you lost the bet, fair and square. And we want that group in the corner as payment."

"Okay, let's just nip this one in the bud, shall we?" She leaned closer. "You didn't steal one of Carmaron's eggs. Because if you did, the lower realm would be buzzing with the news. And it's not so easy to hide a dragon egg in the Ordinary world, now is it?"

James smirked. "It is if you know where to hide one. Valley Green, sis. Mile marker six by the first small cataract. The egg's on the other side of the trail buried in demon flame. And if you hurry, you just might find it before it hatches."

Eve froze, staring at her brothers in shock. "You're telling me you actually stole an egg from the freaking queen of the dragons, a viable, spawn-producing offspring?"

"Yep. And in another few hours, that little sucker is going to hatch wanting mommy. I'm afraid if you don't hurry, it might even, gasp, die."

Eve stuttered, not knowing what to say. James had always been more mischievous while Duncan reveled in vengeance. But neither ever sought to permanently harm the innocent. To kill a creature for want of a bet just didn't seem in character for either of them.

"We're kidding, Evie." Duncan chuckled, relieving her. Suddenly, the redhead from the corner passed their table, and Duncan paused to make eye contact. She blinked and looked twice, then visibly sashayed, *invitingly*, toward the rest room. "Oh, no, not about the dragon egg," he said when he noted Eve's obvious relief. "The egg's sitting in a safe, warm nest on the other side of the Wissahickon River. It's nowhere near death. It probably won't even hatch for another few days. Right, James?"

James nodded absently, still taken with the blond couple waiting on the redhead. "Screw the rules. I'm going to just say hello. And if they invite me to stay, so be it."

"You two have to be the biggest assholes this side of hell." Eve huffed a stray lock of dark hair from her face and stood. "Tainting innocence is not going to please Dad, let alone the angels hanging around what they consider their territory."

"Conshohocken?" Duncan raised a brow and chuckled. "Right. Maybe Amish country, but Evie, Philly and the burbs are ours."

"Desperate housewives and all that," James agreed.

She wanted to bash them both over their rock-hard skulls. "I'm not just talking about those idiots." She waved to the corner. "The dragon egg is unborn, pure as snow, and more dangerous than Dad on a rampage. Carmaron isn't that happy with us at the moment as it is, not since one of the water demons tried to seduce one of her females. And we have enough to deal with having the angels in a tizzy over your last stunt with the now-damned Sister Margaret."

"But that's the beauty of it." Duncan leaned close, James following. "We made it look like the *angels* took it. And it's a real looker, Evie. The egg's blue and gold, with lines of red bursting through it. I'm sure it's royal. And won't Carmaron be pissed when she thinks Michael stole it?"

He had a point, and the hell of it was that their father would no doubt laud them for their creativity. Incriminating the angels and such.

"The *point* is that dragon babies don't belong here. The Ordinary needs to stay ordinary." She mentally planned her route to recover the egg. Her brothers would be more a hindrance than a help, and she had a feeling she'd be blamed for the hassle at the end of it all. Somehow, she always ended up in the middle of their messes, left holding the bag. And now wasn't the time to push her father any further. She just had to find a way to return the egg before Carmaron knew it had been stolen. "When did you take it?"

"This morning. So forget it, Evie. She most likely knows it's been stolen by now." James cocked his head and smiled. "Oh yeah. Did you hear that?"

Eve focused and heard an angel's cry and what sounded like a dragon's snarl beneath the clamor within the bar. Angel cry could be heard for miles to those of the Ethereal. And though the pitch was too high to be heard by the humans within, the dogs outside immediately began howling.

"A bet's a bet, Evie. We have a dragon egg, here in this realm. Now pay up."

She gaped, unable to understand how they could both be so casual about the situation. "You've started another war with the angels, interfered with the dragons, and might have seriously injured a dragon's young. I'll pay up, all right," she growled, "just as soon as I've taken care of the egg."

She flew out of the bar, the patrons instinctively making way for a snarling woman—a demon in a fury.

"Think we should have told her the whole of it?" James stood and stared hard at the two in the corner. The woman raised her head and met his stare, smiling in invitation.

"Why? And ruin her chance to save the universe one dumb creature at a time?" Duncan shook his head. "That desire to save the world is what got her in trouble in the first place. No, let her stew in her juices for a while before we take it back. Besides, it'll do Gabriel and his boys good to knock around with the dragons. They've been getting soft on all that redemption crap."

"True." James turned back to Duncan and snickered. "But I'd still like to see the look on Evie's face when Ranton shows up with that fiery sword in his claws."

Duncan paused. "Ranton? I thought you said you'd worked out the details with Teban. I didn't tell Ranton about this. I told Teban."

"Why the fuck would you do that? Teban can barely hold a thought in his horny head. He's normally too busy screwing anything that moves."

"And he'd play along with us because he loves annoying his mother and his brother to no end. He's not bad, for a dragon. But Ranton has no sense of humor, especially not when it comes to Carmaron's bidding. Why do you think she has her youngest in charge of the legions instead of Teban? Because Ranton lets his sword do the talking."

Both Duncan and James realized their sister was in serious trouble and raced out of the bar...only to find Uriel, Zhephon, and a half dozen pissed off angels waiting with clenched fists.

"Talk about utterly stupid," Eve muttered as she sped on her Harley toward Valley Green Park.

She loved her brothers, but honestly, they played too much when they should have been taking inventory of the souls needing saving. Their particular job, in the hierarchy of the Ethereal, was to assess and beguile those on the brink of Decision. To test those whose souls who teetered between eventually going to heaven and going to hell. Existence in either plane was the goal, because living in limbo screwed with the balance of everything.

Though no one soul was ever wholly good or wholly evil, one temperament or the other weighed predominantly in every creature. Even in the self-possessing dragons.

She grimaced and increased her speed. The dragons, like many of the mythical creatures purported to exist at one time or another on Earth, were, in fact, real. They lived buried in the deeper recesses of the world—in the lower realm near the demons—closer to the Earth's core which provided the necessary heat for their precious eggs to survive.

Unlike the humans, dragons knew about the realities of hell and heaven, and remained free to live in whatever realm they chose. Many often took the form of humans to roam above ground, in the middle realm—in the Ordinary. Like her brothers, they lived for mischief, and for anything that glittered. Partial to gold, they also had appetites far exceeding that of a normal human. They took what they wanted when they wanted, and answered to no one, that she knew of.

And the angels thought they were the favored race....

That her brothers had whisked the egg away from its nest, from its precious heat, meant one of three things. One, they had misjudged the egg's ability to survive without its birthing fire. Two, they had seriously conned her—which didn't mesh considering she'd heard that dragon's angered roar in the bar. Three, and this option seriously sucked, they knew something she didn't, like that the egg had already hatched.

Imagining a baby dragon making a meal of the greater Philly area, she whipped her bike onto one of the main graveled parking lots of the park and made a left down the wide running/biking trail. Luckily, the lateness of the hour, as well as the steady drizzle of rain, had forced many outdoor nuts inside. The few that still ran stared at her in disbelief as she roared by.

Great. Now she'd have to hurry the rescue so the police wouldn't be on her ass. So unfair. And all to right a wrong.

Huffing and cursing her brothers again, she stopped when she saw a marker denoting the number six.

She parked and leapt off the bike, swearing when she realized she still needed to cross the river. Not deep, it would nevertheless be cold despite the late summer night. Seeing a ridge of rocks, she raced across the slippery surface with the preternatural agility of her kind and hurried into the woods on the other side.

Once there, she stilled, listening, and felt a pulse that didn't belong in the Ordinary.

Climbing several feet over the small finger of land, she found a tiny, contained blue glow, and within, a round object with the blue, gold and red markings described by her brothers. This egg, however, was the size of an ostrich egg, much, much smaller than the typical dragon eggs she'd seen.

"What the hell?"

Staring down at it, she cocked her head, hearing a strange, haunting sound. Unearthly welcome and a powerful joy sent shockwaves throughout the woods caging the small egg. Trees creaked, wind howled, and the water near them swirled, rising in direct proportion to the rising volume of dragonsong.

Enamored and utterly moved, Eve slowly dropped to her knees and took the egg in her hands, dousing the small fire with a nod. The minute she touched the egg's smooth, polished surface, her body lit with ecstasy—a feeling not unlike that she received when she'd made a successful sway.

*I'm keeping you.*

She felt it, heard herself think it, realized she meant it...and knew she was utterly screwed. Demons and dragons didn't mix. And what the hell was she thinking wanting to keep Carmaron's precious young? Dragons weren't pets. They were malevolent, vicious killers with an appetite for destruction. Pleasant, to her way of thinking, but they had a thing against siding with Ethereal forces.

*An appetite for destruction....* When the sky suddenly darkened and a shadow covered her, she didn't flinch, expecting the worst.

Cradling the egg against her chest, she glanced up. What looked in shadow like a winged angel suddenly showed itself for a furious, fire-breathing dragon. In a human male's body with large, expansive black wings, Ranton, commander of the dragon legion, made an impressive entrance as he lowered to the ground.

He wore black jeans and boots and a clingy black T-shirt through which his wings commandeered wind. His dark black hair and blazing red eyes sat in a face that any woman would consider handsome. Roughly hewn cheekbones and a strong nose complemented thickly lashed eyes and a stubborn chin. He could have passed for a giant human, save for the fifteen-foot expanse of wings and the red flames of anger burning in his gaze.

Seven feet of enraged male glowered down at her, more ferocious than even the demons of war. "I've come for what's mine," he growled, flame curling in his eyes, in his hands and sputtering from his mouth. His fingers elongated into talons as his flesh hardened into black scales, obscuring his clothing. Impressive, beautiful even, but for the fact he meant to do her some serious harm.

*Don't do it. The egg's safe now, give him back.* But Eve found it impossible to listen to her inner voice of reason. She sighed as she pooled her power, prepared to defend her tie to the new life against her chest with her every fiber of her being. To the torturous bowels of hell, or, God forbid, the starry heights of heaven. "Of course you have. Well, Ranton? Bring it on. I'm ready."

# Chapter Two

Ranton blinked in confusion, thrown by the small demon's statement. Ready? Ready for what? To die, or to fight for the precious life she cradled so tenderly against her chest?

His eyes narrowed, staring at her chest, and at the egg glittering with a strange contentment. That the small life inside had recognized safety confused him. Demons, by nature, were cruel. And this female seemed typical of the race. A true beauty, with blue-black hair and ice blue eyes. The demons never chose to appear physically distasteful in human form. They were very much like the dragons in that respect.

"Where did you get that?"

His voice echoed in the night, but she sighed, appearing not at all threatened. Again he stared, bemused at her calm acceptance of his presence. Angels and demons alike quaked when Ranton charged. Yet this female held her ground, ready for what, exactly?

"A pretty bad prank was played on the dragons, with no ill-intent toward the egg. I'm afraid someone played a joke at my expense." He frowned and she added quickly, "Look, none of this is my fault," pleasing him that she'd sensed the precariousness of her position. With one well-placed swipe, he could send her on a painful return to the lower realm, sans body. "I was planning on returning the egg to Carmaron."

"With no one the wiser," he guessed.

She nodded, her eyes glowing, her body throbbing with energy as she readied for his attack. Oddly, her defensive posture stoked a need to press forward, to taunt her into flight.

And he wondered at his sense as he pondered the idea of stalking and taking the little thief as his prize.

"If not your fault, then who stole the egg from its rightful place?" he asked softly, hearing her indrawn breath. The egg told him she spoke the truth about not stealing him from his nest. But she knew. The demon knew who'd stolen a precious egg, his charge. By damn, she'd tell him the truth. And the irony of his thought wasn't lost on him.

"Tell me, demon, who stole the egg?"

"I don't know."

"Liar."

"Look, I'm going to return it. Does it matter who took it?"

Ranton clicked his talons together, and the female watched them as if mesmerized. "It matters that my warriors are wasting their time kicking angel ass. It matters that one of my kind was tampered with by the unclean."

"*Unclean?* I'm as clean are you are, jackass." Her eyes swirled, red mixing with the bright blue in anger. The fury he felt from her made him dizzy with...lust?

He blinked several times and lowered his hands, curling his wings against his back. "Did you just call me a jackass?" No one, no one living, had ever referred to him as such. And much as he wanted to spank her ass for daring to insult him, he couldn't help admiring her spirit.

"I...ah..." she stammered and paled, apparently realizing what she'd done. Instead of recanting, however, she looked down at the egg and blew warm breath over it.

"What are you doing?"

"What does it look like I'm doing? I'm holding the egg. And for the record, he's fine. He wants me, not Ja—the jerks who stole him, to take him back."

Ranton stared hard at the egg, feeling the same thing. "He, you say?"

She shifted and he couldn't help noting the plump softness of the breasts cushioning his charge. The demon was of average human height, with slim hips, a trim waist and ample breasts. Her sultry features made him think of the impetuous succubi, and he wondered at her nature.

For a dragon to cling so stubbornly—as his little charge did lying so peacefully against a *demon*—meant the female had something the dragons would want. Burning curiosity warred with Ranton's need to mete out justice. Still, she knew the identity of the culprits responsible for his charge's abduction. And he couldn't let the slight pass.

"You want to return him? Fine. Come here."

He held out a large hand, withdrawing his talons into mortal fingers as he did so. Still, the demon looked to flee, and the pleasure that afforded bothered him.

"If you run, I'll find you," he growled. "I'm losing my patience, little demon. Take my hand or suffer the consequences."

A stubborn look flashed in her eyes, and he huffed a breath of fire, absurdly pleased she'd prove difficult.

"Look, Ranton. I understand you're not happy. But this isn't my fault. I'm going to return him to Carmaron's nest. Hell, you can follow me if you want. But stop telling me what to do and back off."

Ranton studied her form in comparison to his. Less muscle, more curves, and no doubt more pleasure packed into her tense frame.

Smiling, he showed curving white teeth, and watched as she hissed in response, her eyes flashing as her body began to shimmer, surrounded by blue flame. Most demons possessed some control over fire. But he'd never seen blue flames from the lower realm before. He'd never seen anything so intriguing, and had an uncontrollable urge to touch her.

"Back off?" he repeated softly. In the blink of an eye, he had her wrapped in his arms, her delicious scent making him almost lightheaded. She smelled like sex, like fiery passion, and he made a spontaneous decision. "I think not. It's time you and your kind learned not to play with fire, little demon."

She struggled, but not as hard as she might have had she not held the egg. Startled anew that she meant to protect his charge with her own safety, he held her tightly and flexed his wings. He allowed his scales to armor the outside of his body and his face, not questioning his resolve to maintain his softer, more comfortable flesh against the female, and took to the sky.

117

Her gasp of outrage, and if he wasn't mistaken, fear, made him grin. If she thought flying a problem, wait until she suffered her punishment soon to come. Cries and screams wouldn't do then. Nothing but unquestioning surrender would suffice.

Eve held onto the egg with all her might, trying her best not to freak out as she hurtled through the air at what felt like a hundred miles an hour. At least the dragon holding her close provided some much-needed heat, as well as a smattering of security. She hated heights and always had, and hoped Ranton would rather torture her slowly—on the ground—than drop her what looked like a bazillion feet to a painful, physical death.

The large, black dragon was every bit as impressive, and intimidating, as she'd heard. The rumors didn't do the arrogant beast justice. She calmed a bit, considering. No, Ranton wouldn't let her go so easily. Falling to her mortal death wouldn't do much more than send her into another human body. The terror would be severe, but not particularly satisfying for a male so commanding. His heart thudded against her chest, his body's massive blood flow only increasing his incredible strength.

Though it hadn't been smart, when he'd thrown out commands, she'd rebelled. Eve hated being ordered to do anything, and she knew she and Ranton would butt heads. He shifted and she swallowed hard. If the erection prodding her belly was anything to go by, they'd be butting more than just heads.

Heat infused her, and Ranton clutched her tighter, pressing her firmly against his groin. The egg sighed with contentment, taking her mind from her sexual abductor, if for only a moment.

*I'm keeping you* resounded in her mind again, and she realized the thought hadn't come from her, but from the being inside the egg. He, and how she knew it was a "he" she couldn't explain, was in ecstasy sandwiched between her and the giant black monster taking her to hell-knew-where. Not that she didn't feel a similar pleasure being so close to Ranton.

Not that she would ever admit it.

Seducing humans into finding their path through life was tolerable. Despite her human body, the demon within it needed more than physical contact to experience true pleasure. And though sex with demons could bring both physical and emotional bliss, it had never stirred her to an honest craving for another. Yet being so close to Ranton made her come alive in ways she couldn't fathom.

*Maybe I'm as much a perv as James. He's Mister "Try Anything". Maybe that's my problem. I want what's taboo. Dragons now, then what's next? Angels? Ech.* "That'll be the day I depart the Ordinary for the lower realm for good." She scrunched her nose. Angel sex sounded so...icky.

"Easy, demon. We've not yet come to my home. Save your terror for what awaits you there," Ranton snarled over the wind.

She glanced up, taken with his pitch black features textured with glittering scales. His eyes were completely red, no irises or pupils showing. His nose had lengthened into a kind of snout. And when he spoke, she could see sharp, white teeth as long as her pinkie finger.

The alien contrast of his features to the soft skin covering muscled flesh enthralled her. Ranton could kill her very easily and held that strength in check. An incredible turn-on, and she couldn't help looking away, confused, and more than wary at her deep attraction. Sure she was overpowered, but when it came to manipulating males, Eve was the expert. So why such concern over mastering a dragon?

Ranton slowed and circled over a dense area of rock on the ground. Glancing down, Eve could barely see more than rocks and a few trees under the glint of moonlight.

"What—"

He seemed to stop dead in the air, and she shrieked when he hurtled head first toward the ground. Everything blurred around them, and she closed her eyes tight, her body heating, pulsing with bursts of fear spiked with rage. Before she could share her unhappiness, however, they met the ground...*and continued to move.*

Falling into what felt like never-ending darkness, Eve felt anything but calm. Despite the similarities of this seeming limitless cavern to her ancestral home, the sensation of falling took away any hope of appreciation. Her stomach churned, her heart beat so loudly she swore she could hear it, and fear drowned her senses.

"Almost there," Ranton growled, his large body like a flesh and bone prison.

A few more minutes passed, and Eve's fear swelled to feverish proportions. The waiting, the anticipation of impact made her want to smash something. *No, not you.* She hugged the egg, soothing it with her fingers. The pad of her thumb accidentally brushed Ranton's chest, and she tingled at the contact. *Him. Ranton. That's the one who'll pay for this.*

Gradually, Eve noticed that their descent seemed to slow, and a faint light took her attention when she was finally able to lift her head. Orange and red fires flickered along the sides of the cave and dotted areas of what looked like solid ground.

The closer they grew, the more she was able to view her surroundings. Dark brown dirt and gray stone mottled the floor upon which they finally landed. At several intervals around the large, oval-shaped chamber sat several torches and fire pots highlighting the scarred walls. Adding to the marks, Ranton held up a taloned hand and ran a nail along the carvings. Then he blasted it with a breath of fire. Apparently he was marking his entrance into the catacombs, the dragon's main keep in the lower realm, a place she'd always wanted to see.

Her curiosity warred with her need to make Ranton pay. She never, ever, wanted to experience flight with him again. Falling for so long and from such a great distance felt like her personal hell come to life. And had she not known better, she might have thought Ranton in league with her father.

Glancing up, she saw him watching her and stiffened. She might be a "little demon" compared with his behemoth size, but she had one hell of a temper when riled. Setting her egg—*the egg*—down near one of the ground-set fires, she turned back to Ranton and willed her fury made flesh. Unholy fire consumed her, and she smiled with demon's promise, her body bathed in ethereal flame.

"What?" Ranton asked with mock innocence. He changed back into the appearance of a man, disconcerting her. "You didn't like the flight?"

His sarcasm pushed her past the tenuous limits of her control. Hellfire shot from her eyes and he swore as his skin began to burn. In the blink of an eye, black scales replaced his flesh. Red fire danced in his eyes, but he stared at her with more than anger. Curiosity, and a bit of...admiration...lingered in his gaze.

"That demon fire stings. And it's blue. Not natural."

"Screw natural. We demons lived here on earth long before dragons existed."

"You have a temper, don't you?" He crossed his arms, his eyes glinting with misplaced humor. "What's your name?"

"Fuck you."

"Your name, or an invitation?" He narrowed his gaze when she hit him with another blast of blue flame. "That's twice, demon. Twice you've burned me, and twice I've let it go. I want your name, and I want the names of those who tried to steal my charge."

They both glanced at the egg, and Eve felt the impulse to pick it up again, to pet it in soothing strokes of reassurance. *Mine.*

When she looked back up at Ranton, she saw his eyes had cleared and narrowed. Now black with striations of green and white, his eyes looked like hard agates. "Why is it he's so taken with you? What do you have that calls to mine?"

"Mine? This is your egg? I thought it was Carmaron's." From what she knew of the dragons, Carmaron ruled their sect. A queen without a king who'd birthed two sons still living. Ranton led her warriors, ruler of the Legion. And his brother, Teban, reigned as prince in the mountainous region of the lower realm, over his kind and those banished from the Ordinary thousands of years ago. The blood elves, dragons and havoc lived in relative peace, or at least kept their discord private from their neighbors, the demons. The dragons cared little for demons and angels, and even less for the Ethereals' responsibility, the humans.

So why had Ranton been above the earth? He couldn't have tracked her idiot brothers so quickly. Could he?

"The egg is in my charge for protection," he snarled, showcasing several blade-sharp teeth. "For that reason I'm not at all hesitant about doing whatever it takes to find my answers. Tell me what I want to know and I'll set you free."

*Bullshit.* The look on his face promised a harsh punishment, one he no doubt relished giving. "My name is Eve."

121

"Eve." He hummed her name, the reverberation of his voice like a cool caress in the stifling, humid air. "Do you know who I am?"

She shrugged. "Ranton, ruler of the Legion, son to Carmaron, and all around obnoxious dragon. I'm suitably impressed."

His nostrils flared, and his body flexed, tensing muscle making his scales flash under the firelight. Her intention to distract him from questions about her brothers had worked. But at what cost?

"Impressed, are you? And I've yet to show you the real me." He took several steps closer and walked around her to the egg. Picking it up, he held it to his heart and closed his eyes, breathing deeply. His skin rippled, and the egg's blue deepened until it looked almost black. "He wants you to see him home."

She refrained from smirking. "I told you that before."

"Well, what are we waiting for?"

The damned dragon did it again. In a preternaturally quick move, he grabbed her in his arms, set the egg in her hands, and flew down several overlarge corridors, past dark shapes blurred by the speed at which they traveled. Nearly dizzy, she didn't realized they'd stopped until he held her by her arms to steady her.

"A demon who doesn't like heights or speed. Odd." He chuckled and once more reverted to a fully human form. "Place him in that bed there." He pointed to a small fire burning within a nest of soft, nonflammable cloth that lay next to a gigantic square bed. Move over king-sized. That sucker was at least ten feet by ten feet.

"Eve?"

She started when he called her name, and realized she'd been focused where she shouldn't have been.

"Don't worry, Eve. We'll get to that soon enough."

She glared, but walked to the egg's nest and set him down gently. The minute the egg settled she felt as if a heavy weight had been lifted from her shoulders, and sheer joy lit her being, remnants of the egg's shared feelings.

"How does he do that?" She had to know. Eve knew several psychic demons, but she, like her brothers, had been born with other talents. Telepathy wasn't one of them.

Ranton studied her, his intensity unsettling. Hunger had settled over his expressionless features, making him seem the ultimate predator. Yet he still hadn't changed into his true dragon form, and she felt that omission more a warning to beware.

"Jentaron is my future king."

Oh shit. Her brothers had really grabbed the wrong dragon.

"Nothing to say, Eve?" Ranton took a step toward her, and she had to force herself not to back away. She knew better than to show fear to a vicious predator. After all, she'd been standing up to her father for years.

She cleared her throat, aware the scent of him drifted closer, inviting her to step in his direction. "So royal dragons can share thoughts?"

"Some can." He stepped closer. "My little king likes you, Eve. And if he could see, I could definitely understand why. Your human flesh does you justice." He caught a strand of her hair. "Such soft, dark silk. And such bright blue eyes. A heady combination, especially in conjunction with your fire."

She swallowed, hard. "I, ah, I wonder that you aren't in your normal form. I thought dragons hated humans."

"Some do. But I've found them exceptionally suitable for my needs."

*Don't ask. Don't ask.* "Needs?"

He smiled, a predator's grin having successfully captured its prey. "Sex, Eve. A human performs the sexual act with great pleasure. Dragons are violent, functioning with a basic need to procreate. But in this form, the carnality of mating is intense." He closed the distance between them. "The pleasure extreme. Surely you've found that to be the case in your work."

"I'm not a succubus. Let's get that straight." She tried to step back, pride bedamned, and found her way blocked by a wall. How did that get there? "I've had occasional sex with humans, but only in order to sway them one way or the other. I hate to break it to you, Ranton, but humans overrate sex."

"Oh?" He toyed with the neckline of her T-shirt, causing flutters of want to course through her blood.

"Hands off." She slapped at his hand, and he caught it and held it above her head, pinned to the wall. "Ranton, I—"

"—will tell me everything I wish to know about yourself, and about the thieves that stole dragon property."

"Property?" She sucked in a breath when his fingers caressed the swell of her breasts. Pure, erotic fire burned at his fingertips. "Jentaron is a life, not a property."

"Semantics." He shrugged. "What should you, a demon, care for dragon young?" His eyes narrowed into hard emeralds and she gasped when his fingers grazed her nipples. "Tell me, Eve, what does my charge see in you?"

"I don't know."

He trapped her free hand pushing at his chest and added it to the one above her head. His large palm easily held both her wrists in place against the wall.

"Perhaps I see what held Jentaron in thrall," he murmured and nuzzled her neck.

Eve wanted to run, fast and far. The incredible eroticism of his every touch should have been enough to warn her away. But the feelings engendered by the happy little egg sitting so near, as well as the unfamiliar tingles in her own heart, made her wonder what kind of dark spell this dragon weaved over her.

Ranton licked at her neck before nipping her, marking her, and her knees buckled. Her panties felt more than wet, her nipples pebbled into knots of need, and her womb ached for...Ranton.

None of it made any sense, but when she felt his knuckle brushing against the inside of her thigh, she instinctively spread her legs to grant him better access.

"That's it, Eve." The heat of his breath only added to his allure. "You're hot, wet, and you smell incredible. Maybe that's what captured little Jentaron. Your *heavenly* scent."

"Not funny." She tried to quell the moan building in her throat...and failed.

"Was that a moan I heard? From a demon no less?" Ranton chuckled. His hands left her and she heard his zipper rasp. He shifted his hips and she felt something hard, hot and heavy brush against her cloth covered belly. "Tell me, Eve, why you couldn't leave the egg. Why didn't you flee when you saw me? Are you as innocent in this deception as you say?"

She barely made sense of his words, her physical needs overtaking common sense, too focused on regenerating the pleasure of his touch.

Taking him by surprise, she fused her mouth to his. Hard lips met hers, and she gave no quarter as she snaked her tongue into his mouth, capturing his attention as she baited the dragon, tempting the beast.

He tasted like chocolate, a pleasant surprise that stilled her actions, giving him that spare second to take charge. And take charge he did. He groaned into her mouth, pressing his body firmly into hers as he thrust his tongue into her mouth, stabbing again and again with wanton accuracy.

"Fuck," he muttered as he licked into her mouth. And she felt what he didn't say. She was lost to the feelings he provoked, and to the helpless response of her body as she surrendered fully to a creature more enemy than friend.

# Chapter Three

Ranton hadn't expected the devastation of her taste, or he would have tried to prevent the connection growing between them. Her scent, the touch of her flesh upon his, of her soft lips against his mouth, made him want to devour her whole. By the embers, he'd never tasted such temptation before, and he highly doubted her claim that she was not a succubus.

She moaned and arched her taut breasts against his chest. His body stiffened, actually froze in desperate need, and he cursed them both as he stripped off his clothing. Her eyes widened as she stared at him, her gaze lingering on his seeping cock. By human standards he was large, and eyeing her slim frame, he knew the fit would be tight. His cock began throbbing, needing to thrust inside her.

"Too many clothes," he growled and sliced them from her body before she could protest. He thought it telling she hadn't done more than stare at him since he'd released her hands. Then again...he greedily absorbed her silken perfection, the creamy white breasts and belly now revealed. Her nipples softly accented her flesh, not a bright red, but a dusky rose, sultry and sweet. Wide areolas dared him to take a bite and he did so with pleasure.

The movement put his entire body in touch with hers, and he ached at holding back.

She squirmed against him and fisted her hands in his hair. "Do it again," she breathed, her eyes bathed in demon flame.

Grinning at the slight female with such strength, he bit her other breast and laved it with his tongue. Unable to help himself, he sought the hot core of her with his hand, hissing with delight when he found her wet and unbearably warm.

"You're wet, Eve. Wet for me." He growled against her breast, teasing the knotty nipples with a burst of warm breath and a raspy tongue. She writhed and moaned, her breasts delightfully responsive. "Tell me what you want."

*No. Tell me who stole the egg. I should demand that.*

She shivered and raked her nails over his scalp, pressing against his temples with rigid little fingers. Jolts of pain added to the tumult of sensation jarring his body, and he hardened like stone.

"Tell me where you want my cock." He lifted her into his arms and she wrapped her legs around his waist, putting her slit directly against that part of him so eager to join her. "In your pussy, Eve?" He slid through her cleft and she sucked in a deep breath.

He lifted from her breasts, forcing her to release her grip on his hair. Staring down into her face, he watched her slumberous eyes narrow further. Her lips parted, and her soft breath fanned his face, an invitation plain as day.

Rubbing his length against her, he gritted his teeth against the welcome feeling of her cream. His balls drew tight, and he wanted nothing more than to shove himself inside her and ride her until she cried out his name.

"Tell me, Eve. Do I fuck your pussy?" He withdrew his assault to position himself lower. "Or maybe your ass? You like it fat and hot in your tight hole?"

She moaned when he prodded her anus, her body slick with need. He pushed harder and she squirmed. Damn, she was tight. He had to force himself to hold back.

"Maybe I just want to suck you with my mouth," she gasped, daring him to respond.

"Oh? Your mouth, hmm?" He shoved her ankles from his waist and pushed her to her knees. Excitement flashed through him, stirring his predatory senses as he took this particular prey to ground. "Suck me then, Eve. I'm going to fuck that mouth, and you're going to swallow my every last drop."

She panted, her features flushed as she stared at his cock.

Not giving her a chance to refuse, he threaded his hands through her hair and pulled her forward. But the little minx took the choice from him. She gripped his shaft firmly, pumping him as she inched her slick lips over his crown. Teasing him, taunting him, she maintained eye contact as she took him deeper and deeper into her throat.

He was panting with raw need by the time she had him balls deep, and her hands massaging his ass only added to the hunger burning bright.

"All of it," he growled, aware he'd lost any sense of control. Nothing mattered now but feeling the release she dangled before him. "Fucking take it."

He thrust in and out, deliberately rough. The demon took all of him, raking her nails down his thighs and her teeth along his shaft. The erotic pain mixed with pleasure and he spurted a few drops before he could hold back.

She groaned, swallowing the small shot of come, and prodded him for more. Her fingers fondled his balls, running along the crease toward his anus. He couldn't help fucking her harder, immensely pleased that a woman who looked so fragile could give as good as he normally did.

"Fuck, Eve," he moaned, ramming with a ferocity that surprised even him. She shoved a finger in his ass and he nearly unloaded.

Her eyes twinkled up at him, those glowing orbs of blue passion erased every thought from his mind but fucking Eve into oblivion.

"You want it, little demon?" he said thickly. She added another finger, stretching his rectum, and he lost it. "You've got it."

He spewed into her mouth, lost in the sensation of her fingers stroking his ass, of her mouth and tongue sucking and swallowing his seed in heaping amounts. Never had his orgasm been so intense, or so large. But Eve, his demon thief, took from him what he'd never expected to give.

His control.

Something within him shattered, and he could only stare down at her, nonplussed that such a deceptively small package could wield such immense danger.

She released him from her mouth and wiped at a small dribble of come on her lower lip. She caught the bead and sucked it off her finger, and his shaft stirred when it should have been wrung dry.

"Oh no." He noted her high color, the jitter of her breasts as she strove to command her own passion. "Don't hide from me, Eve. I fucked your pretty mouth, and now I'm going to eat you up, as all beasts do to pretty little girls."

He grinned, his teeth sharp with the need to bite something.

The fear he would have seen in anyone else showed in Eve as arousal, and he felt as if fate had stepped forward and handed him his future with a cherry on top.

Without another word, he scooped Eve into his arms and tossed her onto the bed. Following her down, he spread her thighs wide, anchoring them with his hands, and proceeded to show Eve what a dragon's tongue could really do.

Eve's eyes rolled back into her head as Ranton licked her from her clit to her asshole with a raspy tongue that had all the earmarks of a pleasure toy specially built for her. As if tasting his addicting flavor wasn't enough, she now had to submit to sexual torture. But what a way to go...

"Ranton, ah, yes," she hissed when he pressed that tongue against her burgeoning clit. He licked and pushed, and was anything but gentle—setting her *on fire*. A thick finger shoved deep inside her. He added teeth, smart little nips that made the blood rush from every other part of her body to pool between her thighs.

He held her legs apart and hard enough to leave bruises. And dear hell, she relished the small pain. His finger pushed so deep she felt a jolt all the way to her soul.

"There it is," he murmured, and she felt him smile against her pussy, his lips brushing against her naked flesh. "So sexy, Eve. Clean and smooth, just the way I like them."

She opened her mouth to rejoin, but could only manage a gasp and his name when his tongue snaked its way through her vagina.

"That's it. Feel me inside you, where I'm going to fuck you soon enough, baby. Soon enough, and then some more. You've unleashed the dragon, Eve, in more ways than one." He laughed softly, but his breath felt like fire against her heated sex, and the eroticism of their startling similarities shook her.

He bore down, his attention centered on her channel and the cream flowing like water from within. He lapped her up and moaned against her folds, his vibrating tongue against her clit like demonic torture. Never had she felt like this with anyone. And that a dragon made her lose her control only added to his allure. Worry, lust and frustrated desire mixed, building upon each other until her nerves stretched so tight she wanted to burst.

"Come, Eve. Come over my tongue. Give me what I need."

She felt the end coming, so close, almost there...

"*Now.*" He clamped down on her clitoris and she exploded, screaming his name over and over as she flooded his mouth with come. He licked her, swallowing it all, and as her nerves screamed, he suddenly mounted her and thrust deep.

He touched the very heart of her womb and continued to push. In and out, pummeling with wild thrusts, he sank deeper and deeper while her orgasm multiplied. Dizzy and confused at how she could still be coming yet spiraling toward another, multiple orgasm, she lay under his mastery and urged him for more.

Alternately snarling and groaning, Ranton fucked her like a demon incubus and came hard, saturating her with dragon seed. She felt his come trickle down her ass and into the bed beneath, and still he shuddered as he unloaded within her. For her part, her body eagerly accepted him, clenching around him to milk every last drop.

Minutes or hours later, when she could finally catch her breath, she saw him staring down at her, their bodies still joined.

Incredulity and suspicion dotted the complete satisfaction in his green and white spotted glare. And much as she should have felt insulted that he thought she'd been playing some trick, she felt too tired to do more than smirk at him.

"Demon."

"Dragon."

"Witch."

"Bastard." She yawned, breaking the mood, and saw him try to hide a smile.

"Might as well rest," he said, withdrawing from her at last. But he held her tightly in place when she would have rolled to the side. "Right here, by my heart where I can track you." He yanked her over his chest and held her fast with his massive arms. "You, my little demon, have a lot more answering to do than you've done. And more surrendering to do as well."

Completely worn out, her huff turned into a sigh. Drifting into sleep, she caught the slight press of his lips on her head before exhaustion overwhelmed her.

ဆၢၥၨ

"Damn you to hell, Daniel," Duncan snarled before smashing his fist into the angel's face, putting him down, hard.

James, the devil take him, didn't look nearly so arrogant now, sandwiched between Annua's open-handed slaps and Zephon's powerful blows. Duncan wanted to slay something, and debated the merits of carving up an angel or his obnoxious brother. They didn't have time for this fighting, not with Evie at the hands of Ranton, a sadistic dragon bold enough to lead a legion of his kind. A creature that fierce wouldn't think twice about hurting their sister, especially if she was anywhere near that egg when he found her.

Though Ranton could do little more than crush her human form, the punishment would be painful for Eve. She'd return to the lower realm a spirit of herself, and need to wait for another human to possess. Thankfully, Duncan, James and Eve had been born human, to Bethany Sinclair, now long dead and sadly, gone to heaven. They had retained their forms for the last four hundred years. Unless they suffered a true human death, their spiritual essence maintained their physical forms. So until someone actually killed them in the Ordinary, they could maintain their human forms, well, forever.

But in fights like these, or with dragons like Ranton, the possibility of losing their physical selves grew strong.

Duncan sneered and shot Uriel into the nearest dumpster with a ball of blue flame. Pleased to hear the angel's echoed curses from inside the metal, Duncan stepped over several angels groaning on the stained tarmac. He fisted his hands on his hips and watched as James' captors pummeled his midsection.

James glared at him between groans. "A little help here?" he rasped.

Duncan shrugged. "I don't know. Did you have any other smart-assed remarks needing said? Or can we find Evie now?"

James flushed but remained silent, and Duncan grabbed Annua by his long red hair and flung him skyward. Not willing to call Michael's wrath, the angel kept his wings hidden and tolerated the rough landing. James, in the meantime, took Zephon by the throat and shoved him down into a pool of what looked and smelled suspiciously like urine.

"Nice place you picked to have a fight, Zephon."

"May the Seraphim grant you their tender affection." Zephon's tone was cold enough to freeze the sun, and Duncan couldn't help grinning.

"Maybe if you flyboys would stop whining so much about redemption, you'd remember how to fight and maybe recognize the beginning of a sucker punch."

"Asshole."

James chuckled and clutched his stomach. "Not that it hasn't been fun, Zephon, because it has. But we have pressing matters to attend to."

"What? One dragon egg not enough? Or were you thinking to seduce that group in the corner of the bar?" Uriel said as he stood in the dumpster. He flicked a rotten banana peel from his shoulder, and Duncan cursed himself for not bringing his phone with him. A picture of the fastidious angel in filth would have been too precious for words.

"Not following."

"You remember, the forbidden innocents sitting inside the bar? The redhead and the blonds." Uriel smiled, his teeth too fucking white for comfort. "The trio is mine. The male's an apprentice, but feel free to break more rules. You've already tainted innocence with the egg, so why not interfere with an apprentice angel, eh?" Uriel sneered. "With any luck, judgment will follow swiftly on the wings of your whole damned family."

Shrugging, Duncan took James by the arm and hurried him toward their parked car along the main drag. "I wouldn't be too sure about your apprentice. He gave James his number."

Shoving his brother in the car and ignoring his hiss of pain, Duncan shot their Mercedes down the street in a hurry.

"I didn't get his number...yet...but the lie was worth it. Did you see the look on Uriel's face?" James smiled around a bruised jaw.

"You should have kept your big mouth shut."

"Give over, Duncan. The angels had it coming."

"Sure they did. But not at Evie's expense. You know what Ranton's going to do to her."

James frowned, rubbing his tender ribs. "You think she'd let a dragon fuck her?"

*"What?"*

"What do you mean, what? Ranton's about as male as they come, and hell, Evie may be our sister, but you'd have to be blind not to see how she affects the opposite sex."

"Just because you're always thinking with your dick doesn't mean the ruler of the Legion is. Did it occur to you he might find just as much pleasure in torturing her?"

James snorted. "Sexually maybe. But I can't see Evie laying down to a dragon."

"Not willingly."

Duncan and James shared a look, and Duncan sped faster toward the park where they'd left the egg.

After a few moments of terse silence, James groaned.

"What? Your ribs?"

"No. Just thinking about what Dad's going to have to say about all this."

Duncan couldn't help squirming in his seat. Their father held firm to some rules, and number one was to always consider family first and foremost. They'd already put Eve in danger with a stupid prank. And rule number two, to keep a low profile while working, had gone by the wayside if the angels knew they'd stolen the egg. Shit, Carmaron probably had an inkling that the angels were indeed innocent. Maybe once he and James found Evie, they'd do best to work some damage control.

"You have a point," Duncan conceded. "It sounded like fun at the time, but maybe that was the liquor talking."

"The rum or the tequila?"

Duncan groaned. "I can't believe we stole one of Carmaron's eggs. Teban has a sense of humor, yes, but he only agreed to our scheme because you two are friends. And weren't you supposed to hold the egg in *your* possession at all times?"

"Oh, yeah."

"That egg is his brother or sister, if you think about it. And if he finds out we left it alone, never mind that nothing could have penetrated that flame around it but one of us, he's going to seriously flip. We should have just fucked with Ranton. That he would definitely have approved of."

"Too late now."

"Yeah, too late for us. Let's just hope Evie's steered clear of the scaly bastard."

# Chapter Four

Pressure woke Eve, that and a steady thrumming in her lower body. She blinked to find herself on her belly, hands prodding at her ass and thighs, spreading her wide.

"What—" She hissed at the sudden fire streaking through her bottom. Pushing up on her elbows, she soon found herself on her hands and knees as Ranton pushed himself inside *her ass*.

"That's it," he encouraged, his voice raspy. "But push out, *sassa*, and this taking will be easier."

"What the hell are you doing?" She groaned, unable to resist doing as he said. As she did, he slid further inside, the discomfort of his size fading under the pleasure of his touch. He stroked her flank with his callused palms, then rubbed circles on her belly before his fingers sought the moist heat of her clit.

"That's what I wanted," he rasped and began playing with the hardening nub. He pushed his cock deeper and deeper still, until his balls rested against her thighs. "Oh yeah, that's it."

"Why are you doing this?"

"Because I have to," he growled and pulled out halfway before slamming deep again. "Because you remain unmarked here, and that's unacceptable."

She didn't understand, but soon found herself not caring as he took control of her body. The feel of his thighs pressed against the back of hers, of his balls slapping against her as he rode her with a mastery that declared his skills as a lover, shook her to the core. Every touch, every caress, sent waves of desire through her body.

His fingers plucked and teased her clit until she wanted to come from that alone. But the rocking of his pelvis, the fullness inside her ass only added to the tension begging for release.

And that scared her. She should have sensed him long before he put himself in her ass. She should have woken and taken control, handling *him* instead of moaning in surrender as he fucked her *again.*

A loud crack scattered her thoughts and she cried out at the slap on her right butt cheek.

"Stop thinking and feel," he rumbled. "Feel the sting of that slap, feel the length of my cock as I ram it into your sweet ass. And feel the mark of ownership, both mine and his." She looked over her shoulder and saw him nod toward the egg beside the bed.

The little egg quivered with ecstasy, his shell glowing with bright blue and green spots of color, intermittent with sparks of red and gold.

"I don't understand."

Ranton groaned and gripped her hips tight with both hands. "You will soon enough."

She wanted to argue, but feeling, a symphony of sound, scent and emotion, flooded her with need. The egg's boundless love rolled through her as Ranton cried out and came, and soon she followed, her body clenching his tightly, her core weeping with the need for fulfillment.

"More," Ranton ordered, and thrust again, pushing her into another orgasm.

Dragonsong filled the room. Ranton continued thrusting, and she couldn't stop coming. When he finally ceased, leaning over Eve with his larger frame, his weight pinned her in place.

"Fuck me," he breathed and rolled off her, taking her with him.

She'd fight him in a minute, as soon as she caught her breath and pushed that harmony from her head. Glaring at the little egg, she gradually realized less of a ringing in her ear as the baby dragon muted his song.

"Don't chastise him too harshly. Jentaron's in love." Humor laced Ranton's words, and she quickly glanced back at him.

His lips twisted in mocking smile, his eyes soft with repletion. Eve stared, enraptured with the look of a satisfied dragon. Despite his human appearance, Ranton looked completely beastly to her, and incredibly attractive.

"How can an egg be in love?"

"How can a dragon love a demon?"

*"What?"* Ranton was in love with her? Her heart wanted to race out of her chest. Dear hell, but she thought she might be feeling the same—

"Jentaron's in love with you—a demon. How that's possible, I don't know."

*Oh, right. Jentaron.* She lay there trying to gather her thoughts while Ranton left the bed. He returned with a damp rag and surprised her by tending to the mess he'd made. His tenderness contrasted sharply with his fierce taking of her ass, and the differences made her wish, for just a moment, that he'd been the one declaring his love.

She ignored any sense of disappointment. "Look, I was supposed to bring him back. I've done that, and a lot more. Now it's time for me to go."

She shifted toward the side of the bed and found herself flattened by several hundred pounds of hulking muscle.

"You don't leave until I say you can leave," he said quietly, his eyes narrowed and intimidating in the extreme. "You're in dragon territory now, Eve. That makes you mine."

"Yours?" she scoffed. "Please. I haven't tried to seriously hurt you because I know you were only protecting Jentaron. But you've taken advantage of the fact—*twice*—and now I have to go. I have a job to do, and lazing around with a beast in the lower realm is not getting it done."

"Your job. What is it, exactly? Tell me."

Another order. She glared up at him. "No."

His brows rose, but instead of looking irritated, he looked amused. "You don't like orders, do you?"

"What gave you that idea, genius?"

His lip curled up in a snarly grin, and she had to convince herself not to notice how cute he looked, especially with those sharp teeth exposed.

"Such a smart mouth. But what soft, ripe lips."

Before she could move, he kissed her. A breath-stealing fusing of the mouths that made her arch up into him.

"That's better." His chest rumbled in what sounded like a purr. "Much better. I wonder that I haven't tried a demon before now. Yes, *sassa*, you're my first demon lover."

"I admit you're my first bout of dragon sex, and needless to say, you're my last."

"It pleases me to hear you say that."

"Well, whoopee for you. I meant that you're too domineering, too arrogant, and too damned big for me. Now get off before I turn nasty. And what the hell does *sassa* mean?"

He shook his head, his soft hair dragging over her shoulders. Funny, but she never would have pegged an overgrown lizard to feel so soft. His hair and skin felt like satin, and she couldn't help rubbing the pads of her fingers over his forearms as she tried to free herself.

"I like nasty." Ranton leaned close to her face and inhaled, closing his eyes. "Oh, Eve. You smell delicious. Warm female, cool demon, and spicy arousal."

She didn't need to look down to see his cock hardening. "What, are you in perpetual heat?" Her loins pooled with want, her cream mixing with the dragon seed still saturating her womb and now her ass.

Ranton merely glanced at the egg again and smiled. "*Sassa* means 'dragon with a demon's temper'. It's often used as a term of affection."

She swallowed hard. "Oh." What did a body say to that? She suddenly felt nervous, especially when his eyes narrowed with satisfaction. "I really do have work to do."

"Work?"

Since he didn't seem to want to let her go, she sighed and told him—but only because *she* decided to talk. "I'm a demon with an important job. Oh sure, succubi and war demons all have their place. But it's my job to help keep the world in balance. Obviously I'm not the only one who does it, but I play an important role in the grand scheme of things."

Ranton eased off of her and rolled to his side, up on one elbow. His eyes remained hard while he listened. "Go on."

"You know the Ethereals take care of humanity. It's our purpose, really."

Far from seeming disgusted with talk of the humans, Ranton looked intrigued.

"Not that you dragons seem to care overmuch, but if the humans go unchecked, they throw the universe off balance. The middle realm is actually quite important. But its occupants have no idea what they're doing. My brothers and I sway those teetering on the brink."

"Brink of what?"

"The brink of Decision. That fine line that separates the souls belonging in heaven and those belonging in hell. And the angels are always trying to one-up us." She grimaced. She still had a bone to pick with Daniel about her last sway. Stupid angel. "The fact of the matter is, both sides of the Ethereal were created to keep order. I can't force a human to decide, nor can I sway one once his or her course is set." *James should really be here listening to this.* "But I can insert myself into a human's life who's in the middle of Decision. We do it all the time when they reach a certain age without having decided the course of their future."

"And the dragons? Why do the Ethereal not bother themselves with us?" Ranton rubbed her shoulder with small, light circles, making her stomach do flip-flops.

"Because you and those in your sect refused us many, many years ago. And there's some question as to whether or not you possess souls. For some reason no one clearly understands, the dragons, blood elves and havoc remain immune to angel and demon interference. I think it's because you live in our realm."

"Whose realm?" he asked softly, his fingers traveling along the slope of her breast to capture a nipple.

She swallowed but refused to back down. "*Our* realm. You might not like it, Ranton, but the demons were here way before the first dragon was even born." She grinned when he frowned. *Finally. Gotcha.* "Legend has it that the first dragon was actually a demon who later changed."

"That's ridiculous." He opened his mouth to say more, but his eyes widened in surprise instead.

"What?" She looked at the egg now mottled with blue. "Did Jentaron say something?"

Ranton gave her a most curious look but said nothing.

"You know, normally I'd hang around and badger you until I get my answers. But I really do have work to do." She thought of her father's reaction when she failed to sway her humans. "And there are consequences if I don't perform."

His fingers on her breast stilled. "What consequences?"

"Asael, my boss, would not be pleased."

"Asael," he murmured in thought. "I know this name. An angel once, now fallen to reign among the demons in the lower region. He's a major demon, and a monster of some skill. My mother was quite taken with him at one time."

*Yeah, that was her father. A real heartbreaker. Literally.*

"Well, if you know his reputation, then you know he's not someone you want on your bad side. I have a certain number of souls to sway in a given work period. And if I don't meet my quota, I end up on his shit list."

"Hmm." He looked introspective, and she took the time to study him as he'd studied her.

Naked, Ranton appeared the very essence of male personified. Broad shoulders, slim hips and long, powerful legs made her want to lick him from head to toe. And then there was the impressive flesh between his thighs, the velvety sack under a long, semi-hard shaft. A pearl of cream clung to his tip and she wanted to lick him, to taste what she'd had only minutes ago.

"Tell me, Eve. Are you any good at your job?"

"The best," she said without hesitation. "I've never met a male I couldn't sway."

"Never, Eve?" He chuckled, surprising, then irritating her.

Without giving him time to prepare, she knocked him onto his back and straddled his waist. "Never, Ranton." She licked her lips, not surprised when his gaze focused there and his cock stirred under her sex, trapped by her position. "Why don't I show you?"

*This time I'm in control. And do I have a few surprises for you.*

Ranton sucked in his breath when Eve fused her mouth to his. By the embers, his little demon knew how to kiss. She sucked on his lower lip and bit him, actually drawing blood. Then she licked the small spot, warming him with demon flame, and took possession of his mouth. He found himself hugging her to him without remembering having lifted his arms.

She squirmed over his cock, her pussy wet and hot, and much as he tried, he couldn't penetrate her without her help. But his frustration faded under the onslaught of sensation in his mouth.

Eve filled him with blue fire, her breath an aphrodisiac. She tasted both sweet and spicy, both hot and cold, and smelled like *citreine*, a scent the dragons were partial to moreso than chocolate. Her tongue stroked his and swept the cavern of his mouth. She licked his elongating teeth, which grew long and sharp when he was impassioned, and neatly avoided getting bitten.

"*Sassa*," he murmured when she left his mouth for his ear.

She nuzzled his neck, the warmth of her breath exciting and stimulating. He felt hard enough to break her in half were she human. Her tongue snaked into his ear, and he bucked against her, needing to thrust hard right now.

"I'm going to ride you, Ranton," she whispered as she settled over him, her pussy's cream coating his shaft. "And you come only when *I* give the word."

Strangely, her dominance excited him. Normally the one holding the power, Ranton had never been held in thrall by anyone or anything. Not the queen or the dragon prince, his brother Teban. Even Jentaron, soon his king, would never *command* his obedience. Ranton would give it because he loved Jentaron, because he had made the decision to honor the new king.

Eve challenged Ranton. She made him think twice about telling her what to do, even though he knew he could dominate her. And her ability to make him question himself intrigued him on so many levels.

Her tongue plunged into his ear as she shifted over him, taking his cock deep.

"Yes, yes," he moaned, oblivious to her manipulations. Fuck, his little *sassa* was so good. Her heat called to his, made him want to fill her with his come, to mark her everywhere and claim her as his. Elemental, driving need pushed him to raw carnality.

She sat up, bringing him fully inside of her, and her eyes sparkled like sapphires. Staring into her knowing grin, he gripped her hips and increased their pace, slamming her on top of him over and over again.

"You want to come inside me, don't you, dragon?" she murmured, cupping her breasts and flicking her nipples. "You want to fuck me until you're spent."

"Hmm." He couldn't think, could only stare as she toyed with *his* breasts, *his* pert nipples. The call of ownership descended, and uncaring that the female he would impress into his being was in fact demon, he pulled her closer, his eyes burning with the need to join them as one.

But Eve leaned forward, breaking eye contact, and sucked on his nipple. Jolted by the erotic kiss, he jerked under her, in thrall to her sensual power. She kissed and caressed, pinching his other nipple while stimulating him into a fury of arousal.

"Yes, you want to fuck. You want me, don't you, Ranton?" she murmured, her words echoing strangely in his chamber.

"I do," he answered honestly, uncaring about anything but the end to his hunger.

"But I won't let you come, not yet," she teased, easing off him before he could protest.

She replaced her pussy with her hand and pumped him, circling the base of his cock with a hard pull when he would have climaxed. Cursing in frustration, he reached for her and saw nothing but a blur. She was there. He felt her touch. But suddenly he couldn't see her, could only feel.

"Quit playing, Eve." Anger grew, anger and frustration. His cock needed to release, and damn it all, he couldn't finish. Not when he had her pussy so close, her ass just a breath away.

She reappeared with a smirk and a kiss. Before he could reprimand her, she'd turned around and had her dripping pussy in his face, her mouth over his cock.

He took full advantage, licking her hard while fucking her mouth.

*So damned good. More.* He felt a flutter of love from Jentaron, his little brother feeding off Ranton's sexual energy with softer, needier emotion. And Ranton suddenly felt a softening in his heart as well.

Eve made him feel things. Around her he was more than the leader of the Legion, but a male in his prime. A dragon to conquer even the most stubborn of females. If only she'd let him.

To have met an equal after living so many years in command over the dragons... He wanted to come, to fill her mouth the way she filled his. Eve shuddered and sucked harder on his cock, to which he added his fingers with his mouth to make her climax. He shoved his fingers in deep, two that stretched and angled for her G-spot, taking her to bliss while he ate her sweet little clit.

But still he couldn't come. And it didn't make sense. Her mouth, her body around him smelled of ecstasy, and he needed to join her.

"Want to come, don't you?" she rasped, letting his cock fall from her lips. "Spill it, let me watch you spew." She wrapped her hands around his shaft and rubbed his head against her lips. "*Come now.*"

He couldn't help himself. He sucked harder on her clit and came, shooting into the air. He wasn't sure where his seed landed, but the utter rapture of release, of tasting Eve's pussy while his come left his body, made him dizzy.

He continued to come, ropy jets of semen landing everywhere while he buried his mouth against Eve. And without understanding how, he lost consciousness.

# Chapter Five

Eve knew she had little time before the big guy woke. Yet she was rubber-kneed, trying her best to overcome the weakness flooding her limbs. Holy hell, but Ranton had taken a lot of effort to put under, and she hadn't anticipated multiple orgasms while doing so.

She used his sheets to clean herself, aware she was dripping with her own juices as much as his seed all over her mouth and chest.

Licking her lips, she tasted him, and found, to her horror, the need to put him inside her again. *Completely freaking nuts.*

With an apologetic glance at Jentaron, she readied to leave...and couldn't.

She hurried to his side and put her lips over the solid blue spot at the top of the egg. "Good-bye, Jentaron." Dragonsong filled the room and her eyes filled. "I love you, too." Glancing back at Ranton's still form, she raced back to him and kissed him on the lips. *And I love you, as wacko as that may be.*

Leaving a protesting egg and an unconscious dragon behind, she tried to recall the many twists and turns they'd made, aware her nudity, and the fact that she was a demon, would draw more attention than she'd want to handle. But she had to return home in order to finish her current sways.

Dragons and demons didn't mix. Ranton led the Legion. Eve helped right the balance of souls. How would the two ever come together save in the bedroom?

A tear slid down one cheek and she dashed it away, mortified she might be crying for a lout like Ranton. Good night, but the male was arrogant, autocratic and too damned big. He'd taken her ass without even asking, as if he owned it. Her butt heated with remembrance and she quickened her stride. Who knew a dragon could be so tender, and so roughly exciting, when making love?

*Having sex, having sex,* she corrected, worried when her mind refused to equate the correlation. Damn it, she'd felt the connection, much as she needed to avoid it. No, she had to return home save her brothers' collective asses before Carmaron, or worse, her father, took a bite out of them.

A sudden roar shook her, and she realized she was running out of time. The beast had obviously awoken and didn't sound at all pleased that she'd escaped.

Sudden pain slammed through her temple before she was lifted in large claws like a rag doll.

"Hmm, what is this? A bluefire demon that smells like my brother?"

She blinked up at a large snout, blood-red eyes spotted with gold, and a green-scaled face. The great beast looked as if he were grinning, but she couldn't be sure. Perhaps that expression was one he used before eating?

"I'm Eve, and I've come to return—"

"Eve? Why didn't you say so?" She dropped twenty feet to the ground and screeched, not at all comforted that he held her now in human arms instead of the dragon's claw from before. "I'm Teban, a friend of James'."

"Great. Look, I'd love to stay and chat, but if I don't get out of here soon, Ranton is going to be all over me."

"All over and inside you, I'd say," Teban said with a grin. "Such a tasty little morsel. No wonder James never introduced us."

"Yeah. And speaking of James, I really have to get back. He and Duncan are probably worried about me."

"That brings up a good point."

She studied Teban as he spoke, noting the differences between him and Ranton. They looked very much alike in human form. Both dark haired and golden of body, Teban was taller yet leaner, his face almost wolfish with a mischievous glint sparking his eyes. He wore nothing but the human skin he

145

was in and looked equally impressive as his cock rose in appreciation of her naked state.

"I'd take you in a heartbeat, but you're already marked. More's the pity."

"Marked? Forget it. I really have to get back."

"I'm afraid you can't. Not yet. Ranton's in a fury, and if he tracks you to the Ordinary, we'll have a major problem."

"You don't seem to understand. Asael gave me a job to do, and if I don't do it, his wrath will fall from me onto you. Now stall your brother, mislead him, whatever. But let me go before hell literally falls in on your head."

"Ah, I see your point." He paused, staring down at her and as he realized he held her in his arms, he quickly let her go and stepped away. "I have to say, Eve, you have the most luscious body."

She flushed, not used to any but her sways and occasional lovers seeing her thus.

"Thanks, I think."

"I'm going to take you back, but you have to promise not to tell anyone who helped you."

"My lips are sealed."

He swallowed visibly. "Let me get you some clothes." He pulled her behind him through a part of the rock wall around her that was in fact a door. A large space lit by flame illuminated a comfortable room. Animal hides littered the floor, as did large, soft cushions in green and gold. Glittering necklaces, baubles and coins were scattered throughout the room, even on the posts of his large bed.

"What is it with you guys? Does every dragon down here have a mammoth bed?"

"Only those of us who prefer comfort and pleasure over crude rutting."

"Ah."

She threw on the oversized shirt he gave her that reached mid-thigh, and waited while he donned black slacks and shoes and a green silk polo. He pointed to a second door away from the one they'd entered.

"Shall we go?"

"Uh, yeah." But before they left, she paused. "You didn't ask any questions, Teban. Almost like you knew why I was down here."

He chuckled. "Your brothers told me all about it. I let them take the egg, knowing James would watch it. And since they only did it to teach you a lesson..."

"What lesson?" She could feel her eyes heating.

"Oh ho, evil Evie, as James likes to say. You really have the most beautiful fire. So blue."

"Teban," she warned, needing to leave, but needing to hear evidence of her brothers' perfidy more.

"It was just a joke, Eve. Except Ranton's involved now, and in case you missed it, he doesn't have the best sense of humor." Another roar shook the walls. "See what I mean? Anyway, James and Duncan told me how you got yourself in trouble trying to save a run-down elementary school from destruction a few months ago. Threatening the new owner of the lot, in public no less, violated several demonic rules, no?"

She scowled. "No one would have paid any attention to it if the angels had kept their snotty noses out of the mess."

"I, for one, liked the fact that you made that bruiser piss his pants. Hey, a little demon fire never hurt anybody, right? But you made all the major headlines. Rumor has it you earned some time in the pit for it, too."

Eve shuddered. She didn't want to relive the torture her father had put her through. Even for a demon, some things, like falling forever through the air covered in spiders and scorpions that liked to bite and sting, could be more scary than hell itself. And her father still had yet to forgive her for that, though she thought it more likely he'd been scared of the repercussions on her had the archangels taken notice. So he'd been extremely firm making a point...she liked to think.

She shook off the past. "So, you're saying James and Duncan tricked me into trying to save a dragon's egg that wasn't in any danger at all?"

"That's about it." Teban beamed. "Ready to go?"

"But what about the egg, I mean, Jentaron? Is he really okay?"

Teban's smile froze. "What did you say?"

"Jentaron. Will he be okay? He was out of his nest for some time."

"But James had him."

She snorted. "Not when he was in the bar making eyes at a stupid blonde. Make that blonds." The minute she said it, she wanted to retract her statement. Teban suddenly looked more like Ranton than she liked. Flames danced in his eyes.

"James left the egg alone?"

"But nestled in our demon fire. Honestly, only he, Duncan or myself could have retrieved him."

The flame in his eyes faded at that. "And you know his name, the name of our new king."

"Uh, yeah."

"How?"

"How what? I knew the egg was a *he* because he told me. But Ranton told me Jentaron's name."

Teban stared, and then he grinned, his mouth so wide he looked to split his face. "This is just priceless. Promise me to hold off your announcement until I'm there. I wouldn't want to miss Carmaron's face when you tell her."

"Tell her my brothers stole the egg?"

"No, definitely not. Never mention that again. And whatever you do, don't tell Ranton about James or Duncan. Now let's get out of here before my little brother finds us."

Before she could ask Teban any more questions, he had her out the door and darting straight up into the air, at speeds that made Ranton's descent into the lower realm look like slow motion.

Ranton had followed her scent until the trail suddenly ended. Odd as it seemed, his *sassa* had vanished. He roared in frustration, his wrath making the rock walls crumble, but he didn't care. That little demon had bested him. *Him,* the ruler of the Legion. And to add insult to injury, she'd left him before he could finish their bond.

The pressing need to find her fueled his fury, and he stomped around the corridors breathing fire and threatening any and all he met for information. But no one had seen her.

He passed another mass of red and black dragons, ignoring their questions as to why he remained in human form. Then he stopped. Teban must have heard his cries, yet his brother had yet to show his face.

Retracing his steps, he found Teban's room and barged in unannounced. The scent of Eve hit him, so strongly he wanted to kill his own brother. The only thing keeping him somewhat sane was the absence of Teban's scent marker, and the clamoring roar of Carmaron.

Shit. She must have learned of Jentaron's disappearance.

*"Ranton, to me now."*

Eve drew further away, yet the queen called. *Fuck.* He was going to seriously paddle his demon's ass, not to mention fuck her senseless, when he found her again. And he didn't even want to think about Teban, lest his rage fly out of hand. Teban had a lot to answer for, thanks to Jentaron's helpful information. No wonder the thieves had been successful in stealing the egg. They'd had his brother's help.

Ranton quickly shredded his human clothing as he transformed into his beast. Thick black scales covered his body, and he breathed fire, inhaling the comfortable aroma of methane and sulfur that lingered under the scent of Eve's touch still clinging to his body.

He flew down several passages, knocking several of his brethren over in his haste to reach an angry-sounding queen.

Entering her chamber guarded by two of his legion, he nodded at them and entered.

"Where have you been?" Carmaron shrieked in greeting. "One of my eggs has been stolen, by an Ethereal, no less."

Ranton did his best not to roll his eyes. For all that he outmuscled and outweighed his mother, she could be a ferocious beast when riled.

"I have Jentaron. He's safely nesting in my chamber."

The terror in her eyes softened and she sniffed, fat red tears streaking down her gold face. "Jentaron? Then he's ready to hatch?"

Ranton allowed himself to smile, pleased beyond measure with his new brother. "Yes. He's ready." Just waiting for a witch of a demon to return so he can sit against her bare breasts, skin to skin, as he grows.

"Then he was never taken in the first place? You had him?" She looked suspicious, but nowhere near the raving dragon he'd heard screeching through the walls.

"Yes. And the rumor about angels or demons taking him was just that." *Oh, Eve, you owe me for this. And you are dearly going to pay.*

"Why, then, are we at war?"

"Not at war. In training. The Legion grows stale battling with tired demons and the blood elves. And the havoc, those monstrous carnivores, are too unstable to engage. Hell, rumor has it they eat their own. We needed a bit of new blood, and the angels provided that relief."

She snorted with amusement. "Good thinking. Uriel in particular can be extremely vexing. He had the nerve to try to sway one of my young a few centuries ago. Can you believe that?"

"No, Mother."

She shuffled toward him on tired legs, and he noted not for the first time how much she'd aged. Though dragons lived a long time, Carmaron had outlived the oldest by a thousand years at least. Her once golden skin now flaked with white, and her scales' luminescence had faded.

Though she'd birthed over ten thousand young, only Ferna, Lier, Teban and Ranton had she kept as her own. And with Ferna and Lier having died years before Teban had been born, she only had two sons now to call hers. When she passed, Jentaron would have to find a queen to carry on the dragon line. Yes, it was time for his brother, the king, to come into the world. If only the stubborn little egg would ignore his need for Eve.

For some odd reason, Jentaron had taken an instant liking to the demon, and didn't want to come into the world without her by his side. Not that Ranton could blame him. But the egg seemed to want her for an altogether, less platonic reason.

Most dragons only had sex to ease the ache of rage. Those anointed breeders did so to procreate, and were only allowed copulation with the queen or one of her approved broodings.

But a few, like Ranton, *liked* the sexual act. He'd tried it in the human form on a lark when he'd reached his teens, and had found, to his surprise, that he liked it. Hell, he more than liked it. With Eve, he craved it.

Departing from his mother with a revered bow, Ranton left with all intention to find Eve. In less time than it had taken to mark her as his, she'd crawled under his skin and refused to leave. He loved the smell of her. Thoughts of her luscious, creamy body made him instantly hard. And the thought of not having her at his side made him want to kill something to ease that unrelenting ache.

What worried him more than anything was the fact that his need for Eve went beyond the physical. How could a dragon ache for a demon? It made no sense. Yes, they both shared a love for things dark and hot. Their world in the lower realm was comprised of black earth, hot, humid recesses of underground lairs and open fields of scorched vegetation. Beautiful in a barren kind of way, yet filled with life. Eve could appreciate a dragon's existence. Yet she had a calling to walk among the humans, a practice banned by Carmaron several centuries ago. Too many of their kind had been killed by the humans—by the very creatures the Ethereal catered to day in and day out.

For his part, Ranton had never much cared either way about the mortals above ground. Looked on as food by some of his kind, the humans had always instilled in him a curiosity. But he'd found a new respect for them when he'd discovered human sexuality.

He hardened and found it awkward to walk as his dick dragged along the ground. Irritated that he had little control over his body, he rose high and flew through the wide corridors toward the main entrance/exit to the catacombs when he heard Jentaron.

*Need to break free. Time to rise.*

"Damn." Another distraction to keep him from Eve. Yet this one he would cherish, the birth of his brother into his keeping, into Guardian claws.

He turned around and flew back into his chamber, lighting every one of the torches in his room with dragon fire. Then he sat in wait, whiling the hours it took to finally watch his brother peck through the egg into a whole new life.

151

He could still remember his own birthing, entering to find Teban waiting on him, the large green dragon's eyes full of love and welcome. A fitting contrast to Carmaron's constant harping and incessant screeching. A wonderful queen and breeder, she was, however, a terrible mother. But for all her faults, Carmaron admitted her failings. And it was with no small gratitude that Ranton thanked her for allowing his brother to raise him.

Jentaron would be his to raise, his to protect. Carmaron had chosen Ranton for that duty, yes, but Jentaron, in the end, had made the final decision. A royal egg, the new king, Jentaron had abilities that would sustain the dragons through the next several millennia.

As the minutes ticked by, Ranton became more and more aware of Jentaron's frantic need to be near Eve.

*Eve. Want my demon.*

Ranton frowned at that, still not sure how to face what was coming all too soon. Jentaron had called to Eve. The king had chosen Eve, a demon, to help introduce him to the world. At first Ranton had thought Eve's mention of demons as the dragon's forefathers as nonsense, but Jentaron had immediately agreed. The little egg had begun singing softly to Ranton, telling him in no uncertain terms that Eve belonged to Ranton, and more, to Jentaron. But Ranton had a feeling his definition of "belonging" and his baby brother's were two different things.

Not sure what to make of Jentaron's feelings, Ranton blew a comforting breath over his brother and focused instead on the changes coming his way. Once Jentaron was born, his duty as commander of the Legion would be split. He would still train the dragon army, but when the time for battle came, his duty would be first and foremost to protect the king. As Guardian, it fell to Ranton to defend his charge, with his life if need be.

He would miss the rush of leading his dragons to battle, but found great satisfaction that he would help mold the future of his kind. Planning took his mind off Eve for a while, and as the hours passed, he fell into an easy rhythm, nudging his brother every so often to stimulate his need to break free from his boundary.

Jentaron continued to cry about Eve, but Ranton tuned him out. Had he not, he might have done something extremely stupid...like taking his birthing brother with him to find the evil woman.

Ranton couldn't help a small smile at how completely she'd manipulated him. Though still pissed she'd knocked him flat on his ass, he felt pride that she'd been able to fool him, the Legion's own general. And what a way to go.

She'd said she had power, but he'd been able to control her fairly easily, at least physically. Now he understood her success rate with her sways. Frowning, he wasn't sure how he felt about her having sex with humans. Clinically, it was her job, to push the humans one way or the other into the Decision. But now that he'd claimed her, she belonged to him.

He glanced at Jentaron, who screeched and fluttered within his shell. Eve belonged to Ranton...and to Jentaron. How that would play out remained a mystery, and that worried him. Ranton had bonded so quickly to Eve, and so fully, he wasn't sure he could share her with another, even with another dragon. The thought of Teban anywhere near Eve still made him see red.

Jentaron cried out and the egg popped, distracting him. He blew a soft breath of fire over the sudden cold penetrating the heat within the egg, and his brother settled a bit.

*Eve. Want my* sassa...

"She's not here, now, brother. Come out and we'll find her together."

*No, want* sassa.

Ranton frowned. *Sassa* was a concept only an adult should understand. He'd told Eve it was a term of affection, and it was. But it was also more than that. *Sassa*—dragon with a demon's temper, keeper of dark flame, conjurer of desire. Most often used in sexual terms, and Jentaron spoke of her as if Eve would belong to him in *that* way. Ranton's blood boiled with jealousy.

He wouldn't tolerate sharing.

*My* sassa.

"No," Ranton growled. "She's mine, you little hatchling. Now stop playing and come on out. And if you want to see her again, you'll abide by my command."

Jentaron sulked but entered the world with one more break of his shell. He glittered, still stained with dragon fire, but looked almost...blue. Ranton stared, incredulous, at the first blue dragon born in over fifteen thousand years. Blue, just like the color of Eve's shining eyes. Ranton grimaced, sensing prophetic doom. But as he stared at his new king, he couldn't help the joy building within his being.

Cradling the tiny dragon in his claws, Ranton puffed a burst of Guardian flame over the hatchling, marking him as under Ranton's protection. Jentaron chirped and fluttered his paper-thin blue wings that began to shine with silvery veins. Then he belched, a small hiss of gas that sparked off the hatchling's claw striking stone.

Jentaron nuzzled his snout along Ranton's, then surprised Ranton by leaping out of his claws to the ground. He watched, bemused, as his brother matured incredibly fast. Almost like a...demon. He had to step back as Jentaron took up more and more space, until the hatchling suddenly grew to a few feet shy of Ranton.

*"Crap, that really hurts."* Jentaron roared his displeasure, but continued to communicate telepathically. He flapped his wings and flexed his fragile claws. *"Now show me how you turn human so we can collect Eve."*

Shaking his head at his brother's one-track mind, Ranton did as asked. His own maturation into a large, fully grown male had taken a year, a full ten years faster than most dragons. His brother, apparently, didn't intend to wait on nature.

Jentaron shifted slowly into a human-shaped body. He looked more like Ranton than Teban. But where both Ranton and Teban were dark, Jentaron had white-blond hair. His eyes, too, were different. Dark blue with silver flecks, decidedly not human.

"You'll have to wear dark glasses if we go out in public." Ranton nodded up.

*"When* we go out. When Eve works above ground, one of us has to be with her at all times."

"Excuse me? One of *us*? Little brother, king you may be, but Eve is mine."

"Technically." Jentaron waved away his concern and tried walking on unsteady legs. "This is so awkward. How do they move about without hind legs? And no wings or tail for balance?"

Ranton snorted. "Yes, but they have many other attributes that more than make up for it."

"I know. Why do you think I matured so quickly?" He grinned, and Ranton saw himself in the gesture. Pride sparked, and love suddenly overwhelmed him. Ah, so this was the Guardian's Bond. After several emotion-packed moments, the imprint began to fade. Ranton took a deep breath, not so quick to deny Jentaron's desires. Love for his brother shone brightly, yet love for his demon, his *sassa*, could not be refuted.

"Jentaron, Eve—"

"Came when I called." Jentaron spoke in a husky voice. "She's yours, Ranton. I claimed her *for* you, so relax. I'm not about stealing her. But a part of Eve is mine as well. I love her," he said quietly, staring into Ranton's troubled gaze. "She's my Guardian as well, brother. Yes," he emphasized, noting Ranton's surprise. "The love I have for her is deep, and different from what I feel for you.

"She's a strong demon, and an even stronger woman. You've sensed her inner fire. She's perfect for you, Ranton, and she'll fulfill her purpose to me and to our sect in more ways than you can know." He forestalled Ranton's questions with an upheld hand. "She's mine too, and I'll say no more about it. But you can blame yourself for this." They both stared down at Jentaron's growing erection. "If your mind hadn't been so strong, I might have been spared this physical hunger. But you've it bad for little Evil Evie." Jentaron grinned. "By the embers, Ranton, you're a horny bastard, aren't you?"

Ranton chuckled, then sighed. The Guardian's Bond had taken away much of his jealousy toward Jentaron. But he still felt the need to own Eve. He needed to cement their bond, and to make sure she knew who was truly in charge of their new family. Jentaron might rule the dragons, but Ranton would rule the roost.

He sighed, watching his brother try to push his penis down. "It doesn't work that way."

"How the hell do you deal with this gnawing hunger?" Jentaron cursed, one of Ranton's favorites. "I need to fuck our *sassa*, and soon, before my brain explodes."

It figured his little brother would be a huge pain in his ass. Ranton grinned wryly. And if he wasn't mistaken, Jentaron would soon be a huge pain in Eve's as well.

# Chapter Six

Eve stared at the human jacking off while she watched with murmurs of encouragement. Before Ranton, she'd found the sight entertaining if a bit lacking in creativity. Now she just wanted him to finish before going home to his wife and three kids. Yeah, George had been easy. Hell would be waiting for this jerk with open arms.

"Thanks, George," she whispered throatily, pleased when he sucked in his breath and did another line of coke. He toppled into his Decision, and she had a brief glimpse of him several years down the road, homeless and desperate while he stole from others to fill his filthy habit. *We'll be seeing you in the Abyss in another thirteen years.*

She picked up her light jacket and left him breathing hard, slamming the door behind her. *What the hell is wrong with me?* Normally buzzing with joy after turning a sway, she found her recent encounter sorely lacking. She rubbed her arms, slightly chilled in the stifled hallway that had to be at least ninety degrees since the air-conditioning had gone out hours ago.

In the catacombs she'd been oppressed with heat, and with a glowering dragon so hot he'd melted her heart.

"Oh hell, I must have it bad. Melted my heart? That is so fucking trippy."

She kicked at a moldy can of something and wondered if Ranton missed her half as much as she missed him. His bold stare, his dominant touch, the tender look in his dragon eyes after watching her come... For all that he'd pushed her around, Ranton had made her feel like she belonged. He'd possessed her, body and soul, and she still couldn't understand how he'd done it.

Sure, he'd fucked her senseless. And she readily admired the fact he could even do that. Maybe that was the attraction. That she'd finally met a male, not a relation, who could manipulate *her*. And his strength. Her sex tingled as she thought about his rippling muscles. The sight of those broad wings, of those thick thighs bunching as he prepared to leap.

She sighed. And his cock felt so damned good. So long and thick inside her. So perfectly right. Power and incredible sex was so...incredibly sexy. She flushed, hoping she didn't look as sappy as she felt.

Now she understood how some of her sways must have felt after sex with her. Utterly spellbound.

Yet it was more than the physical with Ranton. He sneered, he demanded, and he pushed until she surrendered. And he carried her protectively against him, against comfortable flesh when he could have covered himself in sharp scales. The affection he showed Jentaron seemed completely opposite what she would have expected from a dragon.

She knew enough about their species to know Carmaron was a dangerous female, to her own kind as well as to outsiders. Most dragons raised their young to be fierce, proud creatures bent on rejecting any and all but their own kind. And only the strong survived. The dragons possessed intelligence, and as much primitive reason as their ancestors, the drac demons.

But that primitive need to possess, to conquer and keep, turned her on like nothing ever had. To be held in arms strong enough to crush her, by a beast considerate enough to care for her needs before his own, ruined any resistance she might have wanted to have. Her eyes welled and she blinked hard, reminding herself she had no right to a dragon.

Different worlds. He burned and killed. She turned and swayed. He dwelt in the physical; she focused on souls. His kind had been banished from the Ordinary years ago. Her kind dwelled in both the lower *and* the middle realm. How could she sway souls from the lower realm? And how could he live in his natural form in the Ordinary where dragons were anything but?

She glumly turned the corner and screamed when Teban bumped into her, Duncan and James hard on his heels. "Dear hell, Teban. Don't *do* that."

"Where the hell have you been? I told you to wait for me at the bar and bam, you disappear on me. And that was yesterday." Teban glared disdainfully around him at the peeling paper and flea-infested carpet of the rundown hotel. The air of desperation and unsated hunger clung to the walls, definitely out of place for a giant male dressed in Armani slacks and Gucci shoes.

"Evie," Duncan breathed. "We were so worried about you."

"Oh?" She glared at him and James, doing a double-take when she noted James' swollen face. "What the hell happened to you?"

"Evie, I am deeply, deeply sorry." James grabbed her elbow and dragged her down the corridor toward the steps. Duncan took her other arm and Teban brought up the rear.

"Why do I feel like I'm being led to an execution?"

Duncan's eyes darkened, and she stopped in her tracks.

"What's going on?"

"Asael commanded us to bring you back, right before Teban showed up with the 'good' news that he'd found you."

"Great."

"Don't worry, Evie," James said. "I'm going to take full responsibility for this. It was all just a joke. We would have gotten lucky with the trio in the bar, and you would have learned a valuable lesson."

"A lesson we should have followed—not to mess with what doesn't concern the demon world," Duncan finished. "But James screwed up. He planned on involving Ranton, but failed to tell me about it, and I told Teban what was going on instead. The egg was never in any danger."

"No, because James was going to watch it twenty-four/seven, right James?" Teban asked softly.

James looked nervous, and the predatory gleam in Teban's eyes intensified. "Right, Teban. Right. But what I was trying to say was that I'm sorry, Eve. I had no idea Ranton would get to you first." He paused. "He didn't, ah, hurt you, did he?"

Duncan's eyes brightened, a neon blue filled with fire. "Because if he did, dragon or not, he's dead."

Teban shook his head but James stopped him with a look. "Eve?" he pressed.

"No, he didn't hurt me." *He made me come so hard it makes me wet to think about. He made me desire him, to the point that I'm pining for a dragon when I should be focused on my job.* She sighed. "He was very understanding about the whole thing." *And so freakin' scary looking that I fell in love with the beast.*

"*Understanding?*" Teban looked incredulous.

"Oh, well." James coughed. "Then I guess we should say congratulations before we see Dad."

"Congratulations?"

Teban grinned. "I told them that you're now officially dragon property."

"*Property?*"

"Hell, Eve. You knew the sex and name of a royal dragon before he was hatched. That's almost as good as a royal claiming, by Jentaron, mind you. But that won't happen because Ranton marked you. And if he marked you, he's keeping you. It's only a matter of time before he finds you again."

James glanced cautiously around them. "Uh, Eve, if it's all the same to you, I'd rather not draw more attention than we already have. We need to go home now."

She stared at the three males looking so hopeful. What bullshit. As if she had any choice in the matter. Her brothers wanted her to go home, to settle with Asael. Which she could appreciate. And honestly, she didn't want another scandal in the Ordinary centered around her. She'd been gone two days, and she imagined Ranton's fury at having been bested by a female demon had to be extreme.

Though unnerved, she had to smile. What a picture that would make, Ranton in a snit. "Okay, boys. Let's go see Dad."

When Teban moved to join them, she stopped.

"You're coming with us into the Abyss?"

Teban shrugged. "Why not? Besides, I'd like to be there when Ranton tries to explain himself. I can't decide who'll be more fun to watch. Asael or Carmaron?"

"You're a sick bastard, Teban." Duncan shook his head, a smirk on his face.

"So I've been told."

"I'm not following." Eve heard them, but didn't understand. Ranton would try to explain himself? Explain what, exactly, that whole marking thing? Funny, she didn't see anything different in her appearance. And Teban, a dragon, voluntarily asked to join them in demon country?

"Trust me, Evie. When the shit hits the fan, no matter where you are, you'll be right in the middle of it." Trust James to be so succinct.

"Aren't I always?"

ʒʊƧƆ

Ranton growled. Jentaron was turning into the little brother from hell, which wouldn't have been so bad if they hadn't been forced to enter said region. Like most of the lower realm, hell, or the Abyss, as the locals called it, was dark and hot. Personally, he liked it. But the denizens of the Abyss weren't so welcoming to anyone not demonic.

He glanced at the dark red horizon streaked with orange. He had to give it to the demons. The catacombs his kind lived within didn't hint at anything resembling the middle realm. They lit their way using fire, and when the mood struck, they ventured above ground into the humans' world to view the sun and the stars.

But down here, the demons mirrored the Ordinary. A black orb hung suspended in the sky—the miles of open space between the cracked plates upon which they stood and the ceiling of earth and rock above them. Gray-brown rocks streaked with blue and purple mineral dotted the landscape, providing a surprisingly beautiful palette set against the blood-red sky.

Doomed humans grimaced as they passed, led in formation by whip-wielding demons and pleasure-seeking imps. In the distance several demons farmed magic from the land, dropping the stuff into large barrels which would be transported throughout the demon's realm, readied to barter with those needing precious *mana*.

"Tell me again where we're going?"

Damn, Ranton was getting a headache. "If you'd stop whining, we'd probably be there by now."

"Asael? Is that his name?"

"Yes. That's the major demon pulling Eve's strings. Now relax and follow my lead. I have enough to deal with trying to find Eve and protect you from these idiots, let alone yourself."

Jentaron grinned. "Testy. Been too long since you've seen any action, hmm?"

They traveled in human form, to better fit in with those in the Abyss. No wings, no scales, and human attire—shredded cloth barely covering their bodies, like the other souls caught in hell. Problem was, the mortal form made Ranton's urges and sexual needs that much more pronounced. He walked with a constant hard-on, Eve's scent emblazoned on his brain.

"State your purpose here, *dragons*," a uniformed demon spoke from behind them.

They turned to find a faun wearing a green-skinned vest. Hoping he didn't recognize one of his kind over the demon's chest, Ranton sniffed and scented only lizard hide. The demon's tone, however, needed adjusting.

Ranton released his wings and flexed the sharpened appendages, ripping through the ratty T-shirt he'd sported, and rose in height to his normal seven feet, grunting as he did so. "Ah. That smaller form was killing me."

Jentaron sighed and grew as well. "Me too. I guess we're no longer trying to blend in?"

Shaking the faun by the neck, Ranton growled and leaned close. "Where do I find Asael?" He shot fire through his eyes, lighting the faun's beard afire, and the demon quickly told them where to go.

Tossing him several feet away, Ranton slapped his hands together and took to the air. Waiting for his brother, he watched with pride as Jentaron joined him.

"Let's get Eve."

"Our *sassa*."

Ranton cursed under his breath and straightened his unruly cock beneath his trousers. "My *sassa*, damn it."

"Eventually." Jentaron's mouth kicked into a grin, and they sped toward the flaming hill surrounded by shrieking wraiths.

Eve stared at her father's disapproving glare, thankful that, for once, it wasn't directed her way.

"You let your sister take the fall for your antics? Your *younger* sister?"

Duncan remained silent, but James tried to explain himself. "It was a mistake. We were trying to find her when—"

"It was as much my fault as his," Duncan muttered.

Teban stood out of the way in the shadows, not as comfortable in the light of her father's hall. But hell, no one actually liked the light except for Eve, her brothers and her father. Since falling from heaven, Asael maintained a perpetual glow, as well as an otherworldly presence, proclaiming his Descent to all. Fallen angels made the most ferocious demons, because they alone in the lower realm knew what it was to face the abject horrors of His wrath.

"Now hold on a minute. You two stole a dragon's egg, trying to teach your sister a lesson. But you blamed it on the angels?" He stroked his smooth face, the perfection of his features blinding at first glance. Teban, she noted, had yet to take his gaze from Asael. "That I commend. But your job is not to educate your sister. She is as she's meant to be. A bit soft-hearted, true, but pure of heart."

Eve grinned. Apparently, her father had finally forgiven her for the elementary school fiasco.

"That said, you two need to stop using Eve to break the rules. Use a little creativity, sons, and figure out a way to do it without her. Hell and damn. You want an innocent piece of ass, take it the way I took your mother. Find your own loopholes. Do I need to do everything for you?"

James and Duncan glanced away, embarrassed. Teban snickered. A mistake.

163

Asael's eyes shot to Teban, assessing. "And Carmaron went along with this idiotic plan? Come here, little dragon, or should I say, dragon prince. Into the light, if you will."

Trust her father to call Teban little. The dragon had arrived in human form, but she'd seen him as a beast. And "little" didn't describe him, in either form.

"Uh, not exactly. Mother's getting older, so I take charge of most of the day-to-day in the catacombs. But I will say I was misled about the situation." Teban glared at James, who started to speak, then saw their father looking at him and shut up.

"I see. Well, then." Asael glanced down as if in thought, but Eve caught the smirk he tried to hide. "On to justice for all. Duncan, you owe Uriel ten days of service. Ten days with that angel will seem like fifty, and as much as I loathe Uriel, I admire his ingenuity when it comes to punishment. But try to use the time to scout the enemy, if you still have your eyes and ears when he releases you."

Duncan groaned.

"James, you're Teban's to do with as he will. Ten days of service he owes you, prince. Ten days of service you'll receive."

Teban's smile widened, and his teeth elongated past his lips. "Thank you, Asael."

"Try not to scar him overmuch. He is my son, and I hold some fondness for him."

"*Father.*"

"You'd rather the pit?"

James looked at Eve, who shuddered.

"No pit. She's not at fault here," Ranton thundered as he entered her father's main chamber from above, accompanied by another dragon. None of the crude buildings in the Abyss sported ceilings, and Eve had always thought her father partial to the sky in deference to his time spent in the upper realm.

Ranton settled quickly, black scales covering his body, a flaming sword in his hands. The dragon beside him looked like his twin, save he had dark blue eyes and blond hair. Very, very odd.

"Ah, the new dragon king." Asael rose to greet the dragons. He slapped the blond on the back and nodded admiringly at

Ranton's sword. "General, how nice to see you again. I understand that you already know my daughter."

Ranton glanced at Eve, and she was taken aback at the sheer hunger in his gaze. As he stared, the hunger relented to show his anger, which he quickly masked. Her heart raced, and her pussy flooded. Only Ranton could make her both scared and aroused at the same time, the monstrous beast. Oh, shit. She was in for it now.

Her father glanced from her to Ranton and back again, and sat on his throne, his fingers steepled below his chin. Mischief, and if she wasn't mistaken, a spark of satisfaction, danced in his black eyes.

"She's mine," Ranton barked, not even trying to persuade her father of anything.

"She is," the blond dragon agreed. "I called and she came."

Her father's eyes narrowed. "You did?"

"He did?" James and Duncan said as one.

"By the damned," Eve breathed, finally realizing why the stranger looked like Ranton. "Jentaron?"

"Hello, Eve," he said, his voice decidedly seductive.

She blinked and glanced at Ranton, who glared between her and his brother.

"But, you were *an egg* a few days ago."

"Things change."

She couldn't stop staring, and heard Ranton growl. "This is your charge?" She laughed. "You must really have your hands full."

"You have no idea." Ranton's sword blazed. "But I think there's been some misunderstanding. You belong to me."

Asael stood and everyone quieted. He studied Ranton, and she knew what her father saw. A spirit so strong neither he nor the angels could touch it. And a fierceness, a hunger to rival the demons. "So you would take her punishment, then, since her delay was, in fact, your fault?"

"If you would live long enough to give it, yes," Ranton said softly, the threat hanging in the humid air.

Her father stared, unblinking, and soon laughed. But no one spoke, not sure if his laughter meant good tidings or bad. "I

165

like you, Ranton. Full of piss and vinegar, and not a little fire. You want my daughter, hmm? What of Eve's wants? Does she know what being yours will entail?"

Eve stared, openmouthed, at her father. He planned to just hand her over, no explanations needed? And what of Ranton? She was to become "his"? His what? His wife, his mate, his *property*? The last had her glaring and she took a few steps toward the domineering dragon.

"Yes, Ranton, what exactly does being *yours* entail?"

Jentaron smirked and took a step back. "I missed you, Eve."

Ranton breathed fire as he strode toward her. Before he deigned to explain, he kissed her so hard she could barely breathe. "*Sassa,* you will come home with me. We'll live here in the lower region, in the catacombs, and I'll allow you to complete the work of the Ethereals, with some stipulations, of course."

She sputtered, incredulous at his arrogance. "You, you'll allow me—"

"Excellent." Her father beamed. "Make sure to beat her at least twice a week, and if she refuses to see reason, just drop her from the sky once or twice."

"*Father.*"

"Yes, dear. I love you too. But remember, we have work to do. Joining the dragons helps them more than it helps us. So you owe me one, Jentaron. And one day I'll collect."

"Of course you will." Jentaron bowed his head in respect, though his tone was wry.

"But I haven't said I agree." Eve wondered if she made a noise, for everyone seemed to be talking around her. Mating, moving, belonging? So confusing, so why was her heart pounding with...hope?

"The agreement was made for you." Asael hugged her to him and kissed her forehead tenderly. "Make sure to visit often, Eve. And I want one of the fauns to help see to the first of your many birthings."

Now Ranton looked as stunned as she felt. "Birthings? I'm a warrior, not a breeder."

"And she's a demon, not a dragon. Of course you'll breed. And won't that be a battle, to see who wields the Nailiim."

"The what?"

Teban whistled. "The Nailiim. The offspring of dragon and demon. Totally forbidden by the archangel Michael thousands of years ago, today thought more myth than real. Well, this should be fun."

Her father grinned, and Jentaron nodded. "Now I see. Very shrewd, Asael. But rest assured, the hatchlings of dragon blood will remain with my sect."

"And yet those young will breed a new line, and so on and so forth, thinning the hold on your blood, hmm? Then we'll see, won't we?"

"Wait a minute here." Eve's head was spinning. "Hatchlings? I'm a demon, a measure of balance. I don't breed young."

"I know, dear. But you will." Asael sat again and waved to them. "Now this has been enlightening, but I have souls to steal and punishments to mete. Duncan, James, serve out your sentences. Oh, and Duncan, I will be checking with Uriel, so don't try to cheat me out of justice. And try to be discreet when gathering information, okay?"

Duncan swore and disappeared in the blink of an eye.

"You think you're getting off lightly, don't you, James?" Her father laughed, and Eve knew James was in for it. For three hundred years she'd sat by her father's knee. His punishments were swift but fair, and the devil knew James deserved more than his share of retribution for all that he'd put her through. "I know more about Teban than he knows about himself. Good luck."

Teban frowned at her father as he transformed into his beast. Not quite as large as Ranton, Teban nevertheless intimidated with his sharp teeth, fiery breath and glittering green scales. Once turned, his eyes glowed with anticipation, and Eve wondered just what Teban had in mind for her brother, his "friend".

James nodded with deference to Asael, but glared and batted away the claw Teban held out to him. Instead he surrounded himself with blue flame and gracefully mounted

167

Teban's ridged back, waiting with a glum expression, nestled between the gray-green wings.

"A pleasure, as always, Asael." Teban rumbled and turned to Ranton. "I'll see you two at home. And welcome to the world, little brother." He padded to Jentaron and blew fire over the younger male's body.

Jentaron smiled, his grin making Eve's heart race. Damn it all. He looked so much like Ranton, but with blue-gray eyes and blond hair. And that grin made her impossibly wet. He patted Teban on the head, then turned his attention back to Eve. An unnatural hunger burned in his dragon eyes, and she took a step back.

"Oh no, *sassa*. We have some things to discuss at home." Ranton smiled through his teeth and placed his sword at his back. "Asael, until we meet again."

"Good luck, Ranton. You're going to need it. And to you, young king. Blessings of the damned upon your line."

Jentaron nodded. "Thank you, Asael. I'll be seeing you soon, I'm sure. A few years at most before the first of the young arrive."

Asael smiled back. "Exactly."

Eve sputtered, but could say no more as Ranton caught her in his arms and took to the sky. The glitter in his eyes and the speed in his wings told her one thing.

There would be hell to pay.

# Chapter Seven

"If you think that macho display of speed scared me, think again." Standing in Ranton's brightly lit room, Eve glared at Ranton and locked her hands on her hips. Scared, ha. She'd been petrified. But no way in hell would she let him know how much she hated that stomach-in-the-throat maneuver he seemed to have perfected every time she'd flown with him.

"But Eve, we don't want you scared, do we Ranton?" Jentaron said, studying her as if he'd never seen a female before.

Then again, perhaps he hadn't.

"Speak for yourself." Fire darted from Ranton's eyes. "This little demon owes me for what she pulled."

*For what, screwing his brains out?* Eve couldn't help a smirk, and knew she'd made a huge mistake when Ranton's skin began to scale over. Inky darts of color washed over his hands and forearms, and his pupils flamed inside jet-black eyes.

Ranton grabbed her by the shoulders and flame arched over her face. The dragon fire felt more like a caress than a blow, however, and she found herself becoming aroused in the presence of Ranton's rage.

"I want to know what you did to me, exactly. Did you put a spell on me, little demon? And did you really think you could run far enough away that I'd never find you?"

"Yes, Eve," Jentaron added, approaching her from behind. His breath kissed her neck, and she jerked at the sensation of feeling trapped. Angling a look over her shoulder, she swallowed hard. Jentaron's eyes blazed, blue and silver bands of light that looked more demon than dragon. "What exactly did you do to Ranton? Because whatever it was had a definite impact on me as well. I felt a burst of energy just as big brother lost consciousness."

Ranton growled at the reminder and pulled Eve closer, so that she could feel his thick erection prodding her belly. "Why don't you show me again just what you did? And don't worry, this time I'll stop you before I black out."

Ranton glanced over her head, his expression both tense and approving.

"Look, Ranton. I don't know why you think you're the one giving orders around here, but you have to understand—"

She sucked in a breath when Jentaron's lips found the racing pace of her jugular. He sucked, lightly at first, then harder, leaving a mark. And his touch arched lightning through her body.

Staring at Ranton, she saw his mirrored surprise, as well as an evil grin, darkening his face.

"Payback's a bitch, Eve. And you owe us both."

"You left me to hatch alone, Evie," Jentaron murmured and pressed into her backside. He groaned and rubbed against her. "And my hungers have only gotten worse. You have to ease me, Eve. I command it."

Ranton nodded. "And as his Guardian, I can compel you to do so."

Eve blinked, totally turned-on, and totally perplexed. "You want me to fuck your brother?"

"To teach him, instruct him in the ways of human sexuality, and relieve his aches. Love him, Eve, as you do me," he said softly.

Tears welled, confusing her. Her body was on fire, and her emotions jumbled about, desire and love melding within. "I..." She didn't know what to say.

"Show us, Eve. Show us your love," Jentaron whispered, and turned her mouth to his kiss.

Though at an awkward angle, Jentaron's kiss soon had her lost to everything but his unique scent, and the burning pitch of desire. Whereas Ranton's touch commanded her acceptance, made it impossible to refuse, Jentaron's was lighter, more hesitant. And as she understood his newness to sexuality, she also understood he was different than Ranton. Less domineering, gentler. Yet in no way less potent.

"That's it, Jentaron," Ranton murmured, ripping through Eve's clothing with what she imagined a sharp claw. "Take her mouth, love her and own her."

She wanted to deny this talk of ownership, but Jentaron surprised her by plunging his tongue into her mouth. She could feel his erection pressing against her ass, and as the kiss deepened, wasn't surprised when he began pushing against her.

"By the embers, Eve," Jentaron rasped as he left her mouth, trailing kisses down her neck. "I need you so much."

"Easy, brother." Ranton cupped Eve's breasts in his large hands, surprising her that she hadn't felt her clothes fall off. "You've yet to enjoy the taste of her breasts."

Jentaron moved so quickly she had barely blinked before he stood before her.

"So beautiful." His eyes filled, and she glanced from him to Ranton, taken aback at the loving expression in Ranton's gaze as he stared at her.

This was more than possession, more than ownership. Ranton looked at her as if he...loved her.

He smiled, meeting her questioning gaze. "You're mine, Eve. Mine to protect, mine to love, mine to keep. And you're Jentaron's as well." They noted Jentaron's fascination with her body. He had yet to take his eyes from her. "You are his Guardian, like me. You answered his call, and it's now your duty to see to our new king."

She swallowed. "See to him?"

Jentaron took her breast in his mouth and she moaned, the pull of his lips shooting to her womb.

"That's it, Eve. Feel the pleasure, take the offering. You're ours now. Say it."

Ranton moved behind her and ran his hands over her back and around to her belly. Stroking her ribs with feather-light touches, he surprised her with the speed at which he suddenly penetrated her slick channel with his fingers, and she closed her eyes in helpless surrender.

"Say it."

His thumb rubbed her clit while he thrust his digits inside her, and Jentaron continued his loving exploration of her breasts with enthusiasm, bringing her closer and closer to orgasm. Dear hell, but she couldn't help the affection, the love, from spilling over her.

"I'm yours." She opened her eyes to see Jentaron's lit with a fierce hunger.

"Yes, ours." He kissed her again, and before she knew it, she returned his kiss, teaching him how to angle his mouth, how to stroke her tongue with his own, turning his hunger into nearly unquenchable desperation. His body temperature escalated, and she wondered that she didn't feel the burn. But Ranton made it nearly impossible to think.

"Down, Eve," Ranton growled. "On your knees."

He pushed her down as she moved, and she knelt on the hard stone, stimulated by the cold on her hands and knees in contrast to the fiery heat of her lovers. She felt Ranton between her thighs, and tingled when he pushed her legs further apart to settle between them. Jentaron, however, remained on his feet and stared down at her, his cock just slightly higher than her head.

Pre-come glittered at his tip, and she saw the tightness of his sack, the veins prominent on his thick shaft. Jentaron's chest rose and fell, his breathing loud as he stared at Eve on her knees, his brother preparing to fuck her.

"I'll never forget this moment," he said, love in his eyes. "You are so beautiful to me, Eve, so loving. My Guardians," Jentaron sighed. He glanced at Ranton, and she could tell they spoke without words.

When Jentaron left her to walk toward the bed, she watched, anticipation making her wetter and wetter. Ranton played with his cock between her cheeks, and she remembered everything about their last anal play.

"Oh, Eve," Ranton whispered. "You're going to love this so much you'll beg for more. And this is only just beginning. You owe me, love."

"Payback," she breathed, more than eager to settle the score. She wanted Ranton with every beat of her racing heart, and every drop of her heating blood. The demon wanted the dragon, wanted to feel possessed, owned. And Ranton, damn him, knew it.

He rumbled with dark laughter, nudging his cock further into her hole. The heat of him stole her composure, and she angled away, wanting him in her pussy more than her ass. She ached for him, and he meant to prolong her agony.

Jentaron returned quickly, and knelt on two thick pillows he carried.

"What—"

His cock soon met her lips. On the pillows, he aligned perfectly with her mouth, and without saying a word, he pushed for entry, his gaze gone completely silver.

She opened her mouth and accepted him, taking him inch by inch until he was seated fully inside her.

"Eve," he groaned and pulled out, only to slide back in. "That's so good."

Jentaron clenched her hair and began fucking her mouth. Her clit throbbed at his taste, and she unconsciously shoved her ass back toward Ranton. He penetrated her more, and his thickness hurt. But even the pain felt better than the emptiness in her womb. She wanted him to fill her, to be one with her. And her utter need made it impossible for her to succumb to pleasure without him.

She moaned and tried again, failing to capture Ranton between her legs.

"That's good, Eve. Need me, *sassa*. Need me forever," Ranton said thickly and repositioned himself lower. His shaft slid into her with ease, her channel wet and welcoming as he stretched her walls.

"Mmm," she managed around Jentaron's cock. *So good. Give me more, Ranton, Jentaron, more.*

As if he'd heard her, Jentaron grew longer, his size stunning Eve despite her ability to automatically accept him. The demon within her hungered, and Jentaron meant to feed her.

"I can't hold back," he groaned. "Eve, take me."

She pressed harder with her tongue, and raked her teeth lightly along the underside of his shaft. Jentaron cried out and shot, quaking as he filled her mouth with sweet come.

On and on he pulsed, while Ranton fucked her from behind. Jentaron finally stopped and withdrew from her mouth. Ranton continued to pound into her, grunting with pleasure, and she felt her rise toward climax as he hit that spot within her that made her bones melt.

Jentaron leaned down to kiss her. He murmured her name and stroked her hair. He was so gentle, so reverential, and determined to make her crazy with lust. His scent stirred her ardor anew, and when he reached down to fondle her breasts, she rammed back into Ranton's thrusts with a ferocity that increased Ranton's aggression.

"Fuck, Eve. You're killing me," he rasped, his hands clenching her ass so hard he'd leave bruises. The feel of his balls slapping her pussy as he pummeled her made her moan, and his cock felt like pure, dark ecstasy as he took her higher and higher into the perfection of rapture.

Jentaron pinched her nipples and trailed his kisses along her cheek to her ear.

"When Ranton's done, I'm going to fuck you again. I want your ass, Eve, that perfect, round white ass." He thrust his tongue in her ear and she saw stars.

Just as Ranton roared his release, she found hers. Sparks of color lit the blackness suddenly all around her. Her breath froze, her body seized, and pure fire lit her from head to toe, centering in her womb. Ranton's seed dripped down her legs as he came and continued to thrust, until finally, she'd milked all of him.

"Eve," he sighed, and leaned forward to hug her. "Mine."

"Mine," Jentaron agreed, stroking the tears from her cheeks.

"You've both got it wrong," Eve said hoarsely. "Demons rule the lower realm. Therefore, you're both mine."

Jentaron chuckled, but Ranton growled in warning.

"Don't worry, brother. I'm sure we can make Eve see the error of her ways. After all, she was right before. We're all really demons at heart, aren't we?" His eyes blazed, and communication passed between brothers.

Ranton withdrew and came to face her as Jentaron took his place behind her. He chuckled at her face. "Such starry eyes, *sassa*. I think we're wearing her down, Jentaron. But Eve, you still owe me from before."

She glanced down only to see his cock rise again, and her eyes widened. But before she could ask him what he meant her to do, Jentaron slid his cock into her dripping pussy.

"Oh, that is good, Ranton," he said, his voice amazed. "I wish that I—" he paused. "But I won't. Your seed will breed true in Eve. Mine is meant for another."

Eve suddenly understood what he meant when he withdrew and pushed his fingers deep in her pussy. He slid them up and began pushing slowly into her ass.

"No, Jentaron," she protested, his thick fingers stretching her.

"Yes, Eve," Ranton said, amused. "Don't worry, I'll guide him. He won't hurt you...much." His eyes twinkled, and she saw the love shining bright in the sparkles of green and white glowing there.

"You're going to get yours," she breathed hard, harder when Jentaron groaned and replaced his fingers with his cock. "See if you don't find yourself ass-fucked one of these days."

Ranton raised a brow and began stroking himself. He sat in front of her and lay back on the pillows, one hand behind his head and the other on his cock.

"She feels incredible, doesn't she?" he asked his brother.

Jentaron groaned but said nothing, focused on Eve.

"I don't understand how you two make me feel this," she panted, shaking as her body coiled, readying to spring again into climax. "No human or demon ever has."

"Good," Ranton said, his breathing choppy. "Because you were meant for me." He stared over her shoulder and sighed. "For us. Until my king takes a queen. So make sure you teach him right." His eyes glittered. "Now show him how sorry you can be, for having taken advantage of your mate." He glanced down to his huge erection.

"Mate?" she cried, as Jentaron thrust harder into her ass. Good night, she hoped he wasn't planning to grow as large as he had in her mouth. The thought of it made her groan, and she heard him laugh.

"Don't worry, *sassa*. I want only to bring you pleasure as well."

Fire suddenly burned at her clit, a blaze of pleasure that lit her entire body. And she realized Jentaron had somehow spelled her. The pull of Ranton's cock had her lowering her arms and head to his groin as he spread his thighs around her.

At his taste, she shuddered. So male, so incredibly powerful. And her scent lay subtly over his, showing her they were in fact one. She began sucking him, taking him deeper and deeper as Jentaron rammed into her. The exquisite sensation of belonging took her over, and she groaned as she began coming, her thighs wet with bliss.

Jentaron cried out and tensed as he filled her ass, his seed hot as it hit her hole and slid down her thighs.

Ranton bucked as her lips and tongue teased him, taunting him as she controlled his orgasm.

"More, Eve. Suck the head, take me deeper," he groaned, threading his fingers through her hair. He held her, fucking her mouth with surer strokes. "By the fire, I'm coming, *sassa*. Swallow me, love. Take my marker," he hissed as he shot, arching off the floor into her mouth.

Groans filled the air, the scent of love overwhelming as Eve experienced yet another orgasm.

Jentaron and Ranton remained inside her until she'd wrung them dry, then withdrew and cuddled her between them on the cold, hard floor.

"Mmm," she murmured, wanting to protest the cold. But she hadn't the energy to do more than snuggle into her lovers.

Lovers. Ranton and Jentaron, dragons of flame, rulers of power. The love she felt for them both astounded her. Ranton's was pure, dark and decidedly sexual. Jentaron's was filled with desire as well, yet tempered with the need to protect, and to guide. So young, yet so strong already. He answered that need within her to serve and defend, and she sighed at the perfection of her place in life.

"I'm still not sure how we're going to work this out, Eve," Ranton murmured.

"Oh, I've got some ideas." Jentaron chuckled and spooned Eve, hugging her waist. He caressed her skin, his touch comforting. "I love you, *sassa*." He swallowed loudly and continued. "And Ranton, I just wanted to tell you how much I love you as well. You are my brother, my teacher, my Guardian. And I know how difficult it is to share that which you treasure above all else. I'll never take you for granted."

Eve leaned back to look at Ranton's face, and wasn't surprised to see her gruff dragon getting all teary-eyed.

"You're young, but with a knowledge that far surpasses anything I might have imagined. You'll make a fine king, Jentaron. Eve and I wouldn't let you be anything else." He cleared his throat and glanced down at Eve, his heart in his eyes. "And I love you, *sassa*, completely. Both of you, with every flame of my fire." He blinked several times, ridding himself of tears. "Now if we're done with this sentimental crap, let's move to the bed. This frail human form is decidedly uncomfortable on cold rock."

Eve grinned, and had to be carried by Jentaron to the bed. Her legs wouldn't hold her. Once there, she turned to Jentaron, curious.

"So what are these ideas about my future?" she wanted to know.

Moments later, Eve could only stare at him in shock. Angels in the lower realm? Blood elves with souls? Demons and dragons and Nailiim coexisting in the dragon stronghold? Life was about to become much more complicated down here. Chaotic, unruly, and quite possibly more dangerous than life in the Ordinary.

Eve laughed out loud at the thought and smiled at her lovers. She couldn't have been happier.

ಲಏಬದ

Duncan controlled his rage, only barely, learning Uriel had stripped another sway from under his command, effectively stealing another soul for heaven. Damn his father to heaven for putting him through this shit. It ate at his being to watch the angels take souls that should have belonged in hell.

"Thank you, Duncan, for enabling me to save another poor soul from eternal damnation. You know, you'd make a fine angel," Uriel said kindly, pissing Duncan off even more. "You're more like your father than you know—at least, more like the Asael I knew in the upper realm."

"Fuck you." Duncan would have lunged at Uriel for the insult, save for the golden silk binding his wrists and ankles that forced him to remain upright in the middle of the room. Funny thing, he couldn't see what the bindings were tied to, and he imagined he looked like a puppet strung in the air. Fucking angel magic. The glowing brilliance of Uriel's room didn't help either. Marble lined the floor, the walls a pale cream and covered in artwork showcasing the world's judgment, saved by heaven's angels.

"Fuck me? But I though you preferred females." Uriel shrugged, then began to undress. First his trousers, then his long tunic.

The move made Duncan tense, and he tugged harder at the Ethereal ropes holding him tight. "Keep away, asshole, or I'll break the promise I made my father and roast you alive."

"Alive, dead, you're forgetting who you are. Who we are, demon." Uriel grinned, then stood proud and naked before Duncan, his skin so white it was nearly blinding. Duncan had to look away and froze when he felt cool hands on his naked skin.

"Don't worry, Duncan. I wouldn't soil my palms touching a demon." Uriel smirked. "But my apprentices like to work on your kind, to better understand what they're up against."

Duncan gritted his teeth when he saw two dark-haired females petting him. Unbidden, his dick rose, though he wanted none of their angelic touch.

"There we are," Uriel grinned and lay back on his feathered bed to watch. "A demon's pleasure has its own beauty. Let them ease you with the purity of their touch."

Duncan sweated at the effort not to respond to the beautiful women stroking his skin. At least humans encouraged lusts, engaged in the carnality demons breathed like air.

But the angels...their touch hurt, the goodness, the light of their thoughts left pinpricks of pain in their wake. And unlike James, Duncan had never been one to mix pleasure and pain. Yet still his cock rose, and he glared over at Uriel. An angelic spell, no doubt.

"Oh, and Duncan, congratulations on your sister's nuptials."

Duncan stared. "What?"

"Eve made her ties to Ranton official yesterday. Seems she's also taken on the role of Guardian to the dragon's new king, Jentaron."

Duncan nodded, pleased his sister had found such a powerful place in the lower realm. But as Guardian to the dragon king, how would she fulfill her duties to the Ethereal?

"Oh, and Asael sent another message. Eve is going to be occupied watching over the dragons and their cousins, the blood elves. Apparently, there's been a shift in the balance, and some of those in the lower and middle realm, before thought untouchable, actually aren't." Uriel grinned, his handsome features stirring the females to increase their caressing. Now their hands wandered over Duncan's body with a carnal edge, and he strained at his fetters.

"Asael told me to tell you that you and your brother will soon have a new partner to keep order. But in the meantime, I'm to wring every ounce of apology from you that I can."

One of the angels wrapped her hand around Duncan's cock, and he shook from the force of his desire. The perversion of Uriel's minions should have made him sick, at the very least, impotent. But for some unknown reason, he found the angels' touch arousing.

"Sorry yet?"

"When I get free from these, you're going to pay for this." Duncan felt his eyes burn, and knew Uriel saw it as well, for his grin faded.

Uriel rose from the bed, his arousal obvious. "You shouldn't make threats when in the arms of your enemy." He leaned close, his body nearly brushing Duncan's, and Duncan couldn't help the flinch of alarm as he leaned back as far as his restraints would allow.

Uriel laughed and rubbed a finger along Duncan's cheek, the ache scarring him deep. "So pretty for a demon. Behave, Duncan, or I'll let Sara do what she's been begging me for since she laid eyes on you."

Sara, the apprentice with deep, brown eyes, stared hungrily at his cock. Damnation, Uriel wasn't suggesting...

He howled with a mix of rage and pain, and a stunning depth of sexual desire, as Sara took him deep in her mouth.

Uriel sighed. "Ah, the bliss of enlightenment. These ten days won't last long enough, Duncan."

# About the Author

Marie Harte is an avid reader who loves all things paranormal and futuristic. Reading romances since she was twelve, she fell in love with the warmth of first passion and knew writing was her calling.

Twenty-three years later, the Marine Corps, a foray through Information Technology, a husband and four kids, and her dream has finally come true. Marie lives in Georgia with her family and loves hearing from readers.

To read more about Marie, visit Marie at www.marieharte.com and http://marieharte.blogspot.com.

# Look for these titles by
## *Marie Harte*

### *Now Available*
Midsummer Night's Steam: A Scorching Seduction

### *Coming Soon:*
Enjoying the Show
Rachel's Totem

# Wings of Change

*Bianca D'Arc*

# Dedication

To my family for their unfailing support of my writing dream. Many thanks to the good friends I've made through this dragon world I've been privileged to write about for the past few years, especially Megan, Jennifer and Serena for their untiring support and assistance. Thanks also to Angela James for selecting this story, and Summer Devon and Marie Harte, my co-conspirators in the anthology.

# Chapter One

Lucia was more than a little intimidated by the towering castle doorway. Beyond the imposing portal lay the Lair that housed the king's own knights and dragons. It was audacious of her to even walk up to the heavily carved door, but she was on a mission. A life hung in the balance.

Gathering her courage, she lifted the heavy metal knocker. The ornate striker, cast in the shape of a dragon's sinuous body, made an echoing boom as it descended on the plate. It also made her jump, but she scolded herself to be calm. She had to make someone within the castle listen to her.

"What can I do for you, little lady?" A gnarled veteran with a kind smile answered her summons.

She cleared the frog in her throat before speaking. "I need to speak with Sir Kaden."

"Sorry, lass. He's been closeted with the king and council these two days past. The whole castle's in an uproar since the young prince has gone missing."

She should have expected the response. Prince William's disappearance was the talk of the entire city. Her spirits sank, but she refused to give up so easily.

"Perchance, could I talk to Lady Linea?"

"Linea?" The man seemed surprised as he opened the door a bit wider. "Now why would a little thing like you wish to speak with a dragon?"

"And why *my* dragon?" A deep, masculine voice sounded from behind the old man. Lucia looked up, over the old veteran's shoulder to meet the startling ocean blue gaze of what must certainly be a knight of the realm. The door opened wider and the knight stepped to the side of the guard, looking her up and down.

Lucia cringed, knowing what a pitiful sight she made in her rough work clothes, but they were all she had. What she wouldn't give for just one of the many silk gowns she had once owned. But that life was over.

"Please, sir, I know it's a bad time, but I must speak with Lady Linea. A dragon's life is at stake."

"Of which dragon do you speak?"

Lucia was torn. She'd already said more than she should have. "I promised I wouldn't tell anyone, but he asked me to say goodbye—" her voice cracked with emotion before she got herself back under control, "—to Linea and Kaden."

"Kaden?" the knight asked quickly. "Sweet Mother, are you talking about Reynor?" Tears threatening, she nodded, biting her lip. The knight swung the imposing door open wide and took her arm, pulling her into the castle. He led her down a wide hall and Lucia caught sight of other dragons moving here and there. If she'd been in a better frame of mind, she would have loved this glimpse into the Castle Lair, but as things stood, she was too worried about Reynor to notice much. The knight stopped in a small alcove that had seats, but she was too agitated to sit. "Can you tell me what this is about?"

"I'm sorry, milord, but I must speak to Lady Linea. I promised Sir Reynor."

"I'll take you to Linea, but I don't understand why."

Could he really be that blind, she wondered? "They are in love, sir. Linea is his mate."

The knight looked shocked for a moment before a smile dawned over his face. "I had no idea."

"But—" She hesitated as he began walking again, pacing his long strides to allow for her shorter steps.

"Speak freely, mistress. I promise I don't bite." His devilish smile spoke otherwise.

"Well, I thought you were Linea's knight. Did I misunderstand?"

"No, you heard correctly. I'm Marcus, Linea's partner."

"Then how could you not know about—"

He grinned down at her as they turned a corner. "About her and Reynor? Actually, it's pretty simple. The dragons were waiting to tell us until Kaden or I found a mate. Until then, no matter how much they might love one another, they are forbidden to join."

"Really?"

Marcus liked the way the petite maid's eyes widened. She really was the cutest little thing. A full foot shorter than him, she would fit snugly under his chin, should they ever embrace. He liked that idea. Perhaps more than he should on such short acquaintance.

But her words had him worried...and elated at the same time. He was worried about Reynor, but ecstatic to know Linea and Rey were a pair. It gave him some idea who he'd be sharing his mate with when they finally did find her. This cute little wench might even be up for the challenge, though the Mother of All knew, few women were cut out to be mated to a set of knights.

"Because of the way dragon mating affects the knights involved, it is imperative the knights already have a wife of their own before the dragon side of the partnership can be allowed to consummate their union." Marcus gave her the bare bones of the explanation, enjoying the surprise on her lovely face. She had delicate features that spoke of foreign lands. She was intriguing, to say the least.

"Here we are." He opened the large door to the suite he shared with Linea, unsurprised to find the dragon basking in the oval pit of heated sand she loved. Her glistening, pale green scales winked at them in the dim light as just her head craned forward to greet them.

The girl made a deep bow, though her eyes never left those of the dragon. It was a mark of respect and good breeding that surprised him.

"Lady Linea," she said in a strong voice, "it is an honor to meet you. I am Lucia de Alagarithia, last of my line, lately of the Jinn. I bring grave news from Sir Reynor."

*"What's happened to Rey?"*

The dragon's voice rumbled through Marcus's mind, as it always did, comforting and beautiful. He watched the girl carefully to see whether or not she really could hear Linea. It was a rare person indeed who could hear a dragon's silent voice.

"You know already he was injured some time ago. The injury has not healed well and he's been spending a great deal of time at the tavern where I live and work as a serving girl."

Marcus was struck by the exchange. It appeared she really could hear dragons. His curiosity rose another notch.

"We've become friendly," she continued. "I noticed a dimness in his eyes yesterday, and badgered him until he would let me look at his wound. Lady," she paused, stepping closer to the dragon than Marcus had ever seen any stranger dare, "infection has set in and it rages beyond my meager skills. He needs a true healer or I'm afraid..." The girl choked up, her emotion clear. "I'm afraid he'll die." Her whispered words dropped into the silence of the room as she paused. "He made me promise not to tell anyone, but I can't sit by and do nothing. He also made me promise if the worst happened, I would tell you and Sir Kaden goodbye. I came here today to speak to Sir Kaden, but they said he's busy, so I thought perhaps you could do something."

Linea leapt out of her wallow, shaking sand off as she went, clearly agitated. Marcus sensed fear in her like he'd never known before. She was afraid for her mate.

*"I must see him! We must help him!"*

"We will, my love." Marcus stroked one large hand down her neck, trying to calm her. "But let's bring help as well. Can you get a message to King Roland? Kaden needs to know about this, though how Reynor could have hidden the seriousness of his injury from Kaden is beyond me."

*"He feels guilty. He wouldn't even talk to me for the past few days,"* Linea said, anger, frustration and despair in her tone.

Marcus nodded. "They both feel guilty. And it's completely misplaced." He turned back to the pretty girl. "Lucia, you did the right thing in coming here. Come, let's round up the others and be on our way. A stubborn dragon, and an even more stubborn knight, await."

ౠౠౠౠ

Kaden sat with the council, once again stewing over the tragic events of the past few days. The king's youngest brother, Prince William, had been kidnapped. Two young dragons had taken off after him, but no word had been heard from any of them since. Others had been dispatched, but the trail disappeared, and now all the Lairs were on the lookout for sign of the prince and those who'd followed him.

Kaden tried to concentrate on the discussion of efforts to find the young prince, but he couldn't help but think of his own problems and Rey's grievous injury. If he'd been a little faster, a little more nimble, Reynor would have never been hurt. Now, because of his failure, his dragon partner might never fly again. It was the worst fate one could imagine for a dragon. And it was all his fault. No wonder Rey didn't want to see him or even talk to him. Kaden didn't blame him, but he'd never felt so alone in all his life. Without the constant presence of the dragon in his mind, he felt more isolated than ever and his world was without color.

"Kaden!" King Roland shouted his name and Kaden came back to the meeting with a start.

"Yes, my liege."

"Linea tells me Reynor is near death. How could you let this happen?"

"What?" Kaden jumped up from his seat, confused and alarmed.

"A tavern girl from Castleton just came to see Linea, telling her Rey was close to death. You'd better go see what this is about. My wife will go with you. She's tried to contact Rey and he's rebuffing her."

"Sweet Mother! This is all my fault. He didn't want me around, but I thought it was because he blamed me."

At that moment, the queen swept into the room. She was wearing leathers more suited to a knight than a lady, but this queen wasn't your typical noblewoman. "I'm ready to go when you are, Kaden. Tor is waiting in the courtyard."

"Kaden, you and Reynor have serious issues to work out. Don't come back until this is settled." King Roland's expression was unforgiving and Kaden felt the weight of his burdens increase.

"Yes, my liege. I'm sorry." He headed for the doorway to join the waiting queen. "I'm sorry for all of this."

He and the queen headed down the halls at a fast pace. Urgency was required, but if anyone could save Rey, it was Queen Alania. She was a strong dragon healer with a true gift.

"Thank you, milady, for helping Rey."

"You boys have got to start communicating better, Kaden," the queen admonished him. "I can guess what happened. Rey blames himself for his injury while you thought he blamed you."

"I blame myself, milady."

She scoffed. "As I said. Each of you taking blame that should not exist. All dragons get hurt from time to time. It's a fact of our existence. The enemy—if anyone—deserves the blame for this injury, though both of you deserve to be whipped for letting it go this far. The first thing you need to do, once we get Rey back on his feet, is to clear the air between you. Is that understood?"

"Yes, my queen. Perfectly."

"All right then."

They rounded the last corner and came out into a wide courtyard. A giant, sparkling silver dragon waited for them.

"Tor will carry us down to Castleton. Flying is faster than going by land and we haven't a moment to lose."

Another dragon waited, pacing at Tor's side. Linea didn't conceal her impatience well, but her knight partner's eyes were compassionate when they met his. He and Marcus had always been good friends.

"Linea and I will take Lucia," Kaden noticed the small woman hovering in the background for the first time, "and lead the way to the tavern." Kaden was glad Marcus was there to take charge. Just at the moment, Kaden couldn't think beyond the fact that Reynor might die because of his stupidity.

# Chapter Two

Lucia had never ridden on a dragon's back before. Today was indeed a day of firsts. Linea flew beautifully and if not for the dire situation, Lucia would have enjoyed her first flight immensely. The dragon was poetry in motion beneath her, and the strong man holding her by the waist made her feel warm and cared for in a way she hadn't experienced since losing her family all those years ago.

They set down in the tavern yard, the pale green dragon followed closely by the stunning silver beast named Tor. Everyone had heard tales about the royal Ice Dragon who'd been raised by the queen. Lucia strongly suspected the lovely woman riding on the silver dragon was the queen herself.

Jumping down from the dragon's back into Marcus's strong arms, Lucia tried to suppress the little thrill of attraction she felt for the handsome knight. This was no time to start dreaming impossible dreams. Reynor had to come first. His life was at stake here. She led the way into the large tavern—empty now, so early in the day. Part of the old city, the main room had been built on a scale to hold two or three dragons, if they wished to hear some music and join in the merriment of an evening with their knights.

But for the past few days, Reynor had become a full-time resident. Nobody questioned it at first, though they saw to it he had plenty of water. Dragons could go a few days without eating, but everyone knew they enjoyed sweets like melons and bushels of apples, so he had all he could want within easy reach.

Only Lucia would dare go close enough to serve the dragons. She liked them a great deal and had no fear of them, so whenever a dragon deigned to visit the tavern, Lucia was elected to serve them. She didn't mind it at all. In fact, she looked forward to such occasions.

*"Lucy, what have you done?"* Rey's deep voice shivered through her mind.

"I did what I had to do. I brought help." She stood before the shimmering blue dragon, unafraid, with her hands perched on her hips, as if daring him to argue. When he only sighed in defeat and lowered his head to the ground, she walked forward and crouched beside him. "I don't want to see you crippled...or dead, Rey. You're too special for me to allow it. Please forgive me."

*"There is nothing to forgive. You have a good heart, Lucy."*

The queen went immediately to the dragon's left wing. The area near the joint had swollen to three times its normal size and the wound was badly inflamed. Reynor spread his wing at the queen's gentle urging, though not without a great deal of pain. Lucia stayed by his head, stroking his scales soothingly while the other woman worked.

A man she'd seen only a few times before crouched down next to the dragon on the other side, touching the scaled head and looking deep into Reynor's jeweled eyes. Remorse shone clearly on the knight's face. Remorse, fear...and love. Lucia backed off, seeing the two reunited as they should be.

As she moved back, she faltered, but strong arms caught her against a hard chest. Sir Marcus held her waist, tucking her under his chin, her back to his warm, hard front. He gentled her when she would have struggled out of his hold.

"Be at ease, little dragon tamer." His words whispered over her hair. "You've done a beautiful thing by bringing us here. It is a debt we can never repay."

She settled back against him. Sir Kaden lay on the floor, hugging the dragon's neck hard as the queen set about her work. The glow of magic in the air was undeniable. Lucia hadn't seen it since she was a child, but she recognized the subtle scent of ozone and the tingle of strong magic.

When she'd realized how badly Rey was hurt, Lucia had been tempted to try to use the magic talisman given to her when she escaped her homeland all those years ago, but she was too afraid. For one thing, the precious gift was only to be used in the most dire of circumstances, when all other hopes had failed. Such was the credo of her line. For another, Lucia had never used magic before, though she knew some of her family had once been potent healers. They'd been killed before she could learn anything about magic or even discover if she had the ability.

Still, Reynor was a special being and she'd felt desperate as she watched him grow weaker. Unable to stand by and watch him die, she'd done what was necessary to get help for him. The queen was reputed to be a strong dragon healer, though Lucia could see Reynor's eyes cloud with agony as the woman worked. He twitched with pain, but his knight held him and comforted him as best he could.

"I only wish I'd gone to the castle sooner." Her words whispered out on a tragic sigh. She became aware of the green dragon's head looming next to them. Linea, it seemed, refused to be left outside.

*"Will he be all right? Marcus, do you know?"* In her agitation, the female dragon was broadcasting her worries to Lucia as well.

*"The queen has said nothing yet, but she doesn't look too worried to me,"* Marcus replied. *"Judging from her expression I'd say he'll live, though whether he'll ever fly properly again is in the hands of the Mother, I'll wager."*

*"It always was,"* Linea answered. *"The injury was bad enough in the first place, but now those two fools have let it get out of hand!"* The dragon seemed infuriated if the twitching of her tail was any indication.

"May I ask..." Lucia's words were a hesitant whisper. "How did it happen?"

"It was stupid, really." Marcus's hands tightened on her waist, fingers digging into her hips before he seemed to realize what he was doing and released her. "Have you heard about the fighting on the border?" When she nodded, he continued, "We were involved in a skirmish the last time out. Sometimes with these kinds of engagements, you get caught low, within range of ground weapons. It happens." He shrugged. "I saw Rey dodge an arrow. He lost altitude and came within sword distance of a group of cavalry. In such instances, the knight can engage with his own weapons, which Kaden did—and very well too—until one got past his guard and a wild swing took a chunk out of Reynor's wing, down near the joint. It's one of the few places not well protected by scale—it needs to be flexible, you see. A freak of luck for the adversary, though Rey's blast of flame took care of him and his horse soon enough. Still, Rey barely stayed aloft and we had to practically tow him back here. The queen saw to him that night, but the kind of healing he needs is tricky. It's not simply a matter of sewing together something that was torn. A wedge of his wing was actually cut out."

Tears flowed down Lucia's face as she heard the tale, watching the beautiful young queen try to banish the raging infection. Turning in Marcus's loose embrace, Lucia sobbed against the man's chest. She knew she was overreacting, but she couldn't help herself. Rey was so special. He was such a good and kind dragon. She couldn't imagine him crippled for life. It was too painful to contemplate.

"I'm sorry." She sniffled as strong arms settled around her. She wasn't above accepting comfort from Sir Marcus. Men of his station never looked twice at her now that she was a serving wench, though once upon a time...

But fairy tales wouldn't put food in her belly. She'd learned that the hard way when all she'd ever known was cruelly ripped from her grasp. She didn't have much faith in people, but the knights she'd seen in Draconia had begun to make her think maybe—just maybe—there were a few good men left in the world. It was her friendship with the dragons that started her thinking about the men they chose as partners. Surely such noble, magical creatures could see into the hearts of the men they chose to fight alongside.

Lucia dried her tears and cautioned herself to restrain her emotions. Coming apart at the seams did nobody any good. She straightened away from the knight, averting her eyes in embarrassment.

"I'm sorry, Sir Marcus. Please excuse my behavior."

He tipped her chin up until her eyes met his. She was mortified. She just knew her face was blotchy and her eyes were probably red. Oh, why did she have to look like a watery hag when faced with masculine perfection given life?

"You are a puzzle, madam. You look like a tavern girl, but you speak like a lady."

She read curiosity in his lovely eyes. Curiosity and a flicker of interest? Surely not.

"The riddle is easily solved, sir. I am a tavern girl now, but I was once a lady."

A deep, whining moan from the dragon ended their ever-so-slightly flirtatious conversation. Lucia whipped her head around to see what was wrong as Linea shot past, her large green head hovering over her mate. Her long tongue licked out to smooth his ruffled scales with loving attention.

Lucia saw the queen sway on her feet as her power dimmed. Rushing over, Lucia brought a chair for the woman, realizing only then that the owner of the tavern and a few of the other staff were watching the scene from behind the bar. Lucia left the chair ready for the queen and went to the bar.

"Is that lady—?" one of the other girls ventured.

"The queen." Lucia nodded, bustling about as she poured a stiff, restorative ale.

"Imagine that. The queen in our bar." The same girl stared as if star struck.

A commotion near the large door meant for dragons caught Lucia's attention. The silver dragon was trying to fit through the doorway, but he was larger than the others and the place was built to house only two or three regular-sized dragons at any one time. With Rey and Linea already inside, their third, larger friend would be a tight fit.

Lucia went over to him on her way back to the queen. She bowed low, holding her laden tray steady with the impeccable balance that had been trained into her as a child.

"Welcome, Sir Tor. I'm Lucia. I'm sorry, but I don't think you'll fit inside right now. Perhaps you could sit in the yard and crane your neck through the doorway?"

The silver dragon cocked his head toward her. *"Can you hear me?"*

"Yes, milord."

*"Great! I'm Tor."* Lucia couldn't help but smile at the young dragon's enthusiasm. *"Could you help Lana for me? She'll be awfully weak after healing Rey."*

"I guessed as much. This drink is for her. I will aid her in any way I can."

*"You're nice. Thanks."*

"It's my pleasure to be of service." With another bow, she left the giant dragonet in the doorway and moved back to the queen. She was sitting in the chair now, looking exceptionally tired. Lucia approached in a respectful way. "For you, milady. It's the best ale we have. I hope it's to your liking. Or I could get you something else."

Queen Lana reached out with shaking fingers and lifted the glass, drinking deeply. She smiled, her every move dripping with fatigue, as she placed the half-finished drink back on the tray Lucia still held. "Thank you. It's delicious."

"Can I ask? Will Sir Reynor be all right?"

The queen tilted her head, quizzing Lucia with her gaze. "He'll live. Whether he flies again or not is in the hands of the Mother."

"All is in Her hands." Marcus's deep voice came from just over her shoulder. The man could move silently when he wished, it seemed. He swept to one knee before the queen. "Thank you, milady. Lucia told me Reynor and Linea are mates."

With what Marcus had told her about how dragons and knights mated, if Reynor died, Linea might never find another mate. And if she didn't, in all likelihood, neither would her knight. So more than one being's future depended on Reynor's recovery.

Queen Lana reached out and stroked Marcus's hair in a familiar way that annoyed Lucia. Jealousy blasted through her. She'd never felt such immediate, violent possessiveness about anyone before. And certainly not a man she'd only just met. Sure, she'd cried on his shoulder, but that didn't mean she owned him.

Lucia backed away, needing to put some space between herself and the unreasonable reaction. She stopped, though, at the sight of the other knight, sitting now at Reynor's side. He held onto the dragon's neck with one arm, embracing him, offering comfort. Rey's jeweled gaze had more fire now and had lost that worrisome, unhealthy dimness.

Kaden stopped her, catching her hand in his. She looked down at him, surprised by his warm touch.

"Rey told me what a good friend you are, Lucy. I can't—" He broke off, looking away as he blinked rapidly. "I can't tell you how much what you've done means. I can never thank you enough."

Seeing the depth of this man's feelings for the dragon touched something deep inside. She had to get a hold of her own emotions before she started crying again. She stiffened her spine, fighting back the empathy this man evoked with his sad blue eyes.

"Just you take care of each other," she said in a harsher tone than she'd intended. "No more of these misunderstandings."

"Yes, ma'am." Kaden let her go and stood, towering over her, much as Marcus had done. Impulsively, she reached up to move a lock of golden blond hair back from his face. She gasped when his arms came around her. He hugged her close, crushing her against his muscular chest.

"You're a special lady, Lucy." His gruff words drifted past her ear. "Thank you, sweetheart." He surprised her yet again when she felt his lips pause in front of her ear, kissing softly, just once, before he let her go and stepped back.

Lucia looked up at him, feeling the tears gather behind her eyes again, much to her dismay. Before she could let them fall, the dragon nudged her with his snout, breaking the spell. Reflexively, she reached out and stroked his scaly head.

"Are you all right now, Rey?"

*"I've been better,"* he quipped.

"He can't be moved for now. I don't want to undo everything I've just done." The queen stood beside Lucia, speaking to the dragon, the knights and—shockingly—Lucia as well. "Can you work around him?"

Lucia scrambled to answer the queen of all Draconia. "He's been here all week. I know Sir Reynor enjoys the music in the evenings, and many of the customers talk to him, though none can hear him." She lowered her eyes modestly.

"Except you." Marcus spoke from her other side.

She nodded. "Except me." She'd never come out and said she could speak to dragons before, though she knew many in the tavern suspected.

"Then, if it's all right," the queen glanced over to the nodding tavern owner who watched from behind the bar, "I'd like Rey to stay here for a few more days. Will you be here to nurse him and bring water and food to him?"

Lucia curtsied. "Yes, my queen. I would be honored."

"I hope you'll come to the castle and visit with us after Rey is feeling better. There aren't many women who can speak with dragons." The queen sounded tired, but Lucia heard the hint of order in her tone.

She inclined her head politely in acknowledgement. "If you wish, Your Majesty."

"I do." Green eyes sparkled with laughter. "And I want you," the queen turned to Kaden, "to stay with Reynor and work out this guilt between you." She touched both males on the head, joining them with her small, healing hands. "Neither of you are to blame for this. Work it out. Partners should communicate better than this."

Both heads bowed and the knight flushed with embarrassment. "Yes, milady."

The queen sighed and released the males, turning away. She headed for the doorway where the silver dragon waited, pausing only to stroke her hand once over Linea's pale green scales. A few moments later, the young silver dragon was gone and the queen with him.

# Chapter Three

Kaden moved into the tavern that very afternoon, paying the innkeeper a few days in advance for room and board for himself and his dragon. Marcus and Linea stayed near as well. The two dragons lay quietly together, side by side, their necks entwined. Reynor had to be cautious in his movements, but he seemed to do better with Linea at his side.

Lucia went about her business, tending the customers who frequented the tavern. Sir Kaden left on some sort of errand, but Sir Marcus stayed behind with the dragons. Quite a few busybodies came in to see why all the dragons had flown in that day and why, especially, the queen's easily recognizable Ice Dragon had been to visit. Lucia let the other serving girls gossip, but took no part in it herself. She felt self-conscious enough with Sir Marcus's penetrating gaze following her about her duties. She didn't want to make it worse by gossiping about the situation.

Sir Marcus was a handsome devil, but as she learned more about him, he began to remind her painfully of all she'd lost. His courtly manners and polished appearance made her think of things better put away. She could never regain her past. It was better to just forget that, once upon a time, she'd been a noble lady with every expectation of marrying a man much like Sir Marcus.

Oddly though, he didn't seem to mind her fall in stature. To be sure, he was curious about her. That much was obvious from the way his eyes followed her every movement. But he didn't seem to be mocking or judgmental. Mostly, he seemed inquisitive. She feared the questions he'd ask given half a chance and did her best to avoid him, but inevitably, he cornered her at the end of the bar during the usual afternoon lull.

"Tavern work is harder than I realized."

She was polishing glasses when Marcus spoke, surprising her so badly she fumbled the costly glass in her hands and would have dropped it. Marcus caught it before it could shatter, placing it back in her hands with a lingering caress. He didn't immediately let go, making her keenly aware of his warmth and the unexpected calluses on his warrior's hands.

"What?" She'd lost his words to the shock of his appearance. He gazed so deep into her eyes, she thought he might be able to see all the way down into her soul.

"I said you work harder than I thought here in the tavern. I never considered before how much there is to the job."

She pulled away and put the glass behind the bar with its clean fellows. Her limbs trembled as she lifted the next glass for inspection and polishing.

"I know you've been watching me and frankly, Sir Marcus, I don't enjoy it."

Marcus stepped back, appearing surprised by her outburst. She'd surprised herself with the bald truth, but she'd never been one to play games.

"I'm sorry if I offended you."

She tilted her head, considering the glass and avoiding looking at the handsome knight. "Offend is too strong a word, but I accept your apology."

"Please," he edged closer once more, the heat of his presence causing tingles of awareness in her body, "isn't there some way I can make it up to you?" His words sent shivers down her spine, making her think of how his cultured voice would sound in passion. The low, persuasive tone, coupled with his devilishly handsome face should be outlawed. It made a girl think of sex—truly pleasurable, scream-the-house-down sex— all too easily. "I'm already in your debt," he went on, "for the service you preformed for Rey and Kaden. I'd hate to think I owed you even more for my own inept attempt to make conversation."

Gathering her courage, she rounded on him. "And why in the world would you—a knight of the realm—want to *make conversation* with me? Sir Marcus, I know just how far apart our stations in life are." Lucia fought not to let her emotions get the best of her.

"Stations in life?" He seemed genuinely puzzled before realization dawned and he drew closer. "Sweet Lucia, social rank means very little here in Draconia, and to me, personally. It's the measure of the person that really matters. I don't know how it was where you come from, but surely you've seen how it is here? I may have been born of a wealthy family, but there are no expectations about whom I *make conversation*—or other things—with." His smile was downright sinful and she knew full well he meant to be provocative. He succeeded too. Her abdomen rippled with awareness.

"Sir Marcus," she forced herself to step away from him, "I haven't been in Draconia long but even so, I know the difference between a knight and a servant." She raised her chin with a hint of the pride she'd never lost.

Marcus didn't give her a chance to retreat. Right there, in full view of the few people in the tavern, he stepped up and took her into his arms. Before she could protest, his lips covered hers in the most arousing kiss she'd ever known. He conquered her, plunging his tongue into her mouth. His taste was rich and divine, the feel of his strong body against hers like heaven.

But it couldn't last. He reminded her too sharply of the past that was gone forever.

When he eased up, there were tears in her eyes. Hurt and recrimination entered his gaze when he saw her expression, but she didn't want him to feel guilty for something that wasn't his fault.

"I can't apologize." The words were torn from his lips as he held her in his arms.

"I don't want you to, but..."

"What is it, my sweet? Why do you look so sad?"

"It's not your fault." She sighed, resting against his hard chest for just a moment out of time. "It's complicated."

He nuzzled her hair. "Why don't you try to explain it to me?"

"I'm not sure if I can." She pulled away from him and turned so she wouldn't have to look at his too-handsome face. "It's just— You remind me of things, Marcus. You represent a part of my life that's gone forever and it hurts to think of those days, now long over."

When she looked back at the knight, his stiff posture and the muscle ticking in his jaw indicated he hadn't taken her explanation well. Still, she thought she knew him well enough not to fear him. Lucia only regretted the hurt in his eyes.

"I apologize, Lucia." His words were terse. "It was never my intent to bring back your sorrow and I have no idea how to fix it, but know this..." he moved in close, his words for her ears alone, "...I will find a way. I want you, Lucia and I mean to have you."

Lucia tried not to let his ardent words affect her, but they seemed to go straight to her womb. Luckily her trembling knees were hidden by her skirt, but she fought to control her breathing which had grown betrayingly shallow. One thing was clear though, she had to fight fire with fire. This complex man wouldn't take anything less.

"Won't Kaden have something to say about that? Or did I misunderstand the way you knights work your kinky little threesomes?" She kept her voice to a hissing whisper, though there were few people in the tavern and none seemed to be paying much attention to them in the dark corner of the bar.

Her words seemed to set him back on his feet and he regarded her with hooded eyes for some moments before responding. When he did speak, his words offered little comfort.

"You're right. We both will want you in our bed, if you're the woman I think you are. Have you given any thought to how you'll handle that? How it will feel? How good we can make it for you?" With each question, he drew closer until she was almost back in his arms. "I've never shared a woman before, but I've heard accounts from some of the mated knights in the Lair. The pleasure is said to be beyond measure. Especially when the dragons take to the skies in a mating flight. The backlash on the human part of the family is said to be a pleasure like no other." Marcus cupped her ass with one big hand and squeezed.

They were next to the bar where no one could see his groping and she found it hard not to jump at the intimate caress. This knight was less a gentleman than she'd believed, and all man. In that moment he didn't resemble the discrete noblemen of her youth, but more the rough Jinn warriors she'd known since leaving her home all those years ago. He was even more alluring now than he'd been just a few short minutes ago, and altogether much too dangerous.

"One of us will claim your curvy ass, Lucia. Have you ever had a cock up there?" She gasped as he sucked her earlobe into his warm mouth. He let go and whispered into her ear, "I promise, we will make you crave it like your next breath." Then his tongue traced the swirls of her ear, making her squirm. "We'll take turns with you and make sure you never forget how we feel inside you. And when the dragons fly, we'll take you together to a place you never dreamed of."

"Marcus!" It was all too much. No man had ever spoken to her this way. She shocked herself at how hot it made her.

"You'll scream my name in pleasure, Lucia. One day soon. This I promise you." He backed away slowly, his gaze boring down into hers. "But I'll give you time. Time to accept the future and come to terms with the past as best you can. You know now I'm like no man you've ever known before. I'm a knight— nobly born, I grant you—but when it comes to you, I'm a barbarian, Lucia." He chuckled at his own words and stepped back, shaking his head. "Damn, what you do to me, woman. You should be outlawed!"

Lucia sank back against the bar, afraid her knees wouldn't support her. "I was thinking the same thing about you."

He laughed outright at her honest words and she blushed, laughing as well. Things were by no means settled between them, but he seemed to have come to some kind of decision for now. Lucia would steer clear of this all-too-dangerous man, but she feared a reckoning would come in the future, if she stayed in his company for any length of time. That was to be avoided at all costs.

Marcus sauntered away and she turned back to her task, finishing up as quickly as possible. When she'd put the last glass safely on the shelf, she took off for a moment of privacy in her room. At least there, she wouldn't have to feel the handsome knight's eyes on her.

ഊഇഏൽൽ

As Kaden walked back to Castleton after fetching a change of clothes from the Lair, he mentally kicked himself over and over, unable to understand how he and Rey had reached such a point where dragon and knight couldn't even talk to each other. That should never happen in a partnership as deep as theirs. That night—his first in the tavern—Kaden was so tired from grief and worry, he fell into the bed in the small rented room and slept soundly until well after dawn. Breakfast awaited him in the common room, as did Rey.

They talked little, both unable to articulate the problems between them, but just being near each other helped. Linea had spent the night, though Marcus was nowhere in sight. Kaden spent the afternoon gathering more of his belongings from the Lair and bringing them to the tavern. He needed clothes and some grooming supplies for Rey. Dragon scales could dry out when a dragon was ill and didn't get enough exercise. Kaden spent the hours before dinner oiling and polishing Rey's scales in the areas that didn't pain him too much.

Dinner was a quiet affair. Kaden sat at a table next to the dragons and ate in sullen silence while the tavern filled up around them. Most of the patrons were Jinn, as were the proprietor and the serving maids. They were of the working class, but not rough. Merchants, tradesmen and others mingled as a hearty dinner was served, followed by fine ale and even some entertainment. The Jinn were noted for the talent of their minstrels and a few played in the background while the conversations of the customers hummed around them.

Kaden drank a bit more than he probably should have, keeping vigil at Rey's side. The other patrons moved around the tavern, most giving the dragons a wide berth, though some came over to pay their respects and offer melons or other large fruits to the dragons as snacks. Marcus joined Kaden after dinner and sat with him deep into the night. They'd always been friends and he found the other knight's presence both comforting and reassuring.

The only serving girl brave enough, it seemed, to serve the dragons and knights was Lucia. She brought tankards of ale after clearing away the remains of Kaden's dinner. He watched her as the night wore on. Marcus sat with him, watching and speaking little, but it was a comfortable silence.

Kaden noticed how Marcus's gaze followed Lucy. Kaden couldn't help but watch her himself. There was something appealing about the confidant way she moved, and she was a proven beauty—inside and out. No other woman had ever braved the castle gates to summon help for an injured dragon. Only Lucy.

"She's quite a woman," Marcus commented, raising his tankard in Lucia's direction. Kaden realized he'd been caught staring at her. Again.

"I can't figure her out." Kaden sat back, trying to be nonchalant. "She seems comfortable in this atmosphere, but she speaks like a gentlewoman."

"She doesn't really belong here," Marcus agreed. "She was born a noblewoman, but fate has brought her here."

Marcus's words seemed portentous. "For some reason, you think?"

"I do." Marcus lowered the tankard. "I believe she may well be our mate."

The idea shocked Kaden, but he felt an immediate warmth flood his midsection at the idea of bedding Lucia. A wife would be shared between them now it was clear Rey and Linea were mates. Such was the way with dragons. It was rare to find a woman who would willingly live in the Lair with dozens of dragons. Rarer still was the woman who could hear a dragon's silent speech.

"It feels right," Kaden admitted. "She can bespeak dragons. Even in the Castle Lair, not all the women can do that."

"It's a gift," Marcus agreed. "And it's clear she loves Rey already. I think she's fond of Linea too."

"But what about us?" Kaden nearly cursed. The woman had seen him at his absolute worst. She probably despised him for the way he'd seemed to ignore Rey's life-threatening injury.

"Why don't we find out?" Marcus stood, stretching and surveying the quiet tavern. It was late in the evening and most customers had already headed for home. The serving wenches were cleaning their assigned areas, but there seemed little left for them to do. He went across the room, toward the bar where Lucia was washing out tankards in a large bucket of water.

# Chapter Four

Lucia was just finishing up her chores when she noticed Sir Marcus walking in her direction. The man should come with a warning label. He was so good looking, and the way he walked should be outlawed. Long limbs rolled loosely across the tavern floor and his arresting gaze held hers the entire way.

They hadn't spoken since their run-in the day before and seemed to have achieved a somewhat uncomfortable truce. He gave her the patented Marcus melt-your-bones smile that all the other serving girls had been sighing over. It had been nearly impossible to talk to any of the other women at the tavern without being either teased or grilled for information about the knights. Of course, the girls were still frightened by the dragons. No matter how many times Lucia told them the dragons were gentle creatures, the others refused to go anywhere near them. Not even to flirt with the knights.

"Are you nearly done for the night?" Marcus's deep voice rolled over her.

"Just about." She wiped her hands on her apron and untied the strings holding it in place over her simple dress. "Why? Does Rey need anything? Or Linea?" She pointedly left him out of her query.

"No, they're fine. Sleeping, actually." He glanced over his shoulder at the dragons' entwined necks. "I thought maybe you could sit with us—with Kaden and me—for a bit. We owe you much for coming to the castle and haven't had much time to get to know you. We'd like to remedy that."

Surprised and wary, Lucia couldn't ignore the voice inside telling her to grab whatever time she could with these strong men. Such men didn't cross her path at all in the normal course of business, unless she was serving them food or drink. But Marcus and Kaden both had treated her as an equal, not as a servant. The idea was too tantalizing to pass up. It had been so long since she'd sat at a table and shared conversation with an educated man. She missed it. And playing with fire was something she'd always done, regardless of her propensity for getting burned. She went around the bar and allowed Marcus to escort her to the table.

Kaden stood when she neared and pulled out a chair for her. His manners were polite and she was hard pressed to decide which of these men was more handsome. Marcus had a suave beauty to him, a grace of form and movement, but Kaden was pure power in human form. His muscles spoke of long days spent training at arms, while the cunning in his sparkling eyes betrayed keen intelligence.

"Please, Lucy, won't you join us?" Kaden captured one of her hands, lifting it to his lips for a gentle salute.

Barely able to nod at his unexpected chivalry, she took the chair he offered, sitting lightly. If she hadn't felt the scratchy linen of her shift against her skin, she would have thought she'd gone back in time.

The men sat after she did, both focusing their considerable attention on her. She resisted the urge to fidget. Since she'd met him, Marcus had been the focus of her thoughts, but watching Kaden interact with Reynor made her want to understand the more rough-cut knight better. He wasn't quite as effortlessly gallant as Marcus, but had a charm all his own.

"We can't thank you enough for looking after Rey." Marcus poured a bit of the wine they'd ordered earlier into an empty glass and offered it to her.

She accepted, taking a small sip of the fruity vintage. She'd had better, but not recently. "It was my pleasure. Sir Reynor is a sweetheart."

Kaden laughed at that, surprising her with his change in demeanor. Since he'd been here, he'd been alternately worried, dour, sad, or remorseful. Sometimes all at once. It was good to hear his laughter. It touched her, and brought home just how strongly she felt for them all on such short acquaintance.

Of course, talking with Rey over the past days, she'd learned a great deal about his knight. She knew some of Kaden's likes and dislikes, his moments of heroism and the reasons Rey loved him. From the dragon's descriptions, she'd felt she already knew the most important things about Sir Kaden, but meeting him now, she could see there were still depths to his personality to explore and try to understand. And Marcus's warnings of the way they would make love to her tantalized her imagination. She couldn't help the vivid images in her mind as she sat between them, doing her best to keep the betraying heat from her face.

"Were he awake I'm sure Rey would scoff to hear himself described as sweet. He's a fierce dragon, don't you know? You can't call a fire breathing beast *sweet*. It would ruin his image." Kaden's teasing seemed a good sign for the recovery of both dragon and knight.

Lucia chuckled, answering with the same lighthearted air, glad of the distraction from her scandalous thoughts. "Reynor has a heart of gold and he knows I think he's sweet, though like you, he scoffs when I say it."

"How is it you can hear dragons, Lucy?" Marcus asked. "It's not a common ability."

She shifted uncomfortably. "I've always been able to communicate with magical creatures. I grew up in a distant land and we had many different kinds of magic there."

"'Lucia de Alagarithia, last of your line, late of the Jinn'. That's how you introduced yourself to Linea," Marcus said with deceptive casualness. "Perhaps you'll enlighten us. Where is Alagarithia?"

Lucia sighed, remembering days long gone. "Alagarithia is a coastal city in the Doge of Helios's domain. I grew up there, a child of the House of Alagar, ruling line of the city."

"What happened?" Kaden folded one of her hands in his, offering comfort.

"What usually happens when one group wants the power of another? War. And assassination. I was the only survivor, and only just barely. If I hadn't fled the city, I'd be dead as well. For that reason, I don't often publicize who I once was, though I doubt anyone cares to send an assassin this far, after so many years."

"How did you escape?" Marcus leaned forward, listening intently.

"The Jinn hid me in their caravan. They adopted me when it was clear I had no home to return to. They've been good to me."

"But you've never forgotten your origins, or your ladylike manners," Kaden observed, squeezing her hand. "You are Jinn, but not. There's a lot of the lady still in you, sweetheart."

"Much to my dismay at times," she agreed. "It makes me stand out too much from the other girls."

"You would do that regardless." Marcus lifted her free hand in his, tangling their fingers. It felt good to touch both of them, though she was confused by the emotions swirling through her. Sad thoughts of her lost home mixed with the empathy coming from these two wonderful men. "But what magical creatures did you talk to in Helios? I'm not familiar with your city at all, and I've only heard bards' tales of that land. Surely no dragons live there."

"No, no dragons. But there are several kinds of magical sea creatures, and gryphons nested along our cliffs. I used to play with the hatchlings when the adults would let me. They were so soft and fluffy, and while still babies, they couldn't talk yet with their beaks. It takes time for them to learn that skill, so they spoke in my mind, much like the dragons."

"I've never seen a gryphon, but they're said to be deadly and incredibly powerful creatures." Kaden's grip tightened on her hand.

"They are both, but if you know how to approach them from a position of strength, they will sometimes accept you. My father taught me how to gain their respect and a few of the mated pairs allowed me to play with their young. I was just a child then myself, of course."

"So your playmates were baby gryphons?" Marcus looked impressed. "No wonder you're such a formidable woman."

"Me?" She laughed outright. "I'm hardly formidable. I'm only a serving wench after all."

Kaden tugged her closer to his warm body. "You are so much more, Lucy. More than you realize."

His lips settled on hers with delicate urgency, testing first to see if she would accept his kiss. Giving in to her own deepest desires, she settled into the kiss, cataloging every touch, every caress, every sweep of his daring tongue, against the moment when she would wake from this dream.

All too soon, he released her, though he didn't let her go far. One strong hand continued to hold hers, while the other settled at her waist. She could feel the heat of his fingers through her thin dress. It did something to her insides, making her belly quiver in a way that wasn't entirely unpleasant. It felt like magic, only different.

"You taste sweeter than I would have dreamed, Lucy. I'm so glad Rey found you."

The intensity in his eyes was hard to answer. She realized Marcus still held her other hand, and she looked at him with shocked eyes, but he was smiling.

"My impetuous friend may be rushing things, but I'm inclined to do the same. It's hard to hold back when heaven might be right before your eyes." Marcus sounded almost philosophical, but his tone was deep and mysterious, his eyes dancing with lights of pleasure as he leaned closer. Before she knew what was happening, his lips were on hers. Again. When she'd promised herself she wouldn't let it happen. She gave up thinking as his tongue swept in as if it owned her, taking up where Kaden left off and driving her higher still. The two men together were a potent combination.

Was it shameful of her to accept another man's kiss so soon after learning the taste of Kaden? Was it wrong to enjoy them both? Her head was spinning.

An amused female voice sounded through her mind. *"Is it really so hard to understand, little sister? You could be the mate of this family. You could be the tie that binds us all together."*

Marcus ended the kiss, his gaze seeking hers as he drew back. "Don't let her frighten you off. Linea," he addressed the watchful dragon with a glance, "don't pressure her."

The female dragon snorted delicately, a spiral of smoke heading for the high ceiling. *"The girl needs to understand she can have you both."*

The thought tantalized as she looked from one knight to the other. Both of these incredible men were looking at her as a potential mate. The idea was staggering, though her conversations with Marcus should have prepared her for it.

Kaden stroked one finger along her hip. "It's a rare woman that can hear dragon speech. You like Rey and Linea, don't you?"

She nodded, still being cautious. "Yes, but—"

"And you don't hold disgust for either one of us." Marcus's eyes twinkled as he teased her. "Do you?"

"No, but—"

"Then there's no reason for us not to see where this might lead," Kaden said in a determined voice.

"No pressure though," Marcus assured her, as if reminding them all. "We like you a great deal, Lucia. You've already proven your care for our dragon partners and they love you for it. I think the Mother of All put you in our path for a reason, and I don't want to frighten you, but knights often know immediately when they meet the right woman." His eyes sought out Kaden's over her head. He took a deep breath, as if for courage, then went on. "I felt something when I first saw you, but the danger to Rey and the revelation that Linea was his mate had my head spinning. But it feels right to have you here, with us. I think you were meant for us, Lucia. I think I could spend the rest of my life loving you."

Lucia caught her breath at the tender revelation. No man had ever said such things to her, and she realized from any other man, the declaration would have been wrong. But from Marcus...it felt right, but altogether too scary. He still reminded her of the life she'd been forced to leave behind. He'd tried to show her other facets of his personality, but when she wasn't caught up in his passion, she still saw his polish and poise, his rich garments and cultured background. They'd have to work on that before she could ever be truly comfortable in his presence.

Kaden squeezed her waist, claiming her attention. "I owe you gratitude, no doubt, but this feels like so much more. I want to get to know you better and see if you could fit in with our little family. You could complete us, Lucy, and make us the happiest of men—and dragons." He winked at her.

"But there's no pressure." Marcus's words belied the very real pressure she was beginning to feel. He knew it too. The irony in his tone spoke volumes.

She liked Marcus's dry sense of humor, and the fact he acknowledged the depth of the position they put her in made her feel better somehow. Unable to deal with much more, she shook off their hands and stood, looking down at them both. She drew on all her childhood lessons of deportment to face these two with a dignity she wasn't feeling at the moment.

"Gentlemen," she tried to sound stern, "I have no idea why you're teasing me this way."

"Sweetheart," Marcus spoke for both, "we're not teasing. We're in earnest."

"Then," she sniffed and blinked back the tears welling in her eyes, "I have no idea what to say to you. Please," she grabbed the sides of her rough skirt, "give me time to think. I wasn't raised to expect anything like this."

"Talk to Rey and Linea," Kaden advised, catching one of her hands when she would have fled. "Let them explain how it is between knights and their mates if you cannot ask it of us."

Swallowing, she refused to look at either of them as she nodded, though she discovered Kaden's concern was easier to bear than Marcus's. Kaden was rough where Marcus was smooth and he didn't remind her of the painful past, but rather of the protective Jinn warriors who'd put their lives on the line to save hers. Kaden let her go and she took off across the room to the area behind the bar, where her small room—and safety— was located.

"She's magnificent," Marcus said as they watched her flee with a grace few tavern wenches ever achieved.

"And beautiful," Kaden agreed. "Too good for the likes of me, though with your highbred manners, she's a perfect match for you."

"You sound jealous!" Marcus rounded on his friend, teasing in his expression, though underneath there was serious thought behind his words.

"I am, dammit." Kaden swiped the glass off the table and finished his wine in one swallow. "If not for Rey, she would

213

never look at a rough soldier like me. I don't know how to talk to her, how to handle her, how to—"

Marcus cut him off. "But you know how to love her."

That stopped him cold.

He did. He knew very well how to love her. In fact, the seed of love was blooming even now in his heart. He looked at Marcus—the man he'd share Lucy with, if she could handle being their wife.

"You too?"

Marcus sighed and propped his head on one hand, elbow on the table. "In the tumult of the past days, I didn't realize it at first. It just felt so good to have her around. It felt right to have her caring for Rey and talking with him and Linea. Like that was the way it always should be. And then I realized...it probably was. But she fears me, Kaden. Or rather, she fears the memories I bring back."

"How's that?" Kaden was shocked by the sorrow in his friend's tone. Marcus was one of those knights who always seemed sure he could overcome any obstacle. His positive attitude was something Kaden aspired to, but never seemed to achieve, and here Marcus was, as down as Kaden had ever seen him.

"I kissed her yesterday." Marcus rubbed one hand over his face. "Actually, I propositioned her, and grabbed her butt. Damn, she has a fine ass." He seemed lost in reverie for a moment while Kaden seethed. "She nearly ran from me, Kaden. She came right out and told me I reminded her of all that she'd lost and tried to leave. Then I became a barbarian and grabbed her ass."

Kaden laughed. He couldn't help it. It just sounded so ridiculous coming from Marcus in those cultured tones of his.

"It's not funny," Marcus snapped.

Kaden tried to wipe the smile from his face. "Sorry. All right. What happened then?"

"She seemed intrigued, but in the end she ran away." Marcus sounded so glum, Kaden could almost forgive him for making the first move on Lucy.

"So how do we get her to agree to be our mate?"

*"You court her. Woo her. Do whatever it is human males do to show her how good you will be for her."* Linea spoke to both knights. She was resting quietly with Reynor, who slept on, but her jeweled eyes followed the knights.

"Good idea, milady," Kaden said, "but most human women don't expect to have two husbands. The idea of it might be unsettling to her."

*"Judging from the way she kissed you both, I think she's more open to our ways than you believe. Still, it couldn't hurt to show her the Lair. Let her talk to some of the other women. Maybe you could have some of your friends visit here and bring their mates so she can meet them. I doubt she'll want to leave Reynor here while he's still so sick."*

"You are a clever strategist, Lady Linea," Kaden acknowledged, toasting her. "We'll do that."

# Chapter Five

The next day, they put their new plan into action. Several knights and their mates came to visit Rey and Linea throughout the morning and afternoon, the dragons craning their heads in the special, large doorway to see their comrades in the small space. The tavern became more popular than ever, with folks coming in for lunch, dinner and evening entertainment, and to see the dragons and knights up close. It was a treat, even for those who'd lived their whole lives in the shadow of the castle.

Reynor was doing much better physically and seemed to enjoy the attention and well wishes from people he didn't even know. Lucia was kept busy delivering fruit people sent to Rey and Linea as well as drinks they bought for the knights. It was a kind gesture they gladly accepted and returned.

Lucia watched the other knights and their wives, astounded at first by the casual way the threesomes came and went. They were comfortable with each other in a way that spoke of love and deep understanding. Lucia had seldom seen such obvious commitment among lovers, and each new trio seemed happier than the last. After her initial shock, Lucia scrutinized them when they weren't looking, wondering if their apparent happiness wasn't some elaborate hoax. It seemed odd to see so many three-partnered relationships with nary one unhappy member or any hint of discord, but that's exactly what she saw. The thought gave her pause.

"Lucia." Marcus caught her attention as she passed their table. The hour was late and many of the tavern's patrons had already headed for their homes. A quick glance told her the knights had drunk more than their normal share of the libations sent to them as they laughed and talked with their friends. Four other knights and two ladies sat with them, several dragons crowding the tavern yard.

"Yes, Sir Marcus? Is there something you wanted?"

"That's a loaded question, my sweet." He winked. "Can you stop for a moment and join us? You've been rushing around all night long." His tone was disapproving, but she heard the teasing in his words. Still, he was right about the workload. The tavern had been busier than usual, thanks to the attraction of knights and dragons.

The work was more demanding, but the money was good. Increased patronage meant increased gratuities for her, and more income for the owner. He wouldn't begrudge her a few minutes rest now the crowd was dissipating, surely. Not after her actions had brought the dragons and knights—and their windfall—to his door.

"I guess I could sit for a minute or two. If you're sure." She felt distinctly uncomfortable, noting the difference between her rough clothing and the costly silks in which the ladies were dressed.

Kaden took one of her hands and squeezed, offering reassurance in his touch. "Join us."

It was the sparkle in his dark blue eyes that decided her. Allowing him to tug her closer, she took the seat beside him, which placed her next to one of the other women. Lucia looked at the others with some trepidation as Marcus made the introductions.

"Lucia, this is Hal and Jures and their mate, Candis. They're from the Northern Lair, visiting for a few days. And across the table is Bellon and Jeth and their mate, Marta."

Far from turning up their noses at her common appearance, the women made her feel welcome. They shared small talk for a few minutes and Lucia learned that Marta and her men lived in the suite next door to Marcus and Linea. They were neighbors in the Castle Lair, though they appeared older than either Marcus or Kaden.

After a bit, the men started talking among themselves and the ladies turned to her with friendly smiles. Lucia sensed no animosity from either of the women though the difference in their stations couldn't have been plainer. Lucia was a servant.

She'd been waiting on them all night, in fact, but these women spoke to her as if she were an equal.

"So do you have any questions for us, Lucy?" Marta asked. "Is it all right to call you that? Kaden seems to call you Lucy, but Marcus is a bit more formal."

Caught off guard, she smiled and squirmed a bit. "Sir Kaden probably calls me Lucy because Sir Reynor decided early on he liked the sound of it better. And it's fine with me. I actually like it."

"Still so formal? Calling them sir?" Marta looked deflated.

"Well, I'm only a servant, after all. It wouldn't be right—"

"That's garbage." Lady Candis's pronouncement was blunt and sounded rather final. "I was a farm girl when Hal found me. You'll discover we don't care much for rank in the Lair, only that our men and dragons are happy and well cared for. If you can do that, you'll be welcome among us."

"But—"

"They haven't asked her yet, I bet." Marta's glance slid from Marcus to Kaden back to her with a speculative gleam. "The fools."

"Asked me what?"

"To live in the Lair," Marta said with breezy assuredness. "It's clear the dragons already love you. You'd be welcome, Lucy."

"But the key is," Lady Candis chimed in, "do you love them?"

"Yes, of course. Reynor and Linea are both dear to my heart."

"Not the dragons, silly," Marta chided her. "Though that's important, of course. Do you love Marcus and Kaden?"

Stunned by the woman's blunt question, Lucia's gaze shifted to the men. Each was attractive in his own way, though she still feared the memories Marcus brought back. But she couldn't deny his attraction and she had no such qualms about Kaden. Both men had sought her out, made her feel special, and kissed her as if she really mattered to them. Each was unique—Marcus with his debonair flair and Kaden with his rough warrior ways—and she felt deep stirrings of admiration and passion for them both. But was it love?

She didn't dare answer, even in the privacy of her own mind.

"I'm not used to the idea of having more than one lover." She hedged with the ladies who eyed her with varying degrees of expectation.

"Oh, that's the best part." Marta's eyes glowed with mischief. "Two men are most definitely better than one."

"Mmm," Candis agreed with a laugh, "when one makes you angry you can ask the other to punch him in the nose for you."

"But disharmony in a Lair relationship is rare indeed," Marta jumped to reassure her. "The men know if their lady is unhappy, they will both suffer, and the dragons too. And nobody wants to deal with unhappy dragons."

"So that's why all of them looked so happy. But," Lucia lowered her voice, "how does it all work exactly? Do they take turns?" She blushed at her own brazen question but the ladies didn't seem to take offense.

Marta patted her hand again. "Occasionally, but at heart, we're a triple. We do *all things* together."

Lucia shook her head, confused. "I just don't see how it's possible."

"Oh, it's possible, all right," Candis confirmed with a knowing grin. "And darn pleasurable. There's nothing quite like having two men to warm you on a cold winter's night. Two men to see to your every need. Two men to cherish and protect you. And two men to love." Her gaze drifted fondly to her mates, talking animatedly with the other men.

"Give Marcus and Kaden a chance to prove it to you, Lucy. They say you can hear dragons. It's clear you were meant to live in the Lair."

"You can't?" Lucia was surprised by the longing in Marta's tone.

Marta shook her head. "Sadly, no. At times I hear echoes, but I do love the dragons and know they enjoy my company too."

Lucia couldn't imagine what it must be like to live in such close company with dragons and not be able to hear their silent speech. Her heart went out to the other woman.

"Say you'll give it some thought, Lucy," Candis urged. "Come to the Lair and see if you could be happy living there. You'll find a lot of people—and dragons—will be happy to welcome you."

"I will think on it, but they haven't asked. I wouldn't want to be presumptuous."

"Oh, they'll ask." Candis grinned and a knowing smile lit Marta's pretty face as well.

ಶಿ⁂ಲ⁂ಬ

"You know, you two still have to clear the air," Marcus reminded Kaden and Reynor later, after the other knights and their ladies had gone. The tavern was empty now. Only Lucia remained with the two knights, sitting companionably between them.

They'd drunk, perhaps too much, but were reasonably sober as Lucia observed the men and learned more about them. Marcus had been charming. Kaden had been quiet but earnest when he'd worked up the nerve to speak. His reticence was endearing and the way Marcus included him rather than shut him out as other men might have done, impressed her.

Kaden lost all reticence now though, as he sat back and drained his cup. He glowered at his friend.

"It's none of your business."

"Actually," Marcus stared down the other knight, "it *is* my business." He looked from Linea to Reynor and back again with a pointed glance.

"*Leave it be, Marcus,*" Reynor said with a smoky sigh.

"With all due respect, I cannot." Marcus shook his head. "When you and Linea join, what affects you and Kaden will affect us all."

"*If I cannot fly, there will never be a mating flight,*" Reynor shot back. "*Much as it pains me, Linea must seek another.*"

*"There will be no other."* Linea reared her head in annoyance. *"You are my mate, whether you can fly or not."*

Kaden shot to his feet, his eyes wild with a mixture of anger, regret, pain and remorse. "I'm sorry," was all he could choke out before leaving the table. He stormed away toward the back of the tavern and the room he'd rented there.

"Go to him, Lucia," Marcus pleaded, shocking her with the pained compassion in his gaze. "He's hurting."

"What's going on?" She didn't understand everything that had just been said. She felt out of her depth, but her heart ached for the knight and dragon who were so wounded.

"He blames himself for Rey's injury."

*"I don't blame him. I've told him that over and over, but it does no good."* Reynor's voice in their minds was both exasperated and weary.

"He needs to put this guilt behind him and concentrate on Rey's recovery. Perhaps with all of our prayers, Rey will fly again."

*"You will fly, Rey, if I have to throw you into the sky myself."* Linea's loving determination eased some of the tension.

*"If you say so, my love."*

# Chapter Six

Lucia didn't go back to the guest quarters often, and never for social visits. While some of the other serving girls spent time entertaining the guests in a very private manner, it was neither expected nor encouraged. This was a respectable establishment, a tavern first and foremost, with a few guest rooms for the odd traveler. It was not a brothel.

She knocked on Kaden's door with trembling fingers.

"Go away, Marcus."

"It's me. Lucy." Reynor called her that, as did Kaden, though nobody else in this land of dragons used the shortened version of her name. She liked it though. Especially from those two males.

"Lucy." The whisper reached her on the other side of the door. He was in pain. That much was clear from his tortured tone. Daring greatly, she tried the door, finding it unbarred. She pushed it open, peering around the edge.

Kaden sat on the edge of the bed, his elbows resting on his knees, head down in a pose of utter dejection.

"Kaden?"

Bloodshot eyes rose to meet hers. "You shouldn't be in here, Lucy."

She took a step forward, letting the door close behind her. "Do you want to talk about it?"

"No." He laughed, but it had a bitter sound. "Talking changes nothing. My partner is crippled because of me. What kind of knight allows his dragon partner to be so injured?"

"He doesn't blame you." She took another step forward until she was standing right in front of him in the small room.

"I blame myself."

"Then you're the only one. When the queen was here, she said dragons get hurt all the time. It's part of their life. She didn't blame you either."

Kaden shook his head, not meeting her eyes. "You don't understand."

"Then explain it to me." She sat at his side, taking one of his hands. He was such a big man, with big, calloused, warrior's hands. She couldn't stand to see him hurting. It touched her as deeply as seeing Rey in pain and she'd already proven she couldn't just stand by and watch the dragon hurt. The same seemed to be true for his knight.

"If Rey can't fly, he can't truly join with Linea. But dragons mate for life. Linea will never have a hatchling. What's more, she and Marcus won't have the partners in fighting they should. When dragons mate, their knights train together, fight together, live together with their mate. It's a complex relationship. If Rey can't fly, all of that goes out the window. All because of me."

"That's a heavy burden you've assumed." She rubbed his hand as he dealt with a difficult excess of emotion. His expression was full of pain when he could meet her eyes, though he avoided her gaze more than not.

"That's my reality."

"No," she faced him, "that's what your guilt is telling you. It's not the reality I see." She didn't give him a chance to respond. "I see a dragon who loves you. Two of them, actually. Rey needs you to be strong now, when he can't be. He needs your encouragement, not this depression that surrounds you like a cloud. He needs Linea and Marcus...and especially you, Kaden. He loves you."

"I love him too," he whispered.

"Then be strong for him." She moved closer, stroking his cheek and holding his hand close to her heart. "I'm willing to bet he's always been there for you. Now it's your turn. He's full of doubt and fear, but I think dragons don't normally know such emotions. He needs you to help him sort it all out so he can overcome it and learn to fly again. To live again."

"What if he can't fly?"

There it was. The crux of the matter. The fear that ate away at both dragon and knight.

"My father used to say that all things are possible if you believe. I believe in Rey and I believe in you, Kaden. Now you need to believe in yourself."

"Oh, Lucy." He pulled her into his arms. She felt the slight tremble of his muscles and marveled at the emotions this strong man kept bottled up inside.

"I'm here for you, Kaden. For both of you." She whispered near his ear, turning to kiss his jaw lightly. A kiss of affection...and love.

Kaden held her until his emotions settled down. But other things were stirring, such as the hunger that built in him every time she was near. It had been almost unbearable tonight, watching her chat with the other women. He'd wanted so much to take her and claim her as his own, as the other men had done with their mates, but she wasn't his. Not yet.

Perhaps this was the time. She'd come to him. She'd reached out. Perhaps she would welcome his advances. Perhaps she'd come to terms with the idea of sharing his love—and Marcus's—after talking with the other women.

There was only one way to find out.

"Lucy." He pulled back. Holding her gaze, he sought the frayed ribbon holding her tightly braided hair with his fingers. Little tendrils had come out of the braid as she worked, to frame her beautiful face. "Sweetheart, you're too good for the likes of me, but so help me, I want you. I need you, Lucy."

He searched her gaze, hoping for a glimmer of something. What he found made his heart race. Her expression was one of beauty and understanding, and something that looked deceptively like affection...or maybe even love, though it was too soon for him to expect she could feel as deeply as he did.

"Oh, Kaden, you've got it all backwards."

"Backwards? How so?" He leaned his forehead against hers, digging through the braid sections and unweaving her lustrous, dark hair with gentle motions.

"You're the one who's too good for me. I'm just a servant."

Kaden was surprised by her words. Surprised and a little hurt for her. "Servant or queen, you're a special, rare woman, Lucy." He kissed her, unable to help himself. She was soft and pliant against him, womanly and warm. All the things he wanted in his life and had never really had. "Let me love you, sweetheart."

"Yes, Kaden. Yes." Her breathless sighs shot straight to his cock. He was more than ready to show her just how good it could be between them.

But he wanted to go slow. He wanted to savor this first time, for this would be the beginning of their life together— whether she realized it or not. He knew it with certainty, and wanted this time to be special. As special as the woman in his arms.

He laid her back on the bed, coming over her, sheltering her in his warmth. He would have been content just to gaze down at her, soaking in the magic of the moment, but his eagerness won out.

"I knew you were part of us from almost the moment I laid eyes on you, Lucy. Certainly from the moment I saw how you cared for Rey." He kissed her cheeks, drifting down to peck at her lips and under her jaw. "You're so beautiful."

"Kaden." She untied the small closures on her simple dress. He felt like a king at her impatience for his touch. He moved back to help her, revealing the soft swells of her breasts, a bit larger than he'd expected, the nipples rosy and tight with need.

Leaning down, he licked her, zeroing in on one excited bud, tonguing her as she panted. He used his teeth, abrading the soft flesh with the utmost care, his fingers molding and squeezing her other breast as he opened his mouth and sucked gently.

Lucy cried out, writhing in pleasure under him. Kaden felt satisfaction, hearing her whimpers of delight. She was very responsive to him—more so than any woman he could ever remember bedding—and they hadn't even gone very far yet. He couldn't wait to be inside her, but he wanted her to feel everything he did...and more.

He licked her nipple, driving her higher as his hands roamed down her lithe body. He removed her dress with gentle touches that belied the urgency he felt. The simple garment slipped down, revealing a ripe femininity he'd only guessed at until now. She took his breath away.

"You're beautiful, Lucy." He rose over her nude form, his hands circling her generous breasts as he looked at her.

Her legs wriggled under him, making him want to claim her hard and fast. He had to slow down. Lifting away slightly, he gazed deep into her eyes, liking the dazed sensuality in her expression.

"Kaden?" She whimpered.

"It's all right, sweetheart. Just relax and let me love you. I want you to feel nothing but pleasure." He drew patterns on her soft flesh with his fingertips, lying at her side, staring down the length of her lovely body.

"It's all right, Kaden." She smiled at him. "I've done this before, you know. Not too often, but a few times." Her cheeks flamed pink, charming him.

He nipped her shoulder with playful nibbles. "From now on, there will be no others. Only me...and Marcus."

"I don't know—"

"Shh, sweet. No reason to worry about that now. All will happen in its time." He shrugged. "Or not. But know this—after tonight, you are mine."

"Kaden—"

He stilled her with a kiss, sipping the words from her mouth as she turned toward him. She fumbled with the ties on his tunic and he reveled in her unskilled touch. He was glad she wasn't a virgin. He didn't have enough control to bed a virgin and not hurt her. But he was equally glad her difficulty with his laces proved she hadn't undressed too many men in her life. He liked the idea of having her to himself. Well, himself and Marcus, of course.

Though the idea of Rey and Linea being mates was new, Kaden already felt comfortable with the idea he would share his mate with Marcus. He'd always been a good friend and after this latest trouble, he'd proven to be closer than a brother. The formal joining of their dragons would only cement the family ties—if the day ever came when Rey could fly and claim his mate. But Kaden put aside the guilt for the moment. At the moment, Lucy was in his arms, where he most wanted her to be. He'd deal with the mess he'd made of his and Rey's lives later. For now, all he wanted to do was forget his problems in the arms of this giving, tender woman.

"Let me." He stilled her fumbling fingers with his own, rising to stand at the foot of the bed as he dealt with the lacings on his shirt.

Pulling it over his head, he threw it to the corner as she rose on her elbows to watch. Her every subtle movement enticed him. When his fingers went to the lacings on his leggings, she blushed, but didn't look away. Instead, her gaze roamed his torso, focusing finally on his cock straining against the leather to get to her.

When he shucked his leggings, her eyes widened and he felt himself grow even harder, if that were possible. The sexy gasp that issued from her reddened lips urged him on. He stalked over to her, one knee resting between hers as he moved onto the bed. She lay back as he covered her with his body.

He liked her breathless moan when he rubbed his body over her soft skin, so he repeated the move, watching her reaction. It was every bit as gratifying the second time she wriggled beneath him, his chest touching hers, his cock brushing the soft swell of her stomach. He stifled a groan.

"I love how you feel against me, Lucy."

"Come down here, Kaden." She circled his neck and drew his head downward. His name was a trembling sigh against his lips as she kissed him, for the first time initiating intimacy between them. As far as he was concerned, she should do it more often. Her tongue tangled with his as she became more demanding, stunning him and driving him higher.

Her legs parted as he placed both knees inside hers and pushed outward, making room for himself. She was warm and already wet for him. Kaden growled in pleasure as he aligned their bodies, rubbing his aching cock in her slick folds as she rose up to meet him. He broke the kiss.

"Do you want me, sweetheart?"

"Yes, Kaden. Oh, yes!"

"What do you want, exactly?" His smile dared her.

"I want..." She licked her lips, flushing a bit. "I want you inside me, Kaden."

He moved one hand downward, shifting only to tangle his fingers in the curls between her thighs. Sliding briefly around the nubbin that made her gasp, he stroked one finger into her core.

"Like this, Lucy? Is this what you wanted?"

"Kaden! Yes, but—" She whimpered. "I want more!"

"Do you want my cock, Lucy? You'll have to tell me exactly what you want." His words teased, as did his fingers, driving her higher. She was on the precipice as he took his hand from her pussy and slid it upward, circling her nipple with wet fingers.

"Kaden! You're killing me. I need you!"

"Not until you say the words, Lucy." He kissed her, then pulled back to watch her expression. Flushed with excitement and a hint of embarrassment, it was clear she liked his teasing.

"I want your cock, Kaden. I want you inside me. Now. Please!"

"Well, when you put it that way, my love." He positioned himself. "How can I refuse?"

He slid home with a long, powerful thrust. She bore down to accept him, though he could feel the difficulty she had accepting his girth. She may not be a virgin, but her cunt was tight, as if it hadn't been used this way in a very long time. Kaden liked the idea of that, but he knew he'd have to temper his passions until she became accustomed to him. It was all right, though. He loved being inside this special woman. She was tight and hot around him. Warm and slippery, wet and welcoming.

Home.

She felt like home to him. It was a feeling he wanted to keep with him for all time, and if he had anything to say about it, he would. She would be at his side when he and Rey moved back to the Lair. She just didn't know it yet.

"Are you all right, sweet Lucy?"

She made a small humming sound when he stroked just the tiniest bit within her, testing the fit. She was growing used to his presence, her body stretching to accommodate his size.

"I'm all right, Kaden. Please, don't stop!"

"I'll never stop loving you, Lucy. Never." He punctuated his words with kisses as he began to move. He took his time, making small movements at first, then increasing when she urged him on. Her legs rose to wrap around him, her heels digging into his butt.

"I'm sorry, my love. This time it's got to be fast."

"Not fast enough, Kaden!" She cried out as a peak hit her. Kaden could feel her inner muscles working his cock. The spasming of her tight sheath drew him with her, into blissful oblivion as his seed shot into her depths. He shuddered at the last, releasing his pent up fury as his body tightened and then relaxed into a peace he had never before known.

He kissed her forehead with tired lips, rolling with her to their sides. Cradling her in his arms, he stayed deep within her body while one of her knees rode up the outside of his leg to his hip.

"You're mine, Lucy." His breathing slowed as he held her. She fit so perfectly in his arms as he rested his chin on top of her soft hair.

"Kaden." Her whisper touched something deep inside when she fell asleep in his arms.

# Chapter Seven

Lucy woke to movement. Kaden, she recalled instantly.

He was inside her—or perhaps he'd never left. The last thing she remembered before falling into a deeper, more peaceful sleep than she had known in years, was Kaden making love to her. He'd been so strong and gentle, so caring and daring. She'd never been pleasured like that before, though her past experiences had been admittedly few and far between.

"I've been waiting for you to wake up and join me." His growling voice teased her ear.

"Feels like you got started without me."

"Just warming things up, milady." The nibbling kisses he placed in the crease of her neck tickled.

She rolled with him as he took her to her back, sliding deeper inside her slick channel. He felt so good. Like heaven brought down to earth. It was as exhilarating as flying on the dragon's back, only warmer and much more intimate.

Kaden kissed her as he stroked into her with deep, sure thrusts. She pushed back, aligning herself for best entry. He brought her such pleasure there was no question of withdrawal. She was shocked by her own wanton behavior, but Kaden seemed to like it and pleasing him was suddenly very important to her. She came with explosive ease and he followed a moment later.

They lay together, their breath slowing to a more normal rate as Kaden stroked her arm with a trailing fingertip. She felt his eyes on her, watching, measuring. He looked like he was working up to something.

"When Rey's able to be moved," he finally broached the topic that was clearly on his mind, "I want you to move to the Castle Lair with us. I want you to live with me and Rey, warm our home and our hearts for the rest of your days."

"That sounds serious."

"It's very serious, sweetheart." He stroked her hair. "I know it's sudden, but I care for you deeply, Lucy. As does Rey. If the worst happens and he never flies again, you would be a comfort to him. You make him sparkle, Lucy, and you make me happy in a way I've never been before."

She was surprised. They'd only known each other for a few days and only become lovers the night before. But she felt the rightness of it as he spoke the words. He was a good man who didn't deserve the pain he or Rey had been suffering. Her heart went out to him and she was tempted. Oh, so tempted.

"What about Marcus and Linea?"

"In the fullness of time, I hope you might come to accept them too. To let them into our lives and our union. When you're ready. We won't rush you."

"Kaden, I don't know...I just don't know if I can handle two men. It wasn't something I was raised to expect."

"I know. I don't mean to pressure you, sweetheart. Just think about it, all right? And think about coming with us, for a start, when Rey is safe to move in a few days. He needs you. And I need you more than I can say. Besides, if Rey can never fly again..." His expression grew bleak. "Your worries may be for naught. If he can't claim Linea, Marcus will most likely never become an issue. So for now, will you consider living with just me, Lucy? Me and Rey?"

"I'd be leaving behind the only security I've known in years, Kaden. You're asking a lot."

He hugged her. "I promise you'll always have a place in the Lair, whether it works out between us or not. A woman who can hear dragons is rare and special. The Lair folk will welcome you with open arms. Trust me."

"I do trust you, Kaden, but it's an awfully big step."

He spoke no more of it over the next days. Each evening Lucia would sleep in Kaden's arms, making love with him deep into the night. Each day, she would care for the dragon who was quickly becoming the center of her world.

Marcus was there most days, following her with his eyes and making her uncomfortable with his pointed stare. She felt conspicuously like a mouse being sized up by a hawk on the hunt. Given her earlier run-in with Marcus—and the scandalous thoughts he'd planted in her head about lying between the two men—the fact that she continued to be Kaden's lover made her feel self-conscious in the extreme. She knew without doubt all it would take was one word from her and she'd have two knights in her bed, when she was only just getting used to one!

The troublesome idea plagued her, refusing to be put completely from her mind. She served in the tavern during the day, comfortable with Kaden's easy-going treatment and hyperaware of Marcus's continued scrutiny. She couldn't deny she was attracted to both of them. Marcus's courtly manners still brought back memories of times past, though as she got to know him and observed him with Kaden and the dragons, he became more familiar to her and less a reminder of her sad past. Kaden, by contrast, didn't remind her of those things, but kept her with him—firmly in the present. He was good for her in that way, and he was a considerate lover.

Lucia also agonized over Reynor's slow progress and wondered if there was more she could do. Each day, she offered solemn prayers that Rey would heal on his own. Marcus had asked what she was doing on the first day when she placed wildflowers as an offering in the small window above Rey's place on the stone floor. She prayed according to the teachings of her youth, which were different from the way things were done in Draconia. Marcus asked pointed questions, but the next day brought beautiful hothouse blooms from the queen's own conservatory to add to the small vase she'd placed in the sun.

Each day after, he brought a new flower for her offerings—rare orchids and lilies, simple daisies and roses. Each day a new flower and a presence at her side while she offered her prayers over the healing dragon.

Silently, he'd stand with her while they added the blossoms to the growing collection, weeding out wilted flowers each time new ones were added. She was touched he would respect her beliefs in such a way and glad he didn't push for more than friendship, though she knew he hoped for far more. Still, there was Reynor to consider.

Lucia decided to take the chance of moving to the Castle Lair with Kaden. For one thing, she was falling in love with the rugged knight. She already loved Rey and wanted to be on hand to help him work through his recovery. She couldn't imagine being left behind when the dragon left the tavern.

And so, with some trepidation, she let the owner know she'd be leaving the tavern when Reynor and Kaden left. The other girls didn't seem surprised when Lucia packed her few belongings, and each of them wished her well. She was touched by their friendly gestures and the small parting gifts they gave her. A ribbon for her hair from one girl, a carved comb from another. They were small gifts, but dear to her for the true friendship they represented.

When Reynor was able to walk for short distances under his own power without causing more damage, the knights arranged for his removal to the Castle Lair. A huge flatbed wagon was pulled into the tavern yard, drawn by a team of eight sturdy draft horses. Rey walked out to meet it, suffering the indignity of being hauled up to the castle in stoic silence. Wellwishers lined the streets as he was wheeled by, speaking prayers for him and offering their quiet support.

For the second time, Lucia entered the Castle Lair, worry foremost in her mind. Rey had been silent as they moved him. It took some time to negotiate the late afternoon streets and by the time they pulled up to the castle, night had fallen. The cart brought him as close as possible to the large door, where he was able to lower himself to the ground and walk painfully through the Lair to the suite that had been prepared. The other dragons watched his slow progress, silent and solemn. Rey didn't raise his head. He was the very picture of defeat.

Lucia's heart went out to the dragon who'd become one of her closest friends. It hurt to see him this way. He walked gingerly, pain evident in every step as he made his way to an area of the Lair she hadn't seen before.

The Lair section of the castle was constructed in a series of circular ledges with the center being open to the sky above. Stairs for the human inhabitants wound through the inner walls, but it was clear the dragons negotiated the different levels through flight. Rey couldn't strain his wing, so a ground floor suite was set aside for them. Rey didn't speak or even make a sound as he struggled for each step, Kaden, Marcus and Linea following close behind.

Kaden had prepared the way, taking a few hours the day before to move his and Rey's belongings from their old residence, higher up on one of the upper floors. He'd told Lucia all about the new suite. It was larger than their old one, and more luxurious. He thought Rey would like the larger sand pit, and Lucy looked forward to seeing the place he took such obvious delight in.

As the small party slowed, Kaden moved in front of his dragon partner to open a huge door, big enough for the dragon. Lucia noted the mechanism on her way through. Rey could've opened it easily with a stretch of his neck, but perhaps it was too much for his healing hide. Better that Kaden do the stretching for the time being.

A surprise awaited them as the group came to a halt inside the large suite.

"Welcome home, Sir Reynor." Alania, the queen of Draconia and her twin, Princess Arikia, also known as queen of the nomadic Jinn people, sat on the lip of the sandy oval that was clearly Rey's domain. The two women stood, Draconia's queen in leathers, as Lucia had seen her before. Her twin sister wore an ornate green dress that matched her emerald eyes.

Lucia lowered herself in a respectful curtsy, though her eyes never left the two powerful women. She straightened only when the men greeted the two queens. They checked Rey's wounds and the tang of ozone and magic scented the air as they used their healing powers in tandem on his tough hide. After some time, the women moved back and Rey was encouraged to settle into his warm sand wallow.

"The heat will be good for him." Queen Alania faced the knights. "Just leave him be for a while. We've done all we can, but I fear it may not be enough." She looked back at the dragon and Lucia wasn't surprised to see him already asleep. All the activity had no doubt tired him out.

Queen Arikia of the Jinn produced a pot of herbal salve from a low table near the door. "You can use this on the scab. It might help loosen the joint a bit."

Surprisingly, she handed it to Lucia.

"See that he rests. No running around the Lair." Her smile gentled the stern words. "I've heard good things about you from the Jinn, Lucia. Be welcome here and if you need anything, please don't hesitate to ask."

Flabbergasted, Lucia nodded and dropped a small curtsy as she clutched the pot of salve. She remained in that position until the women left.

Linea loomed in the doorway, but backed away as Marcus took his leave. It was clear the other knight didn't want to go, and neither did his dragon, but they did leave, for which Lucia was glad. She had to get used to this new arrangement before she could even consider the three-way relationship the knights proposed. And there was Rey to consider. If he couldn't fly, all her worries might be for naught.

When they were alone, Kaden closed the door. He came up behind her, drawing her back against his chest as they gazed at Rey.

"Will he be all right?" she whispered, unwilling to disturb the dragon's rest.

"He'll be better now that he's back home among his own kind. The tavern was a friendly place, but the good folk who came to see him couldn't communicate with him as we can." He settled his chin atop her head as she snuggled into his arms. "Perhaps it was a good thing for the first part of his recovery, but it's best he's here."

"I hope you're right."

"Come now." He tugged her toward a doorway to their right. "One of the lads brought your belongings to our room. There will be time to unpack tomorrow, but for now, I think we could use a good night's sleep."

"Just sleep?"

"Well, I can think of a few other things to do before we sleep." His roguish smile lit a fire in her womb. "If you're interested."

"I am most definitely interested, Sir Knight."

She tugged him toward the doorway. There was a large bed—larger than any she'd ever seen before—against the center of the far wall, laid with soft blankets in colorful hues. It was one of the grandest rooms she'd seen since she'd left her homeland.

"I arranged to have some things made for you, Lucy. I hope you'll like them."

She spun to the sound of his voice, finding him by a carved wooden closet. He'd opened it and was holding up a whisper thin silken nightgown in a pale blue. It was a costly garment, indeed. Lucia hadn't seen anything so fine since she was a child in her homeland and she'd been too young to own such a daring, inviting garment.

"It's beautiful."

"I want to see you in it." Kaden's eyes flashed at her. "But first, I want to show you our new bath chamber." He led the way to the adjoining room where a large mosaic pool was filled with clear steaming water, waiting for them. Even in her homeland, she'd never seen such a large and beautiful bathing chamber. She stepped forward with some hesitancy into a room, tiled in gorgeous, rich hues.

"How does the water stay warm? Where does it come from?" She looked all around to see if she could discern how they'd managed such a feat.

"All Lairs are designed with a mix of science and magic. This being the Castle Lair, it's probably a bit grander than the others, of course. All the water comes from two sources—one deep within the mountain on which this fortress was built and the other from large cisterns designed into the structure that collect rain and snow and funnel it where needed. The heat is a byproduct of associating with dragonkind. Most often, the resident dragon in each suite will provide heat for his family, but some friends made this ready for us at my request just before we arrived. I wanted your first night here in the Lair to hold every comfort."

That this rough knight would think to do such a thing touched her heart. She turned and kissed his cheek.

"You're a sweet man, Kaden. Thank you."

He tossed the silk nightgown to a nearby bench and grabbed her around the waist, drawing her close.

"I don't know about sweet, but I know I'm a lucky man, to have you here with me, Lucy. If there's anything you want, all you have to do is ask. I tried to think of everything you might need, but with Rey so ill, I'll admit I've been a little distracted. Still, I asked some of the women for help. They stocked our chamber and arranged this." He gestured toward the wall where a series of small bottles were arranged next to a mirror. They looked like lotions and creams, but she'd have to look more closely to see exactly what had been provided. Towels and soaps lay near the mosaic pool, ready for use. All in all, the chamber was fit for a king...or at least a princess. Lucia felt tears gather behind her eyes.

"It's perfect, Kaden. I can't believe you thought of all this. I can't believe you'd do this for me."

He bent to nuzzle her ear. "I'd do anything for you, Lucy. Absolutely anything."

She didn't object when he rid her of her rough dress, discarding it on the floor. She helped him unlace his shirt and leggings, and soon they were both naked, kissing deeply as Kaden edged them closer to the steaming pool. He helped her in, steadying her when she felt the incredible warmth of the water against her skin. It had been so long since she'd had a hot bath, and never one this decadent.

Kaden followed her into the water with a splash. He set about lathering her long hair, rinsing with an ingenious device that sprayed hot water in rivulets over her head. She did the same for him and then they were sliding against each other's soap-slick bodies, cavorting like children as they laughed and played in the soapy water.

Lucia's temperature rose as the water cooled. Kaden produced more than enough fire to keep her warm. It wasn't dragon fire, but rather, the fire of a man who knew how to please his woman. And she was his. There was little question left in her mind as to that. Somewhere along the line, during the worry over Rey and the doubts about her future, she'd fallen in love with Kaden.

# Chapter Eight

She already loved Reynor, so loving his knight shouldn't have surprised her. Still, it did. After losing her family, Lucia hadn't thought she could take the chance of loving anyone ever again, but Kaden proved her wrong. It hadn't been a conscious decision. He'd just worked his way into her heart and now he was there for good. Come what may, her future was tied up with the rugged knight and his dragon partner.

"Out you go now." Kaden swatted her rump with an open palm, making her squeal, but it didn't really hurt. Lucia was taken aback by the spike in her desire from Kaden's playful spank. She looked at him, breathless in her discovery as he smiled, slow and calculating.

He followed her out of the tub and wrapped her in a towel, watching her all the while. She grew uncomfortable under his intense regard, but he wouldn't let her go. When they were both dry, he moved back a pace.

"Put on the nightgown, sweetheart. Slowly."

Her gaze shot to his. He was watching her with a sizzling look of intent on his chiseled features. His masterful words made her stomach flutter in excitement. This was something new. In the few days they'd been lovers, it had been intense, but usually free and easy between them. Tonight, the intensity was even greater, but the easiness was gone. In its place was a commanding man who knew exactly what he wanted and demanded no less than obedience.

Lucia didn't understand why that made her so hot, but it did. She followed his orders, tugging on the nearly see-through garment, fitting it to her breasts as best she could. The gown had probably been sewn for a less well-endowed woman. It hugged her breasts and pushed them upward, and she wasn't surprised to see Kaden's gaze riveted to the spot where she nearly overflowed the plunging neckline.

"Turn around. Slowly." He twirled one finger as he gave the command and she watched him while she moved to do his bidding. His cock was erect and he looked as hungry as she'd ever seen him. His words commanded, his eyes held a fire that was matched by the roiling inferno in her womb. This new, masterful Kaden was something else again.

He reached out one rough hand and smoothed it over the silk at her waist. The fabric was so thin, she felt his touch as if it were against her skin, but with the added tactile delight of the ultra-soft silk. She moaned when his hand moved upward, to cup her breast.

"You're beautiful, little girl." He took her mouth, conquering and demanding a response she was more than willing to give. She would give him anything. Everything. He owned her pleasure. It had never been more clear. When he let her go, he stepped back and put pressure on her shoulders in a clear command.

Confused, but willing to see where he would lead, Lucia sank to her knees. The straining arousal that met her eyes cleared up any questions she might've had.

"I've never done this before, Kaden."

The muscles in his thighs clenched, as did his hands in her damp hair. "Then I'm honored to be the first." There was no question in his voice, no room for argument. His surety made the fire in her belly grow hotter.

"I don't know if I can."

"You can and you will, Lucy. Lick me now. I need it." He exerted light pressure on the back of her head until she was close enough to reach out with her tongue. She'd never imagined doing such a thing, but suddenly she wanted it more than anything. Kaden was so strong and powerful in so many ways, it humbled her to see him tremble at the first tentative brush of her tongue over the head of his cock.

"Oh, yeah. Just like that. Take me deeper."

Warming to her task, she grew bolder. Her gaze flew upward, seeking his approval as she took the tip into her mouth and swirled her tongue all around. His hips surged and pushed him deeper into her mouth, but she didn't mind. In fact, she reveled in the look of bliss on his handsome face as he watched her with half-lidded eyes.

There was no doubt in her mind he was enjoying himself. She liked the feeling that gave her, knowing she could give him such pleasure with such a simple act. Lucia also liked the salty taste of him. His flavor and scent reminded her just the tiniest bit of the ocean near where she'd grown up. They were good memories, wild and free.

He pulsed deeper as she got into the rhythm. Like the ocean, nothing could tame this man, but he could temper himself. For her. Every move he'd made, from the moment they met, had been gentle and considerate. Just once, she wanted to push him beyond that. She wanted to make him wild.

She sucked as he surged, earning a groan from him that made her wet. How she loved this man. Strong, yet caring. Bold, yet thoughtful. He was a generous lover and an even better friend.

"That's enough, sweetheart." He withdrew quickly, disappointing her, but the sparkle in his eye promised even more delicious pleasures to come. He lifted her by the elbows, then scooped her into his arms and carried her to the huge bed. Placing her at the edge of the wide expanse, he parted her legs and stood between. She understood now why the bed was built so high off the ground. His cock was at the perfect height for her pussy without any bending or straining, but he didn't take her yet.

Instead, he sank to his knees, kissing her reddened kneecaps one at a time. "I'm sorry, my love. Next time, I'll remember to put a pillow on the floor so you don't hurt your pretty little knees." She sighed as his hands stroked up the insides of her thighs, spreading her folds to his view. "You sucked my cock so well, I think you deserve a reward. As do I." He grinned with wicked intent as he lowered his head.

The next thing she knew, his lips and tongue were teasing her clit and she could form no more coherent thoughts. Pleasure was her only goal. Her body strained toward a peak, wetness issuing forth as he rumbled approval, but he wouldn't let her come. Kaden sat back and she felt his loss keenly. She rose on her elbows to see what he was about.

"You're the most beautiful, responsive woman I've ever had in my bed, Lucy." His expression was solemn. "I'll never let you go now. You know that, don't you?" Two fingers pushed into her, sliding through her excitement and driving her higher. "I couldn't live without you now, Lucy." Removing his fingers, he stood and pulled her hips forward to meet his cock. He slid home with little fanfare and her body convulsed almost immediately. Then he stilled until she met his gaze.

"I love you, Lucy."

He moved then, as she cried out once more in pleasure. His declaration of love astounded her, warmed her and made her feel whole. She loved him with all her heart and let him know it, crying out the words as he made her come over and over again.

He took her on the side of the bed, in its middle and from behind, making her spasm in bliss many times throughout the night. Just as often, he demanded the words of love, giving them to her in return. By the time they finally slept, there wasn't an inch of her body that wasn't sore—but in the best possible way.

The next days were filled with loving, caring for Rey, learning about life in the Castle Lair and visiting with friends. Linea and Marcus visited often, but there was no overt pressure. Of course, she felt Marcus's gaze following her and Kaden delighted in teasing her about how jealous the other man was. Kaden also began to tease her when they were alone, with enticing descriptions of how Marcus and he would take her, if given a chance. He wove intricate, detailed fantasies of dual loving that started to become more and more appealing.

Her life with Kaden was near perfect, except for poor Reynor. As Rey's injury healed it became clear he would never fly again. The thought broke her heart, and as the days marched forward, she gathered her courage. She knew there was one thing left she could try. It was a long shot, and would be very costly to her, but if it could save Rey's wing—and therefore his ability to fly—she would give anything.

Coming to her decision late one night, she left the wide bed with a final kiss for Kaden. He slept on, oblivious as she retrieved a very special item from her belongings. Armed with only that, she snuck down into the dragon's wallow. Rey was dozing, but woke when she neared. She held the precious gift in one hand and the dragon's head reared when he scented its foreign magic.

*"What is that?"*

"Something from my homeland. Something sacred. Rey, I want to use this on your wing, if you'll give me permission to try."

*"It reeks of powerful magic."*

"Only the good kind, I promise you."

*"I sense that. It's pure and formidable. How can you handle such a thing?"*

"I'm the last of a long line of priestesses. Some in each generation of my family were entrusted the ability to wield this power, to be used only in the most deserving of cases. I believe yours qualifies. Will you let me try?"

Rey shrugged, lifting his injured wing as much as he could. *"It could do no harm. My wing is the next thing to useless as it is."*

She could hear the despair in his words. "Courage, my dear friend." She stood at his shoulder, where the injured wing met his body. A jagged chunk of membrane and bone was missing, crippling him.

The surge of magic caused every dragon in the Lair to take notice. Questions flew from one mind to the next, but Reynor calmed them all. He counseled them to patience as he noted the changes in his wing. Something was happening back there, but he'd be damned if he could feel anything except the delicious tingle of powerful, foreign magic.

He was in no pain, which was quite a change from the past few weeks. Lucy had gone silent, standing behind his wing now, holding a single golden plume over his wound with both hands as if braced against the flow of the energy she commanded.

*"What's going on?"* Kaden's sleepy voice came to him from the doorway of the bedchamber. The knight was rumpled from

sleep, but keenly aware of something strange happening in his suite.

*"Your mate is a priestess of great ability. She's taken the pain away, Kaden. For the first time in weeks, I don't hurt."*

But Lucy did. Kaden could see it on her face as he stumbled toward the edge of the sand pit. Her expression was one of agony as the glow of magic enveloped her. She stood with her feet braced far apart in the warm sand, wielding the longest feather he'd ever seen like a sword that was much too heavy for her.

She staggered and fell just as the glow flared and he was momentarily blinded. When he could see again, Lucy was sprawled on the sand beneath Rey's wing. Rey's *fully healed* wing.

It was a miracle.

But Lucy was down. Unconscious.

Kaden leapt into the wallow, tripping in the sand as he rushed to her side.

"Call for help, Rey!"

Kaden felt a shocking tingle of magic as he scooped her into his arms. It flowed through her petite body so powerfully, he was afraid he might drop her. But no more harm would come to this woman if he had anything to say about it. He took her back to bed, lying her down as the dragon watched from the doorway.

*"Will she be all right?"*

"I have no idea. She's breathing, but I can't rouse her." Insecurity filled him. Was she yet another casualty of his inability to keep Rey safe in the first place?

No less than Queen Arikia answered the summons for a healer. She took one look at Lucy and clucked like a hen, ordering Kaden about as she made her charge more comfortable. Riki was Prince Nico's wife and had a powerful healing talent. Unlike her twin sister, who was more of a dragon healer, Queen Riki had used her healing talent primarily on humans from an early age. If anyone could help Lucy, it would be this woman. But Riki jumped back as if burned when she tried to move the long feather out of Lucy's hands. Kaden hovered near and moved to help, but Riki stayed his hand.

"What is this?"

"I'm not sure, but she used it to heal Rey. She told him it was from her family."

"Then it stands to reason, only family may touch it. Sir Kaden, do you take this woman as your wife?"

"Yes, of course. I love her with all my heart."

Riki smiled. "Good, then. You try to remove the feather."

Kaden reached out and felt only a slight tingle as the feather settled into his palm. He placed it on the long table along one wall, out of the way.

"Darn thing zapped me when I tried to touch it," Riki observed with a small grin. "It's got some powerful magic indeed."

"It healed Reynor completely." Queen Lana's voice came from the doorway. "It did what I couldn't."

*"But what did it do to Lucy?"* Rey was clearly worried.

"From what I can see," Riki spoke as she worked, "it channeled the pain away from you, Reynor, while magic reconstructed what had been lost, but I think Lucy got some of the backwash of pain. She passed out in agony. I can feel the residual in her even now."

"Sweet Mother." Marcus rushed in and fell to his knees at Lucy's bedside, taking one cold hand in his while Kaden watched helplessly. "Will she be all right?"

"It's hard to say. Something similar happened to me a few times before I knew how to channel my power, but this magic came from outside herself. I don't know what that might do to her. My advice for now is to let her sleep it off. Judging by my past experiences, she could sleep for a day or possibly two. I wouldn't worry until then. Chances are, she'll come out of it on her own, none the worse for wear, but wiser about how to use that...thing. Whatever it is."

Riki turned to leave, but Lana had more to say. "She healed Reynor completely. I don't know what kind of magic could do that and I don't know how your mate was able to bring something like that here undetected, but my husband will want to speak with her when she wakes. In the meantime, count your blessings. She's given Reynor—and you all—what none of us could, and suffered for it." She looked over at Lucy, lying so still and pale in the bed. "She must love you an awful lot."

With that, the twin queens left.

Rey stuck his head into the bedchamber as far as he could reach, licking his long tongue out to touch Lucy's cheek. She seemed to settle into a more restful sleep and some of her color came back as Reynor touched her. Dragons had healing in their touch and breath, though they used it only rarely on humans who were not their knight partners.

Kaden put one hand on Rey's neck, the other on Marcus's shoulder as he sat at Lucy's side, her hand tucked against his heart.

"Will she be all right?" Marcus asked in a quiet tone that betrayed his fear.

"She's got to be."

*"Don't worry,"* Rey said to them both. *"We'll all watch over her until she wakes."*

"But what if she doesn't wake?" Kaden's voice was raw with pain.

*"She must."* Linea's voice rumbled through their minds. *"The Mother of All would not have chosen her for you only to take her away so cruelly. Lucy is part of our family now. She'll come back to us. Reynor's been granted a second chance at life. As have we all. That was a gift from the Mother. She would not be so cruel as to snatch your mate from you now, when happiness is finally within our grasp."*

Marcus rose, laying Lucy's hand at her side, and went to his dragon partner, looming in the doorway next to Rey. He threw one arm over her pale green neck. "I love you, Linea. Your faith is stronger than mine, I fear."

*Fear not,* she answered simply. *"Enjoy this moment as much as you can, for this is the moment on which our futures will be built. Reynor is whole again. Praise the Mother."*

Marcus touched Rey's neck. "Praise the Mother, indeed. It's good to see you looking so fit, Rey. It'll be a pleasure to have you back in the skies at Linea's side."

*"It will be good to fly again and when we're all ready, to consummate this union."*

When the dragons flew in their first mating flight, the knights and their mate would be truly joined. Each time after, whenever the dragons mated, the knights would find the same sensual solace with their mate. Dragon sex drive was strong and the knights were so closely linked with their partners, when the dragon half of the partnership felt it was time to play, the human participants had little choice but to follow suit.

"We all look forward to that day," Marcus spoke for them all, "but first we need our mate in good health once more."

*"Agreed. I would do anything for her after all she's done for me. I never thought to feel this way about a human female, but,"* Reynor hesitated, tilting his head to one side as he considered the woman on the bed, *"I find that I love her deeply."*

*"As it should be,"* Linea agreed. *"We all must care for one another if this family is to work. As the Mother of All intends."*

# Chapter Nine

Lucia woke with a persistent, dull ache in her head. Fuzzy with sleep, she became aware of two powerful heat sources on either side of her. One was definitely Kaden. Her legs tangled with his and her cheek rested against his chest. But then what was the other source of incredible heat against her back?

She peered behind her with bleary eyes.

Marcus.

In bed. With her. And Kaden.

She tried to remember what had happened, but drew a blank.

She eased out of the bed, doing her best not to wake either of the men, and headed for the bathing chamber. After relieving her bladder and cleaning up a bit, she moved to the kitchen area, noting the empty wallow where she'd expected to find Rey. The empty wallow reminded her of what she'd done, but she couldn't remember anything after that final surge of magic. Still, she took his absence from the sand pit as a sign that Rey had been healed by her efforts and was now out and about, perhaps flying for the first time in weeks. The thought made her smile.

Going about the steps to make a soothing tea for her headache, Lucia tried to work out some of the kinks in her muscles. She was slow to get going this morning, and didn't remember much after approaching Rey the night before. Her neck and shoulders were stiff and she still felt a little groggy.

Strong, masculine hands settled on her shoulders and started to rub as she sighed.

"Marcus." She knew his touch immediately, so different from Kaden's, but was too weary to be afraid.

He leaned forward and kissed her cheek from behind. "Good morning, Lucia." His arms circled her waist, pulling her backward against his warm chest, just holding her. "By the Mother, I'm glad you're all right. How do you feel?"

"A little stiff. That's all. I guess Kaden put me back in bed last night." She didn't dare ask when he'd joined them. Something odd was going on, but she had a hard time focusing.

"Sweetheart, you collapsed. You've been asleep for three days."

"You're joking."

Marcus released her and she turned. His expression was serious.

"You're not joking." She was shocked.

"Are you sure you're all right?"

"I feel a little sore, and still a bit tired, but otherwise all right. Why?"

"We weren't sure what that magic would do to you." She saw the concern on his face as he cupped her cheek. "We were worried, Lucia. Really worried." He tugged her back into his arms, squeezing her close in a tight hug. "Kaden and I took turns sitting with you all day, each day, but you slept and slept. The only hope we had was because Queen Riki told us what to expect. Still, you slept longer than even she predicted." He kissed her hair. "Don't ever worry us like this again. I don't think I could bear it."

"I didn't mean to." She pulled back. "But I had to try to heal Rey. It was the only gift I had to give."

"You've given us more than we ever could have expected, but you risked yourself too much, Lucy. None of us liked seeing you so still and pale."

"It was the only way."

"What exactly did you do?" He was curious, but she should have expected that.

"Where is the plume?"

"Still on the table in the bedroom where Kaden put it. The darn thing shocked Riki when she tried to touch it."

"Oh, no. Is she all right?" Worry wrinkled her brow.

"She's fine, but what *is* that thing?"

"A gryphon feather."

Marcus stoked her hair. "That's some powerful magic."

"It is." She nodded. "Which is why it's only used in the most dire circumstances. I take it Rey's all right?"

"He's out stretching his wings as we speak." Marcus tightened his embrace, sending a thrill down her spine. Was it wrong to feel so attracted to Marcus? The men wanted her to be wife to both of them, but she wasn't completely sure. Marcus had become less a reminder of her past and more a troublesome temptation of something she dare not desire. Still, being in his arms didn't feel as audacious as she'd once thought. It felt right. Right, and...thrilling.

"Oh, Lucy, I was so worried about you." His whispered words held passion as he lowered his lips to hers. The kiss wasn't tentative, but rather a claiming, a welcoming and a promise of more to come. Marcus swept inside, licking fire along her senses as his tongue explored her mouth, finding all the sensitive spots that cried out for his attention. Lucia moaned as she slid against him, the strength leaving her knees as Marcus seduced her with his masterful kiss.

A moment later, she felt the smooth stone of the kitchen wall against her back as Marcus pressed against her. She didn't mind the hardness at her back any more than she minded the very masculine hardness pressing against her belly. Marcus was built on the long side, if she was any judge, and he was more than eager.

The question remained—could she welcome him into her body as she'd welcomed Kaden? Should she?

As Marcus kissed her, the answer to that question became more and more urgent. The man was on fire and she had to make her decision. Acknowledging the desire they both felt was the first step on a much longer road the men wanted her to navigate. She wasn't at all sure about the future, but the present was becoming more insistent with every moment, every twist of Marcus' hips against hers.

He broke the kiss to meet her gaze. "I realized one very important thing over the last three days, watching you, lying there in that bed." Her temperature soared as he pinned her against the wall with his muscular body.

"What's that?"

"I learned that life is precious—yours most of all. Without you, our lives would be empty. All of us. Me, Kaden and the dragons too. I know we've only known you a short time, but you're part of us, Lucia. We love you. Don't you feel it?"

Slowly, she nodded. "I love you all too."

"But I love *you*, Lucia. I want you to be my wife. Mine and Kaden's."

"I don't know—"

He stilled her words by placing one long finger over her lips. "Don't answer now. Let me show you how much I love you. If, after that, you can still walk away, I'll try my best to let you go, though I can't promise not to beg you to stay." He slid his finger along her lips in a caress. "I love you too much not to fight for you."

"Oh, Marcus, I—"

"Don't say anything now. Just let me prove it. Let me in. Let me show you how good it could be." He placed small, biting kisses over her face and neck as he whispered his words of love, and she was lost.

"Show me, Marcus. Please!"

Marcus growled in triumph as she gave in. He had her pinned against the kitchen wall. Not exactly the most romantic of places to make love for the first time, but he was a desperate man. It seemed, when it came to claiming his mate, he was always going to be more barbarian than nobleman. He couldn't wait any longer.

Blindly, he reached for the hem of the nightshift they'd put her in. Kaden and he had taken care of her while she slept. He knew she was bare beneath the shift and he was glad of it. Right now, he couldn't spare the time to sort through all the bits and pieces women normally wore.

Finding creamy flesh beneath his palms, Marcus slowed. He had the soft cheeks of her ass in his hands as he lifted her higher against the wall. Urging her legs to wrap around his waist, he lowered one hand to test her slick folds.

She was hot and wet, ready for him and so responsive, she stole his breath. She whimpered as he stroked her, gently at first, then with firmer motions. He was glad of her headlong response. Never had he been so close to coming before getting inside a willing wench. At least not since he'd been a raw young boy.

No way would he embarrass himself this time. No, this time he would come inside her the way he'd longed to do for days now. She was willing and he had something to prove to her—his love and devotion, his desire to please her and make her his. His and Kaden's. Never would she be alone again. Between him, Kaden and the dragons, she would have a family again and would never lose them, if he had anything to say about it.

"Lucia," he whispered, nibbling on the lobe of her ear as she shivered in his arms. He loved how responsive she was to his slightest touch. Sparing only a moment, he tugged at the laces on his leggings, freeing his cock and aiming it for the place it most wanted to go. "I'm going to love you now, Lucy."

"Marcus! Please!"

Her breathy tones were music to his ears as he aligned himself and began to shove home. He tried to go slow, lest he hurt her, but she was more than ready. Her slick warmth engulfed him as he moved deeper into her heat. She made alluring sounds of ecstasy as he ground himself into her. When he was fully seated, he stopped for just a moment, savoring the feeling.

Her eyes opened and sought his as she writhed on him. He could feel her inner muscles clenching and holding him, stretching to accommodate his width and length. She fit him perfectly. More perfectly than any woman ever before and he knew it was because this was *his* woman.

"You're mine now, Lucy. Can you feel it?" He leaned in, boxing her against the wall with his large body, kissing her yearning lips as he began to move. It wouldn't be long now. He was too close. And so was she, judging by her breathy sighs and the way her sheath rippled around him. He would fly to the stars with her and then do his damnedest to convince her to let him do it again and again and again. For the rest of their lives.

He thrust harder and faster, trying to watch her reaction as he began to lose control. But he needn't have worried. She was with him. Her cries grew louder as he rammed into her until that final breaking point. The little death. The point between the sky and the stars.

Together they came in a rush of pleasure so intense, Marcus thought his knees would give out. He leaned against her, crowding her against the wall as she writhed in his arms. She screamed at the last, her orgasm taking them both to a point higher than he'd ever flown.

"Marcus!"

"Lucy, my love."

He rocked against her, pulsing more slowly now as he came down from the peak. She continued to ripple around him in aftershocks of ecstasy. The sensation was like nothing he'd ever experienced before.

Moving with caution, he snagged a nearby chair in one hand, pulling it closer. Lifting her away from the wall, he supported her on his cock, unwilling to separate now that he'd finally claimed the heaven of her body. He sank onto the chair with her still seated firmly on him, facing him with his hands on her perky ass.

"Are you all right?" he murmured in her ear as he placed kisses along the side of her face.

"Mmm. Better than all right, if you must know the truth." She tilted her head upward as she smiled at him. "You called me Lucy." Her gaze searched his, but he didn't want to think just yet. Instead, he took her lips in a deep, probing kiss.

She was breathless as she pulled back, her eyes dazed.

"Looks like you two are having fun."

Kaden's voice came to them from the kitchen doorway.

# Chapter Ten

Lucia gasped, embarrassed and guilt-ridden. She tried to scramble off Marcus's lap—and his cock—but he held her there with firm, unyielding hands.

"Don't stop on my account. Marcus has been giving me hell for the past few days because I had you all to myself." Kaden sauntered over and placed a small kiss on the crown of her head.

Confusion replaced fear. Kaden seemed happy to discover them together. The proof was in his actions, his words, and in his eyes. They sparkled at her with approval...and arousal.

"You don't mind?" She searched Kaden's expression.

Kaden shrugged. "Mind? I was waiting for this."

She felt Marcus swelling within her. He was hard and ready, her own body weeping for his renewed possession. Marcus's strong hands at her hips urged her to move and she was helpless against the passion flaring between them once more. Her gaze flew from Kaden to Marcus and back again. Both men were clearly enjoying this and she found herself titillated by the appreciative eyes following her every move.

"Unlace his leggings, Lucia," Marcus ordered in a husky voice. Her womb jumped at his commanding tone. Dare she? Marcus tweaked one nipple to gain her attention. "I want to watch you suck him while I'm inside you." His gaze held hers as she debated the scandalous order. "Do it." He stilled within her tight channel, depriving her of the delicious friction. "I'm waiting."

With trembling fingers, she reached for Kaden. He stood close enough that all she had to do was turn slightly on

Marcus's lap. The twisting motion seated Marcus's hard cock a little differently inside her, hitting a spot she hadn't known about before. It felt good. Damn good.

She squirmed on Marcus while she freed Kaden, stroking him with her fingers. Kaden was wider around than Marcus, though just a little shorter. Both men touched off different kinds of fireworks inside her, though both were incredible, to say the least.

"Lick him, Lucia." Marcus ordered again, his low voice firing her senses.

Leaning forward, she slipped her tongue around the head of Kaden's cock. She liked the deep groan of satisfaction that rumbled through his body. Marcus too, rewarded her by slow, deep movements within her. Between the two of them, she felt incredible. She'd never dreamed of such a thing until she met them, but found she enjoyed pleasing both these special men. And they pleased her as well.

Kaden was hard and ready, but pulled from her mouth minutes later, still hard. She clung to Marcus when he rose from the chair with her still impaled on his lap. His strong arms supported her as he coaxed her calves up around his waist.

"What are you doing?" The precarious position seated her more fully on him than she'd been before, setting off sparks of desire through her womb.

"Relax, little one. We need more room for what comes next." He set off for the nearby bedroom with her riding in his arms, each step driving him into her, shooting her higher. She didn't know if she would last until they reached the bed, but somehow, they managed it. Even then, he didn't disengage while placing her down on the rumpled sheets.

He stood while he stretched her out on the tall bed and untangled her legs from his waist. Holding them up and out, he surged into her, pumping his hips a few times while Kaden watched over his shoulder.

"Now isn't that a pretty sight," Marcus commented to his fellow knight. Just the idea that both watched while Marcus took her sent a rush of warm wetness to her pussy.

Kaden reached out and stroked her clit lightly. "Very nice," he agreed. "She likes you, my friend."

"Hmm." Marcus held himself deep within her for a moment before pulling out completely. Lucy whimpered at the loss. She was far gone and ready for anything these men might ask of her, if they'd only let her come. She was desperate for it.

Marcus moved aside and Kaden took his place with little fanfare, pushing home while Marcus moved onto the bed. He stroked her breasts, watching while Kaden powered into her below.

"Marcus!" She met his eyes as his fingers teased her nipples.

"Oh, I like that," she heard Kaden say. "Tell him what you want, Lucy. Tell us both."

"Keep. Doing. That. Kaden," she panted as he rammed into her. She was close now, but she wanted to take both men with her when she came. "Marcus," her eyes sought his, "I want you."

"Where do you want me, little temptress?" His tone was teasing, but his expression was tight with want.

"Mouth," she breathed, barely able to form the words. "In my mouth. Please!"

Kaden groaned and Marcus's gaze sharpened to glints of blue steel as he moved. "Then you shall have me." He spoke the words like a vow as he positioned himself near her head. All she had to do was turn her head to the side and she had him exactly where she wanted him.

She tasted herself on his long cock, which only reminded her of the passionate moments in the kitchen. She writhed as Marcus fucked her mouth, mirroring Kaden's thrusts into her pussy. Marcus thrust shallowly, but Kaden's cock grew bolder and more forceful as their excitement grew. She whimpered with each coordinated thrust, but was powerless to withhold the small sounds. The men stroked in tandem, faster and deeper now as they approached climax.

Lucia was already there. Her womb clenched on a massive orgasm, every muscle in her body tensing around the men who meant more to her than anything in the world. She came hard, taking them with her. Kaden pulsed warmth into her body as Marcus tried to pull away from her mouth, but she held him there, wanting to taste him. She'd learned how sucking Kaden's cock pleased him, and she wanted to give that same pleasure to Marcus.

"Lucy!" Marcus groaned as he came. She swallowed what she could, but some residual stickiness found its way onto her skin. After a long, hot moment where all three reached for the stars together, Marcus collapsed onto the bed, dragging her into his arms. He stroked her breasts, massaging his come into her skin as she relaxed back against him.

Kaden dozed at their side, drained in the aftermath of their first time coming together as a threesome. Lucy wondered idly if it would always be this way. This urgent, this hot, this amazing.

*"It's good to see you three getting along so well."* Linea's amused voice rumbled through all their minds. Lucy looked over to find the pale green dragon's head resting in the wide doorway.

"I didn't know you were such a voyeur, Lin." Marcus continued to stroke Lucy, holding her securely in his arms. She felt a little uncomfortable with the dragon watching, but the knights didn't seem to mind one bit. Still, she tugged at the blanket near the foot of the massive bed with one foot and Kaden took pity on her, reaching down to lift it over her nude body.

*"Just checking on my new family. I never knew human sex could be so...inspiring. It'll be even better, I think, when Reynor and I can join in the fun."*

"And when will that be?" Kaden asked from his boneless sprawl next to them.

*"Soon,"* Linea purred. *"He's practicing his flying skills even now. He wants to be ready for the mating flight. It's a good thing he was such a good flyer before the injury, and wasn't grounded too long. He only has a small amount of muscle mass to make up."*

"He's been eating like a pig for the past three days," Kaden teased. "A whole cow each day and more besides."

Linea's smoky amusement sent sooty spirals toward the ceiling. *"He wants to gain back what was lost before we take to the sky. It's a good plan. Mating is not to be taken lightly among our kind. You should, perhaps, consider the idea as well. Once we fly, we won't want to stop for a good long while."*

"I don't understand," Lucia voiced her confusion.

Kaden sat up, laughing. "It's simple." He reached out to take her hand, folding it between his. "We're deeply bonded to our dragon partners. When they make love...so must we."

"Every time?" The idea was somewhat startling, though she'd had some indication from what the knights had told her before. Still, she was fresh from her first-ever threesome. Now they were saying she'd be involved—at least on a mental basis—with a quintet of some kind? She didn't quite understand how that could work.

Linea's head bobbed in the doorway. *"Every time,"* she confirmed. *"Fear not, Lucy. From what we've heard, our influence will only increase your pleasure. We can't help the spillover of our passion to our knights, but they will benefit from it in ways that will make you scream in pleasure. Or so the older dragons have assured us. And then later, when the babies come, you and I will take turns mothering our offspring."*

"Babies?" Lucy was floored by the idea. She hadn't thought that far ahead yet, but obviously the dragon had.

*"In time,"* the dragon nodded. *"If the Mother of All so decides to bless us."*

Something wondrous blossomed within Lucia at the thought, but there was also trepidation. The knights—and dragons—would have to be told about her heritage before this went any further. Fear filled her. What if they rejected what she was? What if it conflicted with their allegiance to Draconia?

She hid her thoughts carefully as Marcus settled in to sleep beside her. Kaden dozed as well and Linea remained silent. Watching.

Lucy had to talk to someone about this. But who?

*"The queens are very good at solving problems, if you have one, Lucia de Alagarithia."* Linea's jeweled eye winked at her once before shutting. The dragon, too, dozed as Lucy's mind spun.

# Chapter Eleven

Later that day, Lucia woke to the smell of roasted meat and herbs. Her stomach growled and she realized she was famished. The bed was empty except for her and she wasted no time bathing and dressing, eager to get some food into her deprived body.

When she reached the small kitchen, she was surprised to find two women there before her. Marcus and Kaden were nowhere in sight, and neither were Linea or Reynor. It seemed the two queens had come to cook dinner for her and Lucy realized her moment of truth had arrived. Whether Linea had arranged this or if it was the queens' idea, she didn't know, but the time to reveal the truth—and seek advice—was finally at hand.

"Good evening, Lucy," Queen Lana said. "We thought you'd be hungry after sleeping so long. I hope you don't mind our taking over your kitchen."

"Not at all, Your Majesties. Thank you."

"Oh, please call me Lana, and this is my sister, Riki. We aren't very formal and we'd like to get to know you a bit better, if that's all right."

Lucia knew darn well the two women hadn't been raised in privilege as she had. Everyone in Castleton knew the story of how they'd been stolen from their home and sold as child slaves, only gaining their freedom and birthright as members of one of the royal houses of Draconia in recent months. Both had married into the ruling line. Lana was married to Roland, King of Draconia, and Riki was married to his brother, Prince Nico, King-consort of the Jinn. Riki herself had been crowned Queen of the Jinn just weeks before, in a surprise move that still astounded many of her Jinn brethren. It seemed Riki and Nico had fulfilled some mysterious and ancient prophecy, revealing themselves as the ceremonial heads of the wandering Brotherhood.

The two queens dished up three plates of roasted meat and vegetables, setting them on the table. They sat and Lucia followed suit. She was a bit uncomfortable in the presence of such gifted women. Both were healers of great renown with magical abilities far beyond most people.

"Please be at ease, Lucy," Queen Lana said with a kind smile.

They began eating and her hunger reared its head again. She devoured half her plate before coming up for air. When she did, she met understanding smiles on the faces of the two women. They were watching her closely and Lucia flushed with embarrassment at her poor manners.

"I'm sorry." She wiped her mouth with the napkin. "I guess I was hungrier than I thought."

"Don't worry. We've been in your shoes, Lucy. Healing takes a lot out of you and when you finally wake up and get over the lethargy, you're ravenous. Not to worry. We understand." Riki's green eyes were kind as she continued to eat. "In time you'll learn to channel the energy so you don't wipe yourself out. We can help you learn, if you like."

"Um." She didn't quite know what to say. "I'm not a healer. Not like you are."

"Well, you did what we couldn't and that's saying a lot. You healed Rey completely. All our combined power could do was make him more comfortable, not heal such dreadful damage." Lana's eyes glinted a friendly challenge.

"But that was the plume. Not me."

"Yeah," Riki set down her fork, "do you want to tell us about that feather? That thing packs a punch."

"I'm sorry it zapped you." Lucia blushed again. "It was a gift to my family from a..."

"A gryphon," Queen Lana supplied, surprising Lucia with her knowledge. The queen shrugged. "Well what else could it be, with such power? Besides, the dragons have been gossiping and that's what they've come up with. Were they wrong?"

"No," Lucia smiled, shaking her head, "they're not wrong. My childhood home was near the nesting grounds for several mated pairs of gryphons. My family had a pact with them. For as long as my family was in power, the gryphons would be protected and left in peace. The pact lasted for seven hundred years."

"Until your family was overthrown," Riki guessed.

"Murdered in their beds." Lucia nodded sadly. "I only escaped because I'd stayed the night in the rookery. Nrathrella had just hatched a few days before and her sire allowed me to play with her. For the first few weeks, gryphlets are somewhat nocturnal, so her parents were glad to have me there to help keep an eye on her. Or so they claimed. Looking back," she smiled fondly, "I think they were just humoring me. Ella and I bonded from almost the moment she hatched. She was special."

Queen Lana's hand covered hers on the table. "I know how you feel. Tor and I bonded like that. We've never been apart."

"You're lucky to have him with you." Lucia withdrew, steeling herself to tell the rest of the story. "I had to leave. My father's enemies were looking for me. Syrruss, Ella's sire, flew me away that very night. He left me with a Jinn family he knew and they took me in, hiding me in their caravan. I was passed from Jinn to Jinn, eventually becoming part of the Feather Wing Clan. I've traveled with them for years and when the call to gather went out, I came with them here, to Draconia."

"So whose feather is that and how have you managed to keep it safe all these years?" Riki brought them back to the subject of the plume.

"On the night I left, Syrruss gifted me with one of his plumes as a reminder of my birthright. I've kept it with me, on my person, for all these years and never even tried to use it...until Rey."

"What exactly is your birthright? Are you a princess? A queen?"

Lucia considered. "Perhaps, but my family ruled Alagarithia not by force of arms or political means. We were chosen to rule the human population by the gryphons themselves. It was more of a religious calling than anything else. My ancestors were priests and priestesses of the Lady. You call her the Mother of All. The gryphons serve Her and we serve both the gryphons and the Lady. The gryphon magic was gifted to certain members of my line, down through the generations, to benefit both our races in peace. My mother was the last chosen priestess and she had hopes I would be the next, but I was never consecrated. I don't even know if I would have gained the gryphons' approval once I reached my age of majority. By that time, I'd been away from them and my homeland for more than a decade."

"I feel sure that if you'd been with them at that time, you would have been the next priestess in your line, Lucy. Their magic flowed freely through you and didn't harm you. That's the mark of a truly gifted priestess of any sect." Queen Lana spoke quietly as their meal lay forgotten before them.

Lucia nodded solemnly. "I just don't know if what I did was right. I mean," she was quick to clarify, "nothing could be more important than restoring Rey's ability to fly, but I might have been selfish in my motivations. If Rey can fly, my own future is somewhat assured, after all. I was always taught the power should never be used lightly or purely for personal gain. I'm afraid I may have overstepped, though I didn't see it at the time. And just this morning Linea mentioned children..." Terror filled her heart. "If I am cursed for having misused the gift, then I fear it will pass down my line. I didn't think of that when I wanted to heal Rey."

Riki came to her defense. "No, I'll wager you only thought of Reynor. And Kaden and Marcus. If I were to judge, I'd say your motives were pure, Lucy. Any gift you have may well pass to your children, and if so, it will be a joyous thing."

"Even here?" she challenged the Queen of Draconia. "In the land of dragons? Will gryphon magic be welcome here?"

"Any magic used for good," a deep male voice spoke from the wide archway across the room, "is welcome in our land." Lucy was surprised to see not only King Roland, but Kaden and Marcus standing in the wide opening. They'd heard everything, from the look of them.

The king strolled into the kitchen and kissed his wife on the cheek, motioning for Lucy to stay seated. "I'm sorry to intrude, but what I just heard makes recent occurrences much clearer. Lucia de Alagarithia," his green gaze pinned her where she sat, "guests have arrived to see you."

"Guests?" Lucia was confused.

"Gryphons," Marcus clarified with a teasing grin. "A pair of them just flew in and landed on the battlements. They asked the nearest knight, very politely, for an audience with the king."

"And then," Roland picked up the thread of the story, "they demanded to see you. Seems they only asked for me out of courtesy. Polite brutes they are."

Lucy dashed to her feet. "Do you know who? Who's come?"

"Let's go and see, Lucy," said the king. "I've left them in the throne room, for the time being, with Nico. If they haven't torn him limb from limb yet, perhaps we can find out."

Lucia ran from the room, taking time only to retrieve the golden gryphon plume. Kaden and Marcus flanked her and the royal party came up behind. As they exited the suite, Linea and Reynor joined the group. Lucy walked fast and all scrambled to keep up with her. She didn't even take time to tell Rey how good it was to see him whole and happy once more.

Gryphons had come! She was either in big trouble, or...well, she wasn't quite sure what the alternative could be. Would they want to take her home? Would she dare consider leaving her new family?

Questions raced through her mind, but she knew immediately that no matter what, she would never allow herself to be parted from Kaden, Marcus, Reynor and Linea. They were her family now and she loved them more than anything. But still...gryphons! She couldn't wait to see who had come or what they had to say. Her entire future hinged on the next moments and she was eager to greet them.

Marcus and Kaden guided her through the maze of hallways and into the more public parts of the castle. The throne room was immense and Lucy scolded herself to walk with dignity toward the magnificent beasts that stood facing the Prince of Spies. Nico had a devilish grin on his face and it was clear he was studying the new guests as much as they studied him.

Lucy wanted to run to the gryphons, but she couldn't. She'd been trained since childhood how to approach a gryphon from a position of power. These were strong and magical beings who had strict protocols when it came to dealing with humans. She couldn't show weakness now, though inside her heart cried out at the sight of the male and female gryphons, both showing signs of only recently growing out of their juvenile plumage. She could still see a few stray tufts of downy white where the new, golden, adult feathers had pushed through.

The gryphons must have heard her approach across the massive room. The female's head turned and Lucia was struck by an amazing sense of familiarity. It couldn't be!

She motioned the group behind her to stop as she walked right up to the female. She stood firm, her eyes never leaving the enormous creature who looked down on her with narrowed eyes. Gryphons were about the same size as dragons, but sleeker, with feathers and fur rather than scales. And their beaks were formed in such a way that they could speak, with practice, though some people found them hard to understand.

"I am Lucia de Alagarithia, lately of the Jinn. I greet you, and ask your forgiveness."

One talon rose to push against her shoulder. Lucia knew the gryphon used only a fraction of her immense strength to push against her. Still, Lucia had to brace herself not to stumble back. This was a good sign. The gryphon was tempering her strength. It meant she was willing to parlay.

"Do you not remember me, my friend?"

Lucy searched the gryphon's mobile features. They were so familiar...

"Ella? Nrathrella? Is that you?"

The female gryphon clacked her beak in their version of laughter. "I am grown up. Asss are you, if you are indeed, the Lucccy I remember."

"It's me, Ella. I still have your sire's feather."

"Ah, yess. That iss what bringss uss here. We felt the magic of it dayss ago and have flown long to find you."

"I'm sorry. I had to use the magic. Reynor was injured too badly. He would never have flown again if I hadn't intervened." She was frantic, unable to understand what was happening. These gryphons were acting so differently than she remembered. "Please forgive me."

263

Lucia felt a warm presence at her back. A quick glance over her shoulder showed Reynor moving up behind her. That he would stand with her against two such powerful beings touched her deeply.

"There iss nothing to forgive." The male gryphon spoke for the first time. "To losse the ssky you were born to navigate iss a ssad thing. We do not begrudge your usse of our magic to resstore a dragon to the air."

"We are pleassed that you have found your birthright and that by sso doing, we have found you, Lucccy. I have ssearched for you mosst of my life. Do you not sstill feel the bond?"

"Oh, sweet Mother, Ella. I do. Bless my soul, I do." Lucia moved forward once more, reaching out to stroke the soft feathers of Ella's face as she had when they were little. "I've missed you so much, my sister."

"Asss I have misssed you." The gryphon's voice was as soft as she'd ever heard it. "Thiss iss my mate, Grallorrin. I call him Lorr for short." She winked at the male beside her. "It iss our hope we may sstay here with you, Lucccy. The lasst priesstesss of Alagarithia sshould not be without her gryphon ssisster."

Tears flowed freely down Lucia's face as she beheld the creature who had been her best friend in those last days before all she had ever known was ripped from her life. She'd missed Ella perhaps most of all, next to her family. And now the gryphon was grown, with a mate, and wanting to stay in this land of dragons with her. It was too good to be true.

But there was more than just her own feelings to consider. Now she was on the verge of creating her own family and they had to be included in her decisions, her past and her future, as well.

"*You would be welcome here, Lady Nrathrella.*" Linea surprised them by speaking. "*Lucy should have friends near for her wedding.*"

"Wedding?" Ella's eyes sparkled with delight. "And who iss the lucky man?" Her beak shifted from side to side as she looked from Marcus to Kaden and back again.

Lucia shifted back, unsurprised to find Kaden and Marcus on either side, with Rey and Linea towering behind.

"We both are," Marcus and Kaden spoke in unison as they linked arms with hers. She supposed she should have expected something like this after accepting them both into her body the night before. She cringed inwardly, waiting for Ella's reaction, but unwilling to gainsay either man. They were both hers now—shocking as that still seemed.

Ella and Lorr's beaks clacked in laughter, surprising Lucia. "We had heard about your sstrange wayss, but until thiss moment, I didn't quite believe it," Lorr said. "Congratulationss to you all."

*"Then all that remains is to receive our king's blessing to have you stay for a bit."* Linea took charge again, turning attention to Roland, who stood with his brother Nico and their wives.

"As long as you come in peace, you're welcome in our land. We'd be honored to have you as our guests." Roland was nothing if not diplomatic, though Lucy was certain he'd never expected to be entertaining gryphons in his throne room when he woke this morning.

"You will find, ssire," Lorr spoke in sonorous tones, "that our enemy iss your enemy asss well. I think it iss a good thing to begin relationss between our peopless, before the real battle beginss. We may be the firsst of our kind to vissit, but we will not be the lasst. Even now, your brother makess friendss among our kind."

The king and everyone in the room were instantly alert. "You know what's happened to my brother, Wil?"

Lorr bowed his head in acknowledgment. "If what we ssurmisse iss true, he iss in no danger at the moment. Hiss journey back to you will be dangerouss, but he hass good companionss on his wingss."

The king asked more questions about his brother, young Prince Wil, who'd been kidnapped, and Lorr answered in the same reassuring, but vague way. Finally, the king gave up at his wife's urging, seeming willing to accept for now that these strange, magical creatures meant no harm, but would not say anything further on the subject. Lucia was glad. She'd run up against gryphon obtuseness in the past and knew when to quit.

She was so thrilled to be reunited with Ella. She would concentrate on that happy event rather than the sadness overshadowing the castle since the prince's abduction.

# Chapter Twelve

The gryphons caused quite a stir among the folk of Castleton who saw them flying to and from the castle along with the dragons. They were distinct. Their feathers and fur gleamed rather than sparkled like dragon scale. Their beaks were sharp and hooked like an eagle's and their bodies were those of great cats, tail and all. Their forelimbs were feathered like an eagle's ending in wickedly long talons, while their hind legs were muscular and furred, with massive, clawed paws. Jinn minstrels who knew the tales of gryphon magic were in great demand the next day, though the gryphons stayed some distance from the people of Castleton.

Preparations were well underway for Lucia's wedding. The knights began moving their belongings into a much larger suite on an upper level of the mountain castle that had a sand pit large enough for two dragons and a hatchling or two. Rey was flying and training every day so his wing would be as good as new, or perhaps even better. Having almost lost his ability to fly had made it all the more precious.

Lucia spent much of her time, when not busy preparing her new home, with the gryphons. At first the knights and other Lair folk kept their distance, but she knew they were curious about the visitors. Ella and Lorr had been given an empty suite next to Rey's and Lucia spent the better part of the first day of their visit, speaking with her old friend and learning what had transpired since her departure from Alagarithia.

The following day, Prince Nico and his wife, Queen Arikia, came to call at the gyphon's suite while Lucia was there. Nico insisted on informality and Lucia found it hard to resist his charming ways. Before she knew it, she was chatting with them both as if they were old friends.

"But tell me," the Prince of Spies leaned back in his chair as he regarded the gyphons, "how did you know to come here? I suppose it had something to do with the magic Lucy worked."

"My ssire knew immediately when sshe called on hiss power. Our magic iss linked very clossely to oursselvess. Not like you dragonss."

Nico and Riki both started, though Nico hid it better.

Lorr trilled at his mate, stepping forward. "The dragonkin king sshould have known all of thiss already, but your ssire wass murdered before he could passs along the knowledge." He settled into a sitting position near the Prince of Spies and his mate, eyeing them as a teacher eyes their student. "Dragonkind are not of thiss earth. Like sskithss, you were created wholly by wizard magic. Our kind, by contrasst, originate with two sspeciess that already roamed thesse landss long ago. Wizardkind meddled in our creation asss well, of coursse, but sstill, we are tied much closser to this world, while you are tied to itss people more than the land."

"Fascinating," Nico replied, clearly interested, "but why—?"

The gryphon cut him off with a raised claw. "I'll come to the point ssoon, but you musst know the hisstory firsst." Lorr settled onto his hind paws, sitting comfortably. "The wizard Gryffid created our kind. He took two beastss and merged them into one creation, ussing the power of the land that already flowed through them to make uss what we are. We took our sstrength from the land becausse we were part of it. We love thiss world and will do all in our power to protect it." He sat back. "But becausse dragonkind were not tied to the land, the wizard Draneth ssaw a need to tie them to itss people. He did that by merging with hiss creation. You and your brotherss are the ressult. It wass a good plan." The gryphon nodded as if in approval of the ancient wizard's ideas.

Ella prowled up and sat next to her mate, picking up the story. "But the wizard Sskir grew jealouss of Draneth. They had alwayss been rivals and enemiess. Sskir created the sskithss to kill Draneth and all hiss creationss. At firsst, they were mighty creaturess—even worsse than the sskithss you know today. Many dragonkin died. But sskithss had no tiess to the people or the land. They cared only for themsselvess. Sskir abandoned them when they did not ssucceed in desstroying all dragonss."

"So you're saying," Queen Riki asked, "that both dragons and skiths were created by wizards, but only dragons were made part of the world they inhabit."

"Yess." Ella clacked her beak in approval. "Dragonss have a place here, with the people they have joined their magic to. Sskithss do not. They will alwayss be unnatural and evil. Dragonss may be unnatural, but they will never be evil becausse of the care their maker had for them and hiss willingnesss to become one with them and impart hiss own ssoul for their ssake. Dragonkind owess much to Draneth the Wise. Asss do we all." She bowed her head in acknowledgement of the long-dead wizard.

"The plume Lucccy ussed came from my ssire," Ella said after a respectful moment. "He gave it to her when sshe had to flee. Gryphon magic is part of the land and therefore, sstronger even—in ssome areass—than dragon magic. It iss part of uss. We do not give our magic lightly. It iss tied too clossely to oursselvess. My ssire did not want to losse Lucccy permanently, sso he gave her meanss to both protect hersself and call to him, when the Mother Goddesss deemed the time wass right."

"But why?" Lucy whispered.

Ella reached out a huge paw and touched Lucy's leg. "You are beloved by all gryphonss, Lucccy. Can you not guesss why?"

"Or why the foreign asssasssinss came to kill off your entire line?" Lorr stood, facing her as she sat next to the royals. "They came from Sskithdron, ssent by King Lucan."

Ella rose too. "Lucan sseekss to revive the old warss. He sseess himself as the heir to Sskir, though he hass no wizard blood. Sstill, he iss dangerouss."

Nico leaned forward. "So that's why he merged with the skiths? He sees himself as Skir and he wants to battle all of Skir's old foes?"

Both gryphons nodded solemnly. Lorr spoke. "He wass already opposssed to Draconia. He wantss your land and power for himsself. It'ss why he hass worked for yearss to desstroy your family, but the dragon magic in you hass made it difficult."

Nico's eyes shifted to Lucy. "Skir was also at war with Gryffid, wasn't he?"

Ella clacked her beak. "You are asss quick asss your reputation."

"I don't understand." Lucy was at a loss.

"You are beloved by we gryphonss, Lucccia de Alagarithia," the gryphons faced her, both on their feet, "becausse your line desscendss from Gryffid and the first priesstesss, Leandra de Alagarithia."

Shocking her to her feet, the two gryphons knelt on their forelegs, bowing to her. She well knew gryphons didn't bow to anyone.

"This can't be right."

Queen Riki patted her hand, imparting a gentle tingle of magic that helped calm her. Lucia was glad for the woman's presence and help as panic had threatened to overwhelm her.

The gryphons stood once more, facing her. "It iss right," Ella assured her. "Gryffid placed pairss of uss in sstrategic placess all over the world. We do not call any one land home. Insstead, we care for all landss. When Gryffid vissited Alagarithia, he left two pairss of our kind, but he alsso fell in love with a woman of great power. Leandra wass High Priesstesss of the Lady—what your people called the Mother Goddesss even then—and Gryffid left her with child when he had to move on to the next land to fulfill hiss quesst. He promised to return, but never did. The gryphonss knew he had not abandoned Leandra, but had fallen to his enemiess. He wass not dead, but he wass too weak to return to her. Her love never waivered." Lucia felt tears gather in her eyes for the woman who had been her ancestor. "Sshe raissed their child, a girl sshe named Genfer, and helped look after the firsst of the gryphletss to be born. They forged a friendsship that has lassted through to thiss time. We resspect the fact that you carry Gryffid'ss blood, but we love you for you, Luccccy. You were the playmate of my firsst dayss and I love you asss a ssisster."

Lucia did cry then, feeling tears slide down her face as she moved forward to meet the gryphon. She buried her face in Ella's neck feathers, as she had when she was a little girl.

"I love you too, Ella. I've missed you so much." Her whispered words were for the gryphon alone and they stood together, comforting each other for some time before the storm passed.

Lucia drew back, surprised to see everyone still there, watching her with understanding eyes. Ella stayed near.

"Your marriage is the first sstep," Lorr said from her side. "Our brethren'ss involvement with Prince William iss another."

"Steps in what?" Nico asked. Though it was clear from the tightening of his expression he wanted to know more about his missing brother, he focused instead on the bigger picture. For the moment. Lucia had no doubt he'd do his best to grill the gryphons about Prince William as soon as he saw a better opening.

"Sstepss in uniting the forcess that will be needed to fight Sskir if Lucan managess to free him."

"Sweet Mother!" Nico started, clearly upset. "But I thought the wizards were all dead."

"Not dead. Not all," Lorr confirmed. Sskir wass confined for hiss crimess in a place called the Citadel. He hass sslept in frozen ice thesse many centuriess. Lucan sseekss to free him."

"So that's what his search parties are doing in the north." Nico shot to his feet.

"It iss what we believe. Gryphonss do not ussually fly that far north, but we have ssome friendss among the Ice Dragonss. They are wild, but they help protect the Citadel. It iss what they were created for."

"Roland needs to know." Nico made a move toward the door, but one very large, feathery wing stopped him.

"That iss why we told you, Prince of Sspiess, King of the Jinn. You, perhapss more than any other man, have many piecess of the puzzle already. You, perhapss, know more than even we gryphonss." Lorr trilled, his amusement plain.

"We would create an alliance between oursselvess and the heirss of Draneth, as Gryffid and Draneth were allied in timess passt." Ella cocked her head to the side, watching them. "The Mother Goddesss hass brought the line of Gryffid here for a reasson, we believe. The union of Lucccy with a dragon pair and their knightss, iss the firsst contact, but there will be otherss between gryphonss and dragonkin. Ssoon. This marriage will pave the way for our alliance if, and when, it iss needed."

"I had no idea." Lucia was shocked.

"Neither did we, at firsst." Ella nudged Lucia fondly with her beak. "Eventss have come to passs asss they will. We merely sstruggle to undersstand."

"Well, that makes me feel so much better." Her dry comment startled a laugh out of Queen Riki.

"I know how you feel, Lucy. I only found out a few months ago I was descended from one of Draneth's sons. It's a little confusing at first, but then everything starts to make sense." She turned her attention to the gryphons, a sparkle in her eyes. "Like the way she was able to use the gryphon magic in that feather, when it would probably never respond to anyone else."

Ella nodded. "You are right, my queen. Lucccy carriess Gryffid'ss blood. Only sshe may usse the magic. Her family and chossen matess may handle the plume, though it will sshock anyone elsse who triess to touch it."

Riki rubbed her hand. "Yes, I know." She chuckled and the gryphons trilled as they shared a moment of amusement. They talked a while longer, but Lucia was overwhelmed by all the information. She'd had no clue about her ancestry or her birthright, except as a priestess. Wizard blood, now that was something else again. The idea was startling and scary.

Marcus and Kaden entered the suite, seeking Lucia immediately.

"What's wrong?" Marcus pulled the gauntlets from his hands as he neared her. "We left practice when we felt your distress."

"Already they are clossely bonded," Ella trilled with satisfaction. "Thiss iss a good ssign for the future." She stood and padded past the knights toward the door.

"We sshould talk more with your brother, I think," Lorr said to Nico. "Leave thesse lovebirdss to comfort each other." One large eagle eye winked as his beak clattered in gryphon laughter. He padded after his mate, sharp claws clicking on the polished stone floor.

Riki and Nico left with them, smiles on their faces as they walked behind the gryphons, hand in hand. That left Lucia with her mates. She was glad. She needed their support right now.

She related what the gryphons had told her, much to their astonishment. Marcus held her while Kaden asked pointed, strategic questions about the threat they'd hinted at. Kaden gave up the interrogation when she'd told them all she could, but Lucia hadn't minded sorting through all the startling information with him. It helped calm her nerves, but also reminded her of the true gravity of what had been revealed.

War might well be coming, the likes of which hadn't been seen since wizard times.

# Chapter Thirteen

Lucia sought comfort with her mates that night, sleeping between the two after loving them each thoroughly. The dragons slept side by side for the first time in their new suite, though they had yet to join fully. That would come. Tomorrow.

The wedding feast was set. All the knights and their ladies and dragon partners were ready for the celebration. The young prince was still missing and that sorrow had cast a cloud over the castle for the past week or more, but even the royal family thought going ahead with the wedding was best for all concerned. For one thing, it was important strategically to bring Lucy and her gryphon friends into the family, as it were, but on the purely human side of it, the Lair folk needed something to be cheerful about. Prince William was much beloved and the two young dragons who'd taken off after him, Jenet and Nellin, were sorely missed. Rumors flew as did the dragons, back and forth from all the outlying Lairs, but no one had seen or heard from any of them in days.

Lucia flitted through her day, going over the things she'd learned about the traditional knights' wedding ceremony. It was different than most other nuptial celebrations. There were promises made, which was familiar enough, but afterwards, there were a series of ritual dances. It had been years since Lucia's dancing lessons as a child, but she'd picked up the basic steps very quickly when the women of the Lair showed her. These dances were completely foreign, and very daring, because they were performed with two men. She'd be dancing with both her knights at the same time. And from what the women described when they showed her the layered garments she was expected to wear, they'd be slowly undressing her throughout the ritual.

The other married knights would join in the dancing with their own ladies, and by the time the final dance was performed, the knights and their ladies would be ready to join their counterparts, the dragons, as they took to the air in a mating flight. The human partners would seek their own beds while the dragons would soar into the heavens, but both sides of the partnership would be seeking and sharing pleasure.

The very idea of it took her breath away.

The ceremony was beautiful. Surrounded by dragons, knights and their ladies, plus the royal family and two preening gryphons, Lucia, Marcus and Kaden spoke their vows. Reynor and Linea shared their vows as well and then the feast began in earnest. A lovely dinner was followed by the ritual dancing. By the time they reached the last of the sequence of dances, Lucia was hot in more than one way.

The men tossed her around, leaving her clothed only in the barest necessities. Three by three, the married trios left. The newlyweds ran down the corridor of the Lair as Reynor and Linea took to the air. The other paired dragons followed suit, reaching for the stars together. The single dragons trumpeted and roared, adding their joyous voices to the drumbeat of wings that filled the air all around the castle.

Marcus, Kaden and Lucia barely made it to their suite before they were naked, grasping for one another. The knights were in a frenzy of need, urged on by the dragons' strong connection to them both. Lucia didn't mind one bit. The other women had warned her about the way the dragons' passion would incite the knights. Secretive smiles and teasing remarks had forewarned her about how hard the dragons would drive their lust and how well she would benefit from it.

Trusting her men, Lucia let them carry her, position her, treat her as they wanted. The women had advised letting them have their way this first time, and she wasn't inclined to argue. So far, everything they did only made her want them more.

Kaden lifted her over Marcus, lowering her onto his cock. She was just getting used to the sudden intrusion—though in truth, she'd been wet and ready half the night—when Kaden pushed her forward. The move took her by surprise, but she went willingly. Kaden's powerful hands were rougher than usual, but she found new appreciation of his strength. It made her senses leap higher.

Marcus swept his hands down her body, cupping her ass as he claimed her mouth. His kiss was demanding. More demanding than usual, but altogether enthralling. When he let her up for air, his smile stretched wide and fierce across his handsome face.

"How are you doing?"

"Never better." She jumped when something slick and chilly touched her backside. Marcus chuckled and cupped her ass cheeks more firmly, lifting and separating. The chill came again, but this time she felt Kaden's blunt fingers behind the slick wetness, teasing her back entrance.

"Don't worry, my love." Marcus nipped her lips. "We'll be as gentle as we can. Damn. I've was warned about this, but nothing beats the feelings Linea is broadcasting to me at this moment." His eyes danced with the fire of his passion.

"What's it like?" She gasped as Kaden's finger entered her, stroking the cream inside, stretching and preparing her.

"It's like feeling echoes of a love so strong, it would kill you to stand in its full glory. It's..."

"Amazing," Kaden said as he slid two fingers into her. He loomed over her shoulder, biting down gently on her neck as he stretched her. "How are you doing, sweetheart?"

"Kaden!" She cried out when he twisted his fingers, but it wasn't in pain.

"Good?"

"Oh, Kaden," she gasped.

"We can't wait any longer. I'm sorry, love." Kaden knelt between her and Marcus's splayed thighs, coming over her. He'd removed his fingers, and now sought to replace them with something a little bigger. Make that a *lot* bigger.

She felt their fire rise as Kaden began a slow, careful entry. She'd never done this before, but the women had warned her about it and she thought she was ready. Nothing though, could prepare her for the incredible feelings Kaden was causing. Marcus lay still, only pulsing occasionally, when he couldn't help himself, while Kaden breached that place that had never been breached before.

Lucia accepted their ardor, just as she accepted their love. Kaden wouldn't hurt her. It twinged a bit, but she knew they would bring her bliss.

The dragon's lust drove Kaden onward as he joined fully with Lucia. Marcus was in her pussy and he felt the other man through the thin barrier separating them. It was a new sensation, but not unpleasant.

Hell, with the way Reynor's fire was pushing him, Kaden would do anything at all to be one with his mate at this moment. Her love, her acceptance, her joy in their partnership made this all worthwhile. Without her, Kaden would never have been able to stand the heights to which Reynor's passion forced him. It was an echo only, but it was stronger than anything Kaden had ever experienced. Now he understood why fighting dragons were not allowed to mate unless their knight partners had a love of their own.

He felt the deep bonds of love tying him to Lucy, and through her to Marcus as well. The bonds were snapping into place, never to be broken. They were strengthening with each moment and would form indestructible links between their souls. It was beautiful and breathtaking.

Almost as breathtaking as the echoes of dragon lust driving him to claim his mate in a frenzy of need. He felt the moment Linea and Reynor became one. Rey's triumphant cry as he finally joined with his mate was echoed by Kaden as he slid fully home within his new wife. Moments of blinding fury—a firestorm of passion and lust followed. Then, as Rey came, so did Kaden. Fast, hot, strong and longer than he'd ever come in his life. The dragon echoes affected the knights, pushing them to feats of endurance and virility no human man could achieve naturally.

Kaden collapsed, welcoming the spasms of his mate's body around his that let him know she'd climaxed hard and was still feeling her own pleasure. At the last he'd been blinded to all but the dragons and his own scorching finale. It would get more manageable in time, they'd been told by older, wiser knights, but for right now, Kaden didn't think life could get any more perfect.

He rolled away, disengaging himself carefully from Lucy. Marcus rolled her between them and both knights stroked her soft skin. She was a miracle.

"Are you all right?" Kaden's voice was rough.

"Give me a few minutes to revive and I'll let you know."

"That good, huh?" Kaden rose on one elbow to look at his lovely mate.

"That devastating." She raised one tired hand to cup his cheek. "I love you."

He placed a kiss in her palm. "I love you too, my wife." He stared at her a moment before rising. He moved into the bathing chamber and cleaned himself, then returned with soft cloths to bathe his mate. His wife. Kaden couldn't stop smiling.

Marcus was kissing her when he returned, both of them exchanging words of love. Kaden felt his heart expand in his chest, welling to include both of them, and the dragons as well. His new family stunned him. They were his. Finally, he had a family to call his own.

He stared a moment more, then bent to his task. He would have to take care of Lucy. They had much more ahead of them this night and in the days to come.

ഊഗ♠♣ന

The newlyweds—both dragon and human—spent the next few days lost in each other. The dragons flew almost constantly and when the dragons caught each other in the sky and reached for the clouds, so too did their human partners.

On the second day, Lucia took a few minutes in the afternoon to visit her gryphon friends in the suite next door. She sat with Ella while Lorr was out stretching his wings, flying with some of the dragons in their training flights.

"Lorr and I want to move," Ella pronounced carefully.

"You're leaving?" Lucia felt her heart break.

"Not leaving, ssilly chick. Jusst moving. We will nesst on the mountain, with the king's permission. This warm ssand iss nice, but not what we like for our hatchlingss."

"Then you're—?"

"Pregnant. Asss are you, my dear. Our babiess will grow up together, asss we did."

"I'm—?" Lucia stuttered in her excitement.

"Did you not ssusspect?" Ella chided her with clacking gryphon laughter.

"I'd hoped, but I wasn't certain."

"Be certain."

"Oh, Ella!" Lucia hugged the gryphon's neck tightly in joy. "I have to tell Marcus and Kaden!"

"We heard." The men stood in the large archway, both wearing identical expressions of stunned amazement.

Congratulations and hugs followed, with much time spent fussing over the expectant mothers—both human and gryphon. In the days to come, another female joined the others in expecting her first offspring. When Linea told her family about the egg that would soon be deposited in the warm sand to incubate, their joy was complete. For the first time in centuries a gryphlet and a dragonet would grow up together, as friends.

It boded well for the future, uniting the magical creatures and the people who loved them, and were loved in return. Lucia still feared the resurrection of an ancient war, but with her knights at her side and the children who would depend on them all, she knew she would persevere and prosper in this land of dragons and knights.

# About the Author

To learn more about Bianca D'Arc, please visit www.biancadarc.com. Send an email to Bianca at bianca@biancadarc.com or join her Yahoo! group to join in the fun with other readers as well as Bianca D'Arc! http://groups.yahoo.com/group/BiancaDArc/

# Look for these titles by
## *Bianca D'Arc*

### *Now Available*
Dragon Knights 1: Maiden Flight
Dragon Knights 2: Border Lair
Dragon Knights 3: The Ice Dragon
Dragon Knights 4: Prince of Spies
Ladies of the Lair: Dragon Knights 1 & 2 in Print
Lords of the Were
Forever Valentine
Resonance Mates 1: Hara's Legacy

### *Coming Soon:*
Sweeter Than Wine
Dragon Knights
FireDrake
Resonance Mates 2: Davin's Quest
Resonance Mates 3: Jaci's Experiment

*Dragons.*

*Just the word conjures visions of a dreamworld filled with magic.
Fiery passion. Love without boundaries.*

# I Dream of Dragons II

In Kathleen Scott's *Dragon Tamer,* Serrah and Darion race
against time to find out what is killing the precious dragons of
Cambry.

Nina Mamone's *Hard to Guard* forces two dragon guardians
into a reluctant partnership to track down a kidnapped wyrm.

*Are you ready for this world? Get ready to be swept away
on the wings of dragons.*

Warning, this title contains the following: explicit sex,
graphic language, violence, narcissistic wyrms, steamy dragon
love, .

*Available now in ebook and print from Samhain Publishing.*

*The untrained skills coursing through her might kill a man... but what a way to die.*

# Revealing Skills
## © 2006 Summer Devon

When Gilrohan, shapeshifter and king's man, is thrown into a dank prison cell, his only option is clear—turn himself into a rat and escape. But fleeing the iron bars is easier than escaping the quick hands of the woman who captures him—and undoes his magic. Her undiscovered power is a rare gift, and unknown even to her.

Tabica lives as a slave to her oversexed overlord. Life seems grim until the furry tesslerat shifts into a sleek, naked man beneath her hands. Gilrohan wants to explore her power, and she wants to explore him. Together, they discover that magic can actually work between two people whose lives and love should never have intertwined. But her awakened skills land her into a new existence that threatens to be as dreary as her old one.

*Available now in ebook and print from Samhain Publishing.*

*Duty wars with affection when Racor's greatest spy must
decide who to trust, the evidence against her
sexy suspects, or her heart?*

# A Scorching Seduction
## © 2007 Marie Harte

*A Midsummer Night's Steam story.*

Lt. Col. Trace N'Tre and Assassin Vaan C'Vail are hiding
out in the only place the military can't touch them—on a
pleasure planet in an island resort owned by Vaan's cousin.
Gathering evidence on the outside, they know it's only a matter
of time before they'll have to face their accuser, a high official in
the Racor government.

Unbeknownst to them, Myst, Racor's greatest spy, has had
her eyes on them for some time. The puzzle of these two alleged
traitors doesn't fit, and Myst has made it her mission to find out
why. But when the tables are turned and she's caught spying
under the planet's hot summer suns, pleasure and affection
confuse the issue, making her wonder who to trust—her heart,
or the evidence against her lovers.

Warning, this title contains the following: explicit sex, frank
language, ménage, m/m action, and hot sweaty adventure.

*Available now in ebook from Samhain Publishing.*

*Prince Nico is a cunning master of stealth, but can he master a maiden's fragile heart?*

# Prince of Spies
## © 2007 Bianca D'Arc

*Fourth book in the Dragon Knights series, but can be read on its own.*

Prince Nico is known as the Prince of Spies for a reason. Not only is he the Spymaster of Draconia, but he's a cunning shapeshifter able to take the form of a dragon at will. The gift of his royal heritage comes in handy as Spymaster for the king, but it's a great secret known only to a few.

Riki lives in misery, chained up to serve a mad king's perverted magic. Forced to use her draining healing skills to keep King Lucan of Skithdron alive, Riki is a shadow of the woman she should be.

Nico knows Riki is the woman he's been searching for and wastes no time breaking them both out of the enemy palace. Thus starts an adventure that will take them across two countries, through peril and danger, and the discovery of an undeniable love and mutual respect. Will Nico have the courage to let her fly free, trusting she'll return to him, or will his love smother the fledgling beauty who is breathing free air for the first time in her tragic life?

*Available now in ebook and print from Samhain Publishing.*

# fly Away

### Discover the Talons Series

5 STEAMY NEW PARANORMAL ROMANCES
TO HOOK YOU IN

Kiss Me Deadly, by Shannon Stacey
King of Prey, by Mandy M. Roth
Firebird, by Jaycee Clark
Caged Desire, by Sydney Somers
Seize the Hunter, by Michelle M. Pillow

AVAILABLE IN EBOOK—COMING SOON IN PRINT!

samhain
publishing Ltd.

WWW.SAMHAINPUBLISHING.COM

# hot
# STUFF

## Discover Samhain!
THE HOTTEST NEW PUBLISHER ON THE PLANET

Romance, fantasy, mystery, thriller, mainstream and
more—Samhain has more selection, hotter authors, and
everything's available in both ebook and print.

Pick your favorite, sit back, and enjoy the ride!
Hot stuff indeed.

WWW.SAMHAINPUBLISHING.COM

# GREAT
# Cheap
# FUN

## Discover eBooks!

THE FASTEST WAY TO GET THE HOTTEST NAMES

Get your favorite authors on your favorite reader, long before they're out in print! Ebooks from Samhain go wherever you go, and work with whatever you carry—Palm, PDF, Mobi, and more.

## Samhain Publishing ltd